AFTER THE EXODUS

-THE HALLOWED STAR SERIES-

Book One

First Edition: 2024

Cover and Book Illustrations by Elizabeth Jenney

Edited by Lillian Owen and Lucy Connery

ISBN: 979-8-9897512-0-4

Second Edition, 2025

To my parents, Fran and Bob, for always supporting and encouraging me to read.

To my partner, Liz, for an incalculable amount of things, including listening to me talk about these characters like they're my real-life friends for the past 24 months.

PROLOGUE

Like most people, I dream often when I sleep. But as I get older, there is something very different about my dreams than anyone else I know:

They come true.

Some of them do, anyway, and it's an immense burden. Imagine waking up after experiencing someone you know dying in your dream but having no way to know when it's going to happen. Do you tell them? Do they even want to know? Is it even true?

Some days it feels like enough to break me, but most days we're just trying to survive to the next one. Everyone left on Earth is on the edge of an emotional collapse, and it's often hard to tell what is spiking my anxiety on any given day.

So tonight I will fall asleep, I will see the future, and tomorrow I will once again be able to do nothing about it.

CHAPTER 1: COMETS

Every time a comet flashes across the night sky, I wonder for a brief moment if that's them, coming back for us. I know in my heart it's not quite right. The blinding ball of light is too bright, the speed too quick. Yet hope flickers for one fleeting moment.

Esha and Garven always tell me to knock it off, to quit dreaming about being rescued. Garven's a bit older than Esha and me and remembers the first ship leaving us behind more clearly.

"Oh, they promised they weren't just leaving us here. That just because we were poor, we weren't being stranded, but you knew the minute they stepped on those ships, they were never coming back—"

Esha cuts him off.

"None of us could have known that. We all have friends and family on those ships, *you* have family on those ships, Garven. I'm sure they miss us just as much as we miss them."

"If they're even alive," mumbles Garven.

The phrase echoes in my mind for a while. "If they're even alive." I have no family that I'm waiting for. My only connection on the ships is with Garven's family, and most importantly his sister, Auryn. Auryn was the love of my life. We were together for four years before she and the rest of Garven's family left Earth in the search for a new home.

Still, I find myself dreaming often about what's out there. I wonder if people's friends and families made it to their new homes. For those of us left on Earth, struggling every day to survive? Yeah, you could say a lot of us are bitter about it.

I was 15 when the first ship left in 2129 from Toronto. Those were the people that bought their freedom with money or favor. The rest of the spots on the ship went to the well-connected, politicians and members of their families, and then a lot of doctors and scientists.

It was over three years ago, and it really felt like the beginning of the end for those of us left on Earth. More vividly, I can recall every detail of the second ship taking off because it left from Cleveland, my hometown.

I remember seeing the ship being built. It was the biggest thing I had ever seen in my life, higher than the largest skyscrapers and wider than 10 city blocks. It cast its shadow over the neighborhoods that weren't even going to have passengers on it.

I watched as Auryn and her family left this planet. I had invited Garven to come to our building and watch with us, but he refused.

From the roof, where we watched, we could feel the low rumble of the rockets secured tightly to the ship. The sparks, and then flames, filled the ground below it. A few moments later, they unleashed a heat you could feel a half mile away and finally, a quarter mile radius of smoke that ever so briefly hid the ship from our view. Within moments, the rocket was out of the atmosphere without any of us knowing if we'd ever see them again. As it disappeared, I whispered:

"Goodbye for now, big penguin," toward the sky.

I remember no one clapping or celebrating. Our elderly neighbor from down on the first floor, Bhavishya, who had his son carry him up to watch, wiped a tear from the corner of his eye as he looked over toward the rest of us at the small gathering.

"Us old people got to see some of the world at its best, but you young people," he says while looking at Esha and me, "you young people are just so unlucky."

With that, he nods his head toward his son, who picks him up and begins to carry him down the 12 stories of crumbling brick and exposed wiring. The building itself is tight against other buildings in the same dilapidated shape, or worse.

Generations of families making the slow walk down the stairs, if able, or taking the dangerous elevator if they had to. I wrapped my arm around my dad. With his failing health, we're about the same height now, 5'10". His was an unsteady walk. The weight of his body leaning on me felt like the weight of the world, and in some ways it was.

We made it to our floor, and I unlocked the door with one hand while keeping my father standing with another. Esha held my mom's arm. She was a little less steady than my dad, but much prouder. As much as it pained her to wait while I fumbled for my keys, she'd never show it.

Finally, I opened the old wooden door to our apartment, pushing on the bottom metal kick plate in the same worn-down spot that's been hit thousands of times before. For a moment, my mom stood there, all 5'7" of her, with thinning gray hair underneath a red bandana and her green eyes as fiery as ever. I could tell she was struggling by the way her hand gripped firmly onto Esha's shirt, a black tank top fraying at the bottom, pulling the fabric toward the ground. My dad turned and smiled at her, the way he always had for the last 25 years of their marriage. They held each other's hands, and in sickness, they walked down the hallway to their bedroom to lay down.

Sure, the trip to the roof exhausted them, but I think life itself is what they needed a break from.

Now, with Garven, Esha, and I laying on the ground, looking up at the night sky, what I wouldn't give to see them one last time: my mom as stubborn as ever, and my dad using every ounce of his energy to smile at her. I can't help but keep the belief that one day that comet up in the sky will be a ship, that ship will be here to save us, and maybe, just maybe, some lucky families will get the reunion I never will.

CHAPTER 2: SURVIVAL

We left the city of Cleveland a few weeks back on our way to hike 190 miles to Buffalo. Garven has some friends there that can help us get to our final destination: Toronto.

Cleveland, Buffalo, and Toronto are the only three cities left in North America with any sort of population. Over the past few years, it's been tougher and tougher in Cleveland to survive, so a lot of people are heading over to Buffalo.

The reason we're headed to Toronto, though, is because it's the agreed upon landing place for any of the three ships that can make it back and pick us up. Auryn promised she would be on the second ship when it came back, and for a while it was the only way I could get Garven to even consider making the near-200-mile hike.

The first year after Garven's family left, Esha was the one who kept both him and me from falling apart. With my parents passing away, both out of my life over the course of just a few months, and Auryn, the only love I had ever known leaving on the second ship, I was overwhelmed and fell into a deep depression.

It was Esha who made me come along to search apartments for food. It was Esha who, sometimes literally, picked me up off the floor, put me in the tub, and ran the makeshift room temperature shower over me after days — and sometimes weeks — of being too numb to clean myself. During this time my anxiety medication, that I was hoping would last me a few years, dwindled quickly.

It wasn't just me, though. Garven had wild mood swings. He would yell angrily, to no one in particular, about how unfair it was that so many of us were just left behind to fend for ourselves. In the next breath, he would say how much he didn't even care that he was left behind.

Without Esha, I truly believe that we wouldn't be here, currently hiking toward a new city and a new life. It's amazing how strong someone can be while being pushed to the brink. All 5'5" of her, I would trust her with my life.

Eventually, the Raiders became more aggressive and it was easy for everyone, including Garven, to see that there was no longer a place for us in Cleveland. So, we packed up what we could; food, my backpack with water filter, clothes, and my most prized possession, my notebook.

Before she passed, my mother made it for me, finding old, unused, or partially used scraps of paper from the decades before I was born. By the time I was born, there had already been so much damage done to the planet that there weren't enough trees, or people, to run paper mills any more.

But my mother always kept scraps. From what my dad said, she had seen the warning signs about Earth so much earlier than most people. So, she saved everything she thought might be useful. Water filters that might have a little more use left in them, clothes that were torn to shreds were repurposed and saved, and canned food long expired were put into closets. Plus, those scraps of paper that became my most prized possession. These things filled up an entire room in our apartment. It was so full I had a hard time opening the door when I was little. I would shove and shove, until I could barely squeeze through.

Inside, there were towers of old books, stacked higher than my height at that age. Boxes filled with cans of soup and bags of rice. Shelves of old music records and a small record player in the corner. Every time someone moved a box, you could see the dust through the sun rays from the window. When days were especially bad, or when my panic disorder was starting to ramp up, all I wanted in the world was to smell the old paper and dig through the boxes.

Once, when I was a little bit younger, maybe nine or ten, I wedged my way through the door and a tower of boxes crashed down into it. I was trapped, but I didn't mind. It took my dad a solid 15 minutes before he was able to get it open again. It always drove him crazy, all this seemingly useless junk. He always talked about what else we could do with the space.

"Wouldn't a nice reading room be great? Somewhere quiet and," he paused to look at me, "maybe a little more peaceful?"

My mom loved to tease him toward the end.

"What good would a reading nook have been while the world is on fire?" She'd say to him.

He chuckled because it did, in the late 2120s, seem so ridiculous, the idea of a reading nook. The last people on Earth are scraping along, trying to survive, and my dad is there, reading his books in an otherwise empty room. Now, though? What I wouldn't do for a safe room to read in.

None of it was surprising though, he always thought of himself as an academic. His plan was to go to school to become a professor. He certainly looked the part, from the few old pictures of him I saw. Always standing up as straight as a book spine, smiling a wide grin, with his glass's half fallen down the bridge of his nose.

My mom said that when she first met him, he was,

"Handsome, quiet, and 5'11": the three things I was looking for," she had a big laugh at that, before he interrupted her,

"Salia, my dear, you know I was six feet tall."

She rolled her eyes and mouthed "No he wasn't" in my direction.

"Of course you were, Burton," she replies, as she patted him on the head and walked toward the kitchen.

Remembering this brought a smile to my face, which hasn't happened much in the last few years. Recalling them as their funny, self-deprecating selves instead of what they became toward the end.

Without much medical care left on Earth, those who were a little older or with health problems didn't have many options in terms of treatment. All the doctors and surgeons were preparing to leave on the ships, and most of them on the first and second ones. So when my mom was diagnosed with cancer in the late 2120s, we knew she didn't have a lot of time left. Shortly after, my dad became sick and they tried doing everything they could, for the rest of their lives, to get me on a ship to another planet.

They were turned away again and again. Without money or connections, they had no way to get me on a ship. To the people in charge, they were just two sick, elderly people with a kid who wouldn't be much help either. The only real shot we had was for me to luck into a spot on the third ship as part of the ticket lottery.

Honestly, though? I wanted nothing to do with being on the third ship. The only ship I cared about was Auryn's, the second one to leave, which I had no chance to be on. People on different ships will almost certainly never see each other again. But a ship and someone left here on Earth meeting again? That's possible, and it's partly what keeps me going on those long, wind-filled nights.

Nights like tonight. We've battened down the hatches on our tents, tied them as hard as we could to our stakes and found as secluded a place as possible. We'll often just roll out a sleeping pack, but the wind is picking up and it can get so bad that it hurts your eyes with the dust particles flying in the air. Even though we're already coated in a thin layer of dust and dirt, spending the night in a windstorm and then trying to get clean in the morning? No thanks.

We always pick a place to set up camp off the beaten path, so while during the day we often try to walk along the old interstate system of roads, when we stop, we head a quarter mile or farther away from the road to set up camp and sleep.

Today was an especially long day. The sun was beating down on the concrete all around us, and it made it feel ten degrees warmer than it already was. Most days reach well into the 90s, temperature wise, so walking on the road felt like it was over 100. It's a tough decision to make, because taking this route means the fastest way to get where we're going, but it also means our water packs only last us two to three days since we're sweating so much.

I'll often take off my thin, light tan long-sleeved jacket and drape it over my head and neck for shade. Underneath, I have a green tank top, which has certainly seen better days, with small rips and holes along the bottom. A few months ago, I grabbed a pair of scissors on a whim and made Esha chop my hair. I hadn't cut it since before my parents were sick, so it was almost all the way down my back. She had only ever cut her own hair before, but I trusted her.

When done, she said my cut was a "Voluminous pixie cut for triangle faces."

When she told me that, I burst out laughing and asked her what on earth that meant. She smiled, then cracked up and showed me the magazine page that she looked at to use as reference. It was one of the old magazines my mom kept around.

"You kinda look like the model in this picture, you've both got that same dark brown hair and face shape, that's why I picked it," Esha teased.

"By the way, you've never even asked me the name of my haircut," she says with her smile still spread across her face.

"Well, it couldn't possibly have as cool a name as the uh, large pixie triangle I have," I responded, already forgetting what mine was called.

"It's a wolf cut. I picked it because it sounds badass," Esha says.

Indeed, it does, I think to myself while nodding and looking at her dirty blonde hair glowing the sunlight through the windows.

Keeping cool in all this heat is priority number one when we're traveling, along with being safe, which means avoiding the Raiders at all costs. That's why we camp so far from the road.

Even with all the precautions, we take turns standing guard. 2.5 hours a shift, 3 shifts in total. We haven't seen the Raiders in a few days, but they move as the population moves, and more people are trying to find their way to Buffalo or Toronto, like us. After two full years living in Cleveland after the second ship took off, there weren't many supplies left.

Tonight I have the second shift, the worst of the three. I'm up for the first hour of Garven's shift trying to get comfortable and fall asleep. Ever since I lost my parents and Auryn, I've been a terrible sleeper. All I think about is the few weeks before the second ship took off. Auryn would spend each day with her family, and each night at my parents' apartment.

Most nights, we'd head up to the roof of the building, roll out some mats, and look at the stars. We'd talk often about how before we knew it, Auryn would be flying through all that darkness. The first few days I cried so often. She would put her arm under my head, pull me in tight, and hug me until I had no tears left.

"Don't worry, my little penguin. I'll be back in a couple of years to pick you up and get out of here," she would say.

I loved it when she called me her "little penguin." She told me she read in a book that when penguins were still around, they would mate for life. From that same book, she tore out a picture of a penguin and always kept it on her. It's that thought I finally drift away to tonight.

A little over an hour later, Garven wakes me up for my shift. I'm going to be exhausted for tomorrow's walk, that much I'm sure of, but I've been exhausted for two years, so I'm pretty used to it.

While on lookout, I listen intently to the sounds of the night, which tonight will be the wind whipping against the side of the tents and dead branches being blown around. I set my watch to make sure I wake up Esha when I'm supposed to. It's just precautionary, since Esha always wakes up on her own and she never sleeps through when she's supposed to be awake. For as long as I've known her, she's been the most reliable person I know.

Besides our regular walking tomorrow, we're also going to try and search through some nearby houses to see if we can find anything valuable: Shoes, food rations, soap, rope, and first aid gear. If we're extremely lucky, we might find some left behind water filters. Most people who went on the trips left plenty behind, so when we stay in the areas along the freshwater lakes we get a little luckier finding the necessities.

After setting my watch, I have another bite of my food ration, which I save specifically to eat during my shift of the night. Garven always finishes his entire meal well before we decide to sleep. As Esha and I have heard almost every day since we started all living and traveling together, he gets bad heartburn if he eats right before bed.

I, on the other hand, am hungry all the time, so I try to leave myself a bite to wake up to so that I don't spend my entire watch thinking only about food.

Esha seems to save a lot of food until her night watch duty. It's a small thing to notice but halfway through all her meals, I see her wrap them back up and place them in her backpack. She seems to enjoy eating in the peace and quiet of the nighttime. Her thoughts and her food, her own.

CHAPTER 3: AURYN

The anticipation was palpable. Fourteen months into their journey, passengers on the ship The Amelia Earhart were just one month away from their new home. The usual hum of activity of the people on board grew louder with each passing day. It was especially noticeable amid the quiet sounds of the engines firing and filters humming.

On this day, many passengers aboard were congregating at the front of the ship: A several story wide and four level tall window that, for most of the past year, had shown little but the all-consuming darkness and pin pricks of light from distant stars. Stars that Auryn wished so many times to have habitable planets surrounding them. Anything to get her off this ship sooner. Now, it's showing long distance images of the planet they are going to attempt to make home: Planet B.52.C. Affectionately known around the ship as "The Gray" for the swirling masses of enormous gray clouds that obscure portions of the surface.

At first, the trip seemed like a vacation to Auryn; it seemed just like her grandparents used to describe taking cruises in the 2050s and 60s. Fun activities on board and group bonding exercises to get to know one another. But cruises only lasted a week or two. Here, trapped in this amazing feat of technology, it was starting to feel more like a prison to her now. With constant long lines, breakdowns, and delays for any of the entertainment activities on board, most leisure time was spent frustrated or worse: Bored.

Auryn, feeling as fresh as you can after a two-month cryosleep, was excited to land on The Gray. To be able to finally breathe air that hadn't been recycled through other passengers' lungs a thousand times.

Every passenger on the ship had to cryosleep for two months out of every eight months, for a total of four months on the trip. They were told it was for mental health reasons, but she assumes it's so that the ship doesn't run out of food or supplies. To feed, clean, and entertain 80,000 people on a 15-month space journey in a floating can is a delicate operation, so having 20,000 people in cryosleep at any given time allows for a little more room on the ship.

As far as any of them knew, they could be the last humans left in the universe. Auryn tries not to linger on that thought for too long. She tries not to think about Garven and Finley, left back on Earth. Were they still alive? She doesn't allow her mind to wander too far into that question.

The most she allowed herself to think about that question was when she was preparing for her first cryosleep. There, in her small pod, waiting for the slow release of gas to help her fall asleep, she folded her arms on her chest and hugged her favorite possession: A torn-out picture of a penguin.

She thought about Fin, and about Garven.

Garven was her protective older brother. Anytime she needed to head outside of the apartment, he would go with her. If she wanted to go visit Finley? Garven would just happen to be walking in the same direction and walk along with her. She never actually saw him hang out with other people his age, but he always had a pretend reason to be heading in the same direction that she was.

Even though he was obviously lying to her, Auryn never mentioned that she knew. Auryn liked having him there with her. Not for protection, since she always thought that she could handle herself. Because they all knew that in a few short months, Auryn, her brother Forbin, and their parents Arthur and Alia would be leaving both the planet and Garven behind. Auryn wanted to spend as much time with him as possible before that happened.

Leaving or staying was an impossible decision for a then 16-year-old Auryn to make, so her parents made it for her; they had four tickets for The Amelia Earhart, and she was to be on that ship no matter what. In the grand scheme of potentially saving humanity, it wasn't much of a decision at all, but it was devastating for her. It's part of the reason she took her first cryosleep at the end of the first week on the ship. She couldn't bear to be in her feelings anymore, so a two-month nap felt like the only way to regroup, to stop thinking about what she left behind. Auryn woke up the same way she fell asleep: Holding onto the picture of a penguin, thinking about Finley. It was like no time had passed at all.

Over the course of their journey, several people on the ship tried to get close to her. There was Petyr, the son of her parents' friends. He was a nice enough boy, always gentle and kind to her. Sharing his desserts and walking all the different floors of the ship with her. They would almost always end up strolling through the secondary lounge on floor 41. It was a gigantic space, 500 feet long and almost as wide. It had holographic fountains and benches everywhere to sit.

They would pump in nature sounds, and after so many hours spent there, Auryn knew the pattern and could make the call of the next bird. At first, she thought it funny that she could tell but as the weeks went by, it drove her crazy that they decided to only use an hour of calls before repeating.

As much as Auryn enjoyed the company of Petyr, she knew they would never be more than friends. She wasn't interested in Petyr, or any of the other boys on the ship.

His flirting with her lasted several months, but finally he asked her directly, "Would you want to be with me?"

Auryn has always hated having tough conversations, but she told him she wasn't capable of having the same feeling for him that he had for her. As she expected, he slowly came around less and less, until it was nothing more than a halfhearted wave and weak smile in the hallways.

Auryn's mom was disappointed in her, even if she wouldn't say it directly. Petyr had a future ahead of him. He was good-looking, studied the ship's systems, and was going to help with setting up the new colony when they arrived at

B.52.C. She'd never come out and say it, but repopulating was also of utmost importance once the colony was built and stabilized, and she didn't want Auryn to miss out on *all the good ones* to procreate with when she was old enough.

The thought made her shudder. First, because she had no interest at all in procreating, and secondly, she was going to be on the ship heading back to Earth to pick up any survivors that had left and had made it to Toronto. That was the plan with Fin and Garven. They had 3 years to make it from Cleveland to Toronto. The 15-month trip here, six months to set up the colony and make sure the ship was in good condition, and 15 months back. All told, Auryn was willing to give up three years of her life aboard a spaceship if it meant rescuing her brother and Fin.

But now, growing larger and larger in her view through the window, Planet B.52.C. At least for a little while, she was going to have much more on her mind: Helping to save what's left of humanity.

CHAPTER 4: RAIDERS

As expected, I wake up completely exhausted. I try to stretch my arms out, but my tent is so small that they hit the opening flap immediately. I turn onto my side and realize the pain in my leg that started a few days ago was getting worse.

Reluctantly, I sit up and begin my day by opening the zipper. Esha is up already because she had last shift last night. From how quiet it is, I doubt Garven is up yet.

"Morning," I say, my throat so dry I'm barely able to get out the words.

"Mornin', Fin," she replied. "Ready for a long one today?

"Not really, no," I say while chuckling. Esha gives me a quick smile, nods, and says,

"Yeah, me neither."

As we talk, a rustling noise comes from Garven's tent. We both look over as the zipper slides up. Garven's a pretty big guy, and seeing a muscular, 6-foot-tall dude trying to get out of a tiny one-person tent will always be funny to me.

"Alright, on the list of things for us to find today is a bigger tent for me," he says once he gets to his feet.

With that, he stretches out, and his back pops so loudly both Esha and I can hear it. He notices that both of our eyebrows are raised looking at him.

"That's exactly why I need to find a new tent. I'm curled up like a damn bear cub in there."

Esha and I both nod, and agree we'll keep an eye out when we search through houses today.

For as tired and sore as we all are, Garven is talking a big game this morning about how far we're going to march today. I've never seen him this determined in the few weeks we've been walking.

"We're only a week outside Buffalo now and once we're there, we'll be able to rest for a bit," he says. "We just need to go through houses one more time and fill up our water packs wherever we can. I don't know about you two, but I'm almost out."

"You'll all be happy to know that when I was walking around and patrolling the area last night, I found a small pond not too far from here," Esha says.

"You know you're not supposed to be wandering around alone, Esha, that's not safe," Garven replies.

"I didn't even hear you leave the area, how is that possible?" I ask her.

"See, Garven, I'm so stealthy Fin didn't even know I was gone, and you know how lightly this one sleeps," Esha says while pointing at me.

Garven grumbles to himself and starts to grab the things needed to make some breakfast out of his pack.

"I'm gonna grab some dry sticks. Fin, get the pan ready so we can make a quick hot breakfast. Esha, could you fill up and filter one of the bags from that pond so we can use it to cook?"

"Sí, capitán" Esha replies.

Garven hates it when Esha calls him that. It's her way of letting him know that he's getting a little bossy around us. She loves keeping him in check.

Esha and Garven didn't know each other that much before we became unlikely travelers. Even though she lived with my parents and me the last several years, he almost never came inside our apartment. When I would visit Auryn at her family's place, Esha would rarely come along.

"I want you and Auryn to have some alone time, and that's hard to do with me third wheeling around," she would often say.

I'm sure it was partially that, but I also sensed that she didn't want to leave my parents alone at home either. They took her in when she had nowhere else to go, and she felt forever indebted to them for that. They were really sick and frail toward the end, and she always wanted to make sure she was there for them.

We cook up some breakfast by reheating a couple of our dried food packs, along with some filtered water, over a small open flame. We only do this a couple of times a week because it's so time consuming, but Garven knows that if he wants us to hike an extra-long time in the hot sun, we are going to need more than a dried ration bar.

Once the meals were cooking, we started packing up our tents and camp area. Once we're all ready and the pan is cooled, we can take off. We like to hike for a few hours in the early morning, and then when the noon sun hits, find as shady an area as possible and stop for a few hours. Today, that rest time will be looking through some houses for supplies.

Before we officially head out for the day, we walk over to the pond nearby and fill enough into our packs to last each of us a few days. It was really fortunate that Esha did spot this, as much as we don't want to encourage her wandering off. I only had about a half day's worth of water left as well, and anytime you had to venture to the shores of Lake Erie to fill your packs, you were asking for danger. We've only had to once so far, a few days ago, and it was almost disastrous.

. . .

We were running out of water, and couldn't find a pond or river nearby, so we decided to try the edge of the lake. At first, we hid near some abandoned buildings a couple hundred feet from the shore. We were already going to have our midday rest in them, so it was a perfect location.

They were the types of buildings you could see in almost any town left standing in North America. The outer bricks mostly crumbled, the inner concrete and beams exposed to the elements. All of them stacked up near each other along the waterfront, but not touching. Esha said it was to prevent fires from spreading. Some as tall as seven or eight stories, others low rise buildings stretched hundreds of feet long.

If you got close enough, you could see the old and broken rebar sticking out in all directions, the steel support beams rusting. You'd be convinced that with the mildest of shoves, the entire structure will come crashing down. All the windows were already broken out, either by people sneaking in or the harsh wind and storms blowing debris into them.

Esha climbed up a few stories and was on lookout with one of our few flares. I made sure to tell her to be careful before she went up, because this building looked even worse than some of the others. She rolled her eyes a little, then nodded and climbed up to the top – five full floors. To get up to floor two, she hoisted herself up with pure upper body strength through a crumbled and open area of the wall. She gave the second story floor a solid stomp and yelled back down,

"See? Sturdy as it needs to be!"

It wasn't exactly convincing. One single 5 '5" person, even as strong as Esha is, probably wasn't going to collapse the rebar and concrete floor. It's more the walls and top of the building I'm worried about.

Once on the second floor, she disappeared for a few minutes before we could see her lift herself up on the ledge of the top floor and look out over the lake. Her upper body strength and core never cease to amaze me. Every time we're in a situation where we need to climb, or lift, Esha is the first one to run toward the problem.

Garven and I were in charge of filling the packs, which takes longer than you might expect since it must go through the filtration system. Once it filters out any harmful bacteria, metals, and nitrates, it's safe to go into our water packs.

The packs themselves hold about 2.5 gallons, and we had three of them to fill. We were gonna be here, out in the open, for at least 15 minutes.

While looking out to see if anyone else was around, I noticed something unusual: What appeared to be new tree saplings close to the edge of the lake. Most of the existing plant life and trees around are old growth. They survived as other life dwindled because they were the tallest or strongest and could get to the limited rainwater more easily than the smaller vegetation. Whenever we did see any new growth, it tended to be one lonely, sickly-looking sapling, not a collection of a half dozen or so, already 7 to 8 feet high.

I had to investigate, and Garven was a more than willing partner. We approached carefully, making sure to keep watch on Esha and check back toward the building line, and to make sure no one could surprise us. Although at this point, this far out in the open, there wasn't anywhere to hide if we were spotted.

We got close enough to the trees and the most unexpected emotion came over me: Hope. I immediately started to tear up and tried wiping them away before Garven noticed. He isn't the sentimental type, after all, and I was expecting him to give me one of his patented little lectures about not getting my hopes up.

"Fin," I heard his voice say. My shoulders tensed up as I waited for the rest.

"I get it. I'm not sure I'd ever see trees growing out in the wild again. Not like this, at least."

He didn't further elaborate, but he didn't need to. This wasn't something we were expecting to see, maybe ever. Yet there we were on the shores of the lake, witnessing new life.

"I think this is an Eastern Redbud," he then said. "Make sure you tell Esha that I said that. She's not the only one who knows some plants."

Garven smiled his wide, beaming smile, and laughed.

"We should get to filling," he then said, and I nodded in agreement.

We were chatting away and just wrapping up the second pack when the flare went off. We looked toward the building to see Esha waving frantically and pointing farther down toward the water line.

I turned to look, and our worst fears were confirmed: Raiders, a half mile down the shoreline, making a beeline toward us. I looked at Garven with a panicked look, but he was as calm as ever.

"Get everything, head to Esha, and find a good hiding spot in the buildings," he said.

"You have to come with," I started to say, but before I could even finish my sentence, he had his pack on his back and was making his way down the shoreline the opposite direction of the Raiders, jogging lightly.

We had talked about this on our walks in the prior days, but I was hoping we'd never actually have to do it. He was going to lead them away by staying in their sightline, then double back when we were hidden away and he had successfully lost them.

I flung my backpack over my shoulder, grabbed Esha's by the cloth handle on top, and started rushing toward the large, abandoned group of buildings. When I got close, I saw Esha finishing her scramble down to the side of the building. Using mostly the outside of the building, she got herself down by grabbing onto a ledge and lowering her body down far enough to jump to the next floor down. I hated watching every second of it.

"Follow me, I saw some good spots when I was climbing up," she said, and I nodded.

I used an old crate to boost myself up to the second floor. She then led me through a series of collapsed walls, sunken floors, and open ceilings. I had no idea the building was even that big, but Esha was a pro at assessing a situation and figuring out a solution.

I wonder if she's terrified, I thought to myself, remembering what happened to her and her family. But I couldn't concentrate on that. We needed to find a place to hide right away and then worry about Garven making it back.

Finally, after another minute, she pointed at a collapsed part of the building that we could barely squeeze through. The wall of what was probably a large closet had started to collapse, and it was leaning across to another wall. The gap at the front was no more than two feet wide, and it was so dark inside that I couldn't tell how deep it went.

I shoved my bag and both water packs through first, just barely fitting, and then slid through myself, adding to the scratches and cuts I've already received from a week's worth of sleeping off the beaten trail.

Esha then shoved her bag at me, and the space was getting tight.

"I don't know if I can fit. Stay with our packs and I'll find another spot," she said.

Before I could say another word, she disappeared from my view. There were a thousand thoughts running through my head, but the main one was staying quiet. I was holding Esha's bag and it was heavy. I tried to bend down and place it on the ground, but it slipped from my hand and created a loud, echoing noise.

My shoulders tensed up as the gravity of my mistake sunk in. I didn't mean to drop the bag, of course, but my intentions had nothing to do with whether I get kidnapped. If they heard it and figured out where I was, there was nowhere to run to, nowhere I could escape. Right then it was me, the darkness, and any luck I might've had left.

I took a deep breath and started to listen for any sounds I could make out from the warehouse. The silence was almost immediately interrupted by an unfamiliar voice.

"Come out, come out wherever you are. I heard you in here, my little stowaway," the man yelled. You could hear the words coated in arrogance as he said them.

He used the word "stowaway" entirely wrong, and I hated him immediately for it.

"You can't hide forever; these are our buildings," a second voice said.

I slowed my breathing and tried to think. At least two of them came toward the building, which meant Garven might have three people searching him. I racked my brain for ideas to get out of there, but my anxiety started ramping up, and the ability to think clearly slowly faded. Sometimes my panic gets so bad I black out and fall to the ground. Most often, I get tunnel vision, sweat badly, and breathe loudly, all things you don't want to happen while being hunted by Raiders.

I also get really bad nausea, so maybe I can throw up on them and try to escape, I thought to myself, only half joking.

"We know you're in here, and we're going to get your little boyfriend who ditched you along the water, too. Might as well give yourself up now and we might even take pity on you," the first voice said.

My little boyfriend? I thought to myself in disbelief.

I didn't know Garven that well before the second ship took off. He was four years older than me, and when I did hang out at Auryn's place, he tended to stick to himself. The only thing I really knew about him was how much he liked studying and working out.

He would regularly walk through their living room after doing sit-ups and push-ups in the hallway of their building. Sweat glistening off his muscular black shoulders. Back then, his hair was a little longer on the top and faded as it got toward his ears. Auryn did an alright job cutting it with the supplies they had. I always thought it was unfair how smart and attractive Auryn's entire family is.

He'd give a friendly wave to me, and oftentimes he would tease Auryn about whatever embarrassing thing he could remember. Like all older brothers, he liked to make her feel a little bit uncomfortable around her partner. It was especially easy since we were teenagers, and he was nearing twenty.

I think part of the reason both Garven and Auryn studied so often, and knew so much, was because of their parents. They were some of the smartest people I'd ever met, which didn't land you on the first ship but certainly was enough to get you on the second. Their mom's ability to not only code, but create advanced navigation projections, and their dad's ability to fix hardware issues, made them a near lock to take them and their family on a ship.

Everyone knew that each family only received four passes, and Garven had two parents, and two siblings not old enough to take care of themselves. He always says that he never wanted to be on any of the ships anyways. That it would have been selfish of him to take a spot that belonged to someone who needed it more, but he had to have wanted to leave, right?

Who in their right mind wanted to stay behind and watch the world die?

Who in their right mind would want to be here, fending for their lives, and maybe sacrificing themselves for two people they barely knew two years ago? But that's exactly what he was doing right now.

My racing thoughts were once again interrupted by the voice of the first man, but he was much, much closer this time. I could hear him, strangely, singing. Each step of his movement was a beat for the soft melody he was trying to serenade me with.

He was inching closer and closer until I could see him, not 10 feet outside the crumbled wall and ceiling I was hiding in. Getting ever so close. My heart was pounding, my vision starting to close in. I slowly and quietly pulled my old, rusty knife from my side pocket, and then:

A loud crash toward the other side of the building. It caught his attention, and he changed course and made his way away from me. For now, at least, I can breathe again.

A half minute passed, and I heard the faint sounds of one of the men, I think the one that was by me? He seemed to be yelling from a different floor of the building. Then, the scream came. It definitely wasn't Esha's voice that was screaming, but if I had to bet, I'd say she was somehow involved.

After that, I could hear him running on one of the floors above me, toward the water, yelling obscenities to no one in particular.

"Hey! HEY! If you can hear me," he yelled toward the direction Garven was heading, "Cassian is… He's not okay!" Cassian must have been the other man's name.

Suddenly Esha's face appears in the opening.

"Hand me the stuff, we have to go now," she says.

"What was all that? What happened?" I responded.

"No time. Let's go."

As quietly as I could I handed Esha her backpack, with a mostly empty water pack. After I handed her mine, I slipped out through the rubble, gashing my leg in the process.

I should remember to wrap that later, I thought to myself.

"We have to get out of this building and find Garven, they'll be coming for us here," Esha said.

I assumed this had to do with the yelling from a minute ago, but I decided I'd catch up on the details later. We quietly headed back toward the wall we came in, stepping over crumbled brick and concrete, the gray floor coated in a thick powder of dust. If they were smarter, those guys could have followed our footsteps to exactly where I was. The thought sent shivers up my spine. All the while, the man kept yelling toward the shore and buildings.

"Cassian needs help! We need the med pack!" He kept screaming repeatedly.

As we climbed down onto the crates and reached the ground outside below, we looked toward the shore. In the near distance, we saw the three other Raiders running toward the building. They were running right by the saplings Garven and I were at a measly 20 minutes prior. I froze for a moment, having no idea if they'd spotted us or not. Esha grabbed my arm, and we took off toward the next building over. It was a low two-story building several blocks long.

We made our way through a similar crumbled maze as the first building. Collapsed walls, rusty rebar, and empty crates and machines everywhere. From the looks of it, this building must have made huge parts for something, maybe vehicles or building equipment. I couldn't help but notice some of the machines in there were easily 50 or 60 feet long. The industry along the lakes must have been massive before the Earth started dying.

It wasn't all just the planet warming. In the few history books we were able to get our hands on, I read about rivers being poisoned in the 2020s. That killed farmland and animals. Once that started happening, food shortages became more common, causing yet more fighting over lands between countries. Once populations started moving out, factories like this just shut down, and began the process of crumbling.

We finally made it out to the other side of the building and were immediately startled.

"Man, am I really ugly enough to startle you?" Asked Garven, with a big, joyous grin.

"I've never been happier to see you in my entire life," I responded.

"We'll have time to chit chat later, we still have to get the hell out of here," Esha said sternly.

We quickly but quietly made our way along the building sides, on the opposite side of the lake. Two mostly-filled water packs were going to have to be enough for a few days. Especially considering that the Raiders were that close, we knew we'd have to keep the pace up and walk longer than normal the rest of the day.

As the lake and buildings faded from our view, I asked Esha what had happened. She stayed quiet for a minute, contemplating what to say.

"The guy was right by me, and I saw that the wall between us was about ready to collapse, so I…" she paused for another minute, obviously replaying what had happened in her head. "I took a chance and shoved the wall onto him…" She trailed off for another moment, "he screamed for a second and then just stopped. I checked to see if the other guy was around, and it didn't sound like it, so I took off running to come find you."

Maybe 15 seconds of silence went by. Long enough for my mind to start to wander. She crushed him. Is he dead? Did those other guys dig him out? How pissed are they going to be?

Could they be tracking us right now?

Garven and I looked at each other, unsure of what to say. I've never had to kill anyone, and while Garven had been in plenty of fights, I'm not sure he had either.

"In this world, you have to do what you have to do," Garven finally says. "If it wasn't him, it was you. The sad truth is it might be a lot more like that while trying to get to Toronto."

If that was his inspirational speech, it could use some work, but he was right. They weren't just going to stop looking for us. The best-case scenario would have been they take all our stuff and leave us to die. Worst case scenario?

I literally shuddered at the thought, and Esha notices. She nodded her head. We marched on.

CHAPTER 5: ESHA

Esha's parents and my parents were friends for as long as I can remember, way before either of us were ever born. Our moms were colleagues at work for a while and immediately became friends. There isn't really a time in my life where I don't remember Esha being in it. Birthdays, holidays, playing around the neighborhood during the cooler months, Esha was pretty much always around. She was a year younger than I but was always the more mature one of the two of us.

A year before the first ship took off, there was a surprise knock on our door around 1a.m. A knock on the door at one in the morning is always a surprise, and rarely a good one.

My dad gained the strength to shuffle toward the door, with me not far behind him, clutching a pan I grabbed from the kitchen, trying to look as menacing as a 14-year-old can look. When he opened it, slowly and with a pronounced shake in his hand, there Esha stood trembling, with clean streaks from her eyes to her chin. I'd never seen her crying before.

My dad brought her into the apartment and, as calmly as he could, asked her what happened. Where were her parents? She sat motionless on our couch for a few minutes, trying to sniffle in the snot coming out of her nose. When that didn't work, she took her sleeve and used it to wipe her face, smearing the dirt on her cheeks along with it.

Finally, she looked up, first staring at my dad, then me, directly in the eyes, and in the faintest voice I've ever heard, said,

"The Raiders."

Everyone on earth knew about the Raiders. By the 2110s, as populations shrunk and the last central government in North America was crumbling from a lack of money, resources, and all the things that always keep governments in power, guerilla groups popped up to steal from people and protect their own.

One of the last memories I had with my mom was the both of us wondering aloud how exactly these groups were called "guerilla" groups. Language is funny like that sometimes. What used to be common knowledge becomes the knowledge only of scholars before they, too, pass away, and that knowledge can be lost forever.

By the time I was born, the entire population of the Americas was huddled within a few hundred miles of each other around the last remaining non-contaminated freshwater lakes: Erie and Ontario.

Before the ships took off, the main population centers were the cities of Cleveland, Toronto and Buffalo, but even then, the cities themselves only housed around 175,000 people each. With every passing month, it seemed like more and more people were joining these gangs.

I understood the desire. "Eat or Be Eaten" was painted all over buildings and bridges, the slogan of the Raiders. Even though I'm pretty sure no one had started with cannibalism yet, the principle was the same. So, when Esha arrived at our doorstep that night and uttered "The Raiders," we immediately knew something horrible had happened.

By the early 2120s, they were the one main group had taken over most of the Great Lakes area. Small groups wearing green bandanas, the left arm of their jacket cut off, and with distinct patches. They would roam around searching for the neighborhoods that couldn't defend themselves and steal food, water, anything they could. If your community was large enough, they tended not to come around, but by the late 2120s, our little neighborhood had shrunk to a couple thousand people.

That's when we started to notice them more. At first, they just had people hanging around the streets of our neighborhood in Cleveland. I'd notice the familiar green bandana on the corner of Euclid and 116th, standing there and observing. Probably counting how many adults were walking around. So, our neighborhood started some patrols. My dad said that they wanted to show them they couldn't just come around here and steal from the folks that were just trying to survive.

Then, the announcements about the shuttles were made and any semblance of community that had persevered up to that point vanished. Some neighbors were selected for the trips, some were not. How could you go about holding a conversation with someone who the world deemed "worth saving" when the same courtesy wasn't granted to you? People leaving on the shuttles started pulling less and less of their own weight.

I don't begrudge them, of course. They had decisions to make and training to complete. They weren't going to take the midnight to 4am patrol to ward off the Raiders anymore.

What that meant for the rest of us, though, was figuring out how to either fight or avoid them. Lots of families started moving into close proximity. This included Esha's family moving just a block down from ours. Each building on the block would leave their large, solar charged spotlight on each night so the street was pretty lit up. Anyone who did still want to patrol the streets at night could, but it was sporadic at best. Our shrinking community had become ripe for the Raiders to pick on, so they did.

Slowly we heard more and more stories about nighttime robberies in the streets, then inside people's homes and before long, it became more than robberies. As people weren't willing to give up what little they had left, fights ensued and lives were lost.

Young, old, people who were counted on as providers. It didn't matter, if you had what they wanted, they were going to take it.

Esha has never shared with me what it was the Raiders were coming for that night, but what they left was a young child covered in dirt, wandering the streets in search of the family she hoped would take her in.

CHAPTER 6: CALENDULA

Garven is keeping up a quick pace, even in the blistering sun, but I'm starting to fall behind. I haven't said anything to the group yet, but the cut on my leg that I got from squeezing into and out of my hiding spot in the warehouse is starting to feel rough. Each step is getting harder to take, and I am dreading the moment that's fast approaching when I tell them what's wrong.

I feel especially guilty because Garven already sacrificed himself by the lake in order to draw some Raiders away from us. Esha gave me a good hiding spot and then pushed a wall onto a guy to get us both out. That has to change a person and, through all that, all I did was hide and injure myself.

I'm feeling like more and more of a dead weight each day that we're together, and now this. I'm going to have to stop before we normally would for lunch, just in the hopes that Esha has some sort of miracle plant cure for this damn cut.

Looking ahead, I see the interstate is a slight uphill for the next few miles. Heat lines rise up from the concrete and cars that broke down 30 or more years ago sit rusting sporadically between the lanes. They've been picked clean already, seats and electronics taken long ago. Most of these cars are from the 2050s and 2060s, the last decades they were made on any sort of scale. While they didn't use gasoline like all the antique cars before that, they still produced a lot of waste to make the batteries that they used.

From what my parents said, you could still see them on the roads occasionally until the early 2100s, but their parts were scarce and the only people who could really afford them were a small number of politicians and the rich who were left.

As we pass by one, I look inside. Even though we've passed a hundred or more in the last few days, I was hoping maybe this one had a seat left in it so I could take a break quickly. Just like all the ones I'd seen before it did not, and there's no way I'm going to make it all that way to lunch time without resting first. Finally, I yell forward.

"Hey, I think I need to stop for a moment."

Garven turns around and immediately looks annoyed.

"We've only been walking a few hours, what's the matter?"

I sit against the hot concrete barrier at the side of the road and slowly roll up a pantleg. When it reaches the wound, I wince and let out a small gasp. Looking down, I see that it's definitely gotten worse over the past half a day. Looking at it makes me feel a little bit queasy.

"Fin, what the hell? When did this happen?" Asks Esha.

I sigh deeply; I hate having to tell them.

"When we were running from the Raiders, as I was getting out of the hiding spot, my leg was sliced on some rebar. I didn't think much of it at the time, but now that it's getting worse I thought I should tell you."

"That was like four days ago! Why didn't you say anything before now? We could have had this healed up by now, Fin!" Esha responds.

This might be the most upset I've ever seen her.

"Alright, well, let's do what we can to patch you up now," said Garven.

"I—I don't know if what we have is going to heal it. I have a little bit of calendula and a little bit of chamomile. I'll apply the chamomile while boiling up a little bit of the calendula," said Esha, mostly to herself.

"Alright, let's get off the road. It looks like there are some houses over that way. After you're done patching Fin up, we can look through them since we found nothing from the ones this morning," says Garven.

We all nod and head over toward a rundown old housing development a quarter mile from the road.

I had a feeling Esha would have something to help. Every time we're walking along a path, she is scouring the ground to find any new plants that might be helpful. There aren't a lot, but along the freshwater lakes there are patches where plants I've never even seen are starting to grow.

She said it's because of the wind. The first time she mentioned it she must have seen the confusion on my face. How could the wind be the reason plants from far away areas are growing here? Then she explained.

"The wind can carry seeds such long distances. Especially when there's so much dry land, it doesn't get caught in grass and weeds like it used to. So, it just continues to blow along until it reaches an area that's damp, which for the past 10 years is pretty much only Lake Erie and Lake Ontario."

"Now, a lot of seeds die along the way," she continued, "too hot, too dry, any critters that are left will eat them when they see them. But some of them made it all the way up here, so when I can, I like to grab a few leaves and a few seeds. You never know when you'll need them."

She was right about that. Apparently, the calendula and chamomile will help slow the spread of the infection and even help to heal it a little.

"It's not going to heal quickly, so your leg is still going to hurt for a few days at least, but it will hopefully be enough to get you to Buffalo where we can really get you patched up," she says.

Oftentimes during our hikes, I turn around to see her catching back up to Garven and I, and she lets us know what she's found. Yesterday it was this very chamomile plant, telling us,

"You know, a long time ago this used to only grow overseas, but it's a hearty plant that grows in a lot of places around here now. It needs a certain amount of cool air to grow successfully and even though it's pretty hot in these parts, it's nothing compared to a few hundred miles south. Plus, the soil around the lakes is still nutrient-rich, which it also needs. It's a pretty good time to be chamomile in these parts."

It's one of the few things that she talks about that you can hear excitement in her voice.

"So how long do you think this'll take?" Garven asks impatiently.

"Well, I have to make the chamomile into a paste to apply while the water is boiling for the other stuff, but it shouldn't take more than a half hour, maybe forty-five minutes," Esha responds.

"Well, we might as well have lunch now, then do the house search. Then maybe by 2:30 or 3 we can be back on the road. How does that sound to you, Fin?" Garven says.

"That sounds like a good plan to me, Garven," I respond.

I can tell he doesn't really believe me. He stares at me for a couple extra seconds before his gaze turns toward Esha.

He walks up to her and has a brief conversation that I can't hear. She nods while he's talking, and for a moment they both look over at me.

"I mean, I'm right here guys, you can talk to me," I say.

They both turn toward each other and continue their conversation. It feels like they're my parents and they're trying to figure out what my punishment is.

"Alright, it's settled. Let's have some lunch, have Esha patch you up, and go from there. It's going to be a long one today, and for the next couple of days as well," Garven finally says.

Esha first pulls out the chamomile, which has a round, yellow center filled with seeds and individual white petals overlapping each other, making the whole flower circular. It's a pretty plant when all the tiny yellow seeds are there, but that's not usually the case. She then pulls out the calendula, one of which is yellow, and another is orange. They each have hundreds of small, thin, colorful petals and tiny, long seeds that stick out from the middle in different shades of yellow and brown.

As she starts her process, I begin to pull lunch out from my backpack. Today it consists of some dehydrated meal packs that we made ourselves before we left. Making the meals was one of my least favorite things to do. First, we chopped everything we could: Lots of veggies from rooftop gardens, some proteins, and a small amount of old grains. Then we gathered all the old metal baking trays from all the apartments and started a small fire. We kept it super low, placed each baking sheet above it, and just waited for everything to dehydrate.

Occasionally I would zone out and almost burn the food, but for the most part we were able to shovel those into the silver foil packets and close them up really tight. An arduous process, but one that's given us enough food to last for a few months if we really need to stretch it.

Normally, I like to add a pretty decent amount of water to mine— it makes it easier to eat — but I've been a little more nervous ever since the incident by the lake, so I only add a little.

I eat slowly, so I'm only halfway into the pack when Esha starts applying the first paste. Even though I knew it was about to happen, I gasped audibly when the first amount was wiped on.

"Does it hurt?" Asks Esha.

"The paste, no, the wound, yeah maybe a little," I laugh uncomfortably while I say this.

I catch Esha glancing over at Garven for a moment. The expression on his face doesn't change, no doubt because he doesn't want me to see his reaction.

"It's pretty bad, isn't it?" I ask, hoping they lie to me in a way that makes me believe them.

"Well, it's not great, but you're not going to lose a leg or anything. I have enough stuff to make sure the infection doesn't get any worse over the next few days, but we're going to have to count on you to struggle through and make it to Buffalo with us, alright?" Esha replies.

This is the most Esha has ever reminded me of her parents. Her mother was always so straight and to the point, but there was a warmth to the honesty. If there was a person in my life I'd want to deliver me bad news, I'd choose Esha every time.

The bad news is that the walk to Buffalo will no doubt be slowed down by me. It'll also be painful, but in a week we'll be in Buffalo and, if the rumors are true, they have doctors and medicine over there. So, the best thing I can do is grin and bear it for the next week and rest afterwards.

"Hey, Fin," Garven says, cutting through my slowly spiraling mental health, "settle a little bet for us, will ya?"

"Um, alright, what's up?" I reply.

"Is 'Fin' spelled with one or two 'N's at the end?" As Garven says this, he looks over at Esha. She smirks. Apparently, they've been debating this for a while and have finally decided to just flat out ask me. Now that I think of it, there's been a couple times where they've jokingly asked to see my notebook, probably to see if I signed my name in it. Since no one sees it, I told them no, but now it seems extra suspicious.

"Well, who thinks it's one and who thinks it's two?" I ask.

"We'd rather not say. We don't want you picking favorites," Esha chimes in.

"Well in that case, I think I'm not going to tell either of you, and you'll just have to wonder forever and ever."

Garven and Esha both realize that the grin on my face means I'm telling the truth when I say this. They hate it, only the way friends can hate it.

"Alright, maybe if we get desperate enough, we'll tell you who thinks what," Garven responds.

"Deal," I say.

After Esha applies the first paste, I have to sit there with it on for 15 minutes. She's now busy getting the other plant ready. I feel helpless as she does all of the work.

I've noticed my mood has shifted the last day as well. I'm trying to be my same old self, but I feel more irritable. My leg is so uncomfortable. This log I'm sitting on is so uncomfortable. This heat is so uncomfortable. I just feel generally irritated at everything right now. I want to chug water, but we're never sure we have enough. I want to be in Buffalo already, but there's no quick way to get there.

The frustration I'm feeling is overwhelming. I breathe deep several times, and Esha notices.

"Everything alright over there?" She asks.

"Yeah, everything is fine. I'm fine," I pause. "It's fine."

"So, everything is fine then?" Esha responds, with a bit of a smirk on her face.

"I'll be fine. Just a little crabby, probably because of my leg. Once we're back on the road I'll be—" I catch myself before I say the word fine again.

"Swell."

"Alright, I'm about to put on the second coating on your leg. Are you sure that's fine?" Esha asks, stifling back a laugh.

Normally this would make me chuckle, yet I can't help but feel a little bit of anger underneath it all, so I say nothing.

She puts the plant smear on my leg and once again it begins to throb. Garven asks how long we'll need to stick around before we can go search some houses, and Esha lets him know that it'll be in another 20 minutes or so.

"If you two want, you can go search houses now, and I'll come catch up in 20 minutes. The houses are right there, I can see them all from here; I'll be alright," I say to them.

"That's not a bad idea," Garven replies.

He and Esha talk for a few minutes. While they're talking, I look through the trees and across the street at the row of houses we're going to search. Five similarly shaped houses, all two stories high with a peak at the top. Each one has a crumbled driveway in between them. I can't even imagine having that much room for yourself, or even your family.

On four of them, they have a porch that is entirely caved in and blocking the front door. That could be good news for us because it might have convinced others to not bother checking the insides. On the fifth, the porch is not only not collapsed, but it looks like it's in pretty good shape. I bet someone had lived there more recently than the others.

From here it looks like that house was built mostly in brick, unlike the others. That's probably why it's still in such good shape.

"Alright, we're going to start looking through those houses. Whenever you feel ready, but no sooner than 15 minutes, you can come and help," when saying this, Garven really emphasized the "no sooner" part. Esha hands me the medical bandage I'm to wrap my leg with shortly.

With that, they cross the street and Garven enters the farthest house on the left, Esha enters the one next to it. After staring at the collapsed porch, Garven goes around and disappears toward the back. While at the house, Esha just lifts herself up through a missing window on the side.

I sit here on the ground, bored and waiting for another 15 minutes to come and go. The next house up to be searched is the brick one, right in the middle, and I'm excited for what I might find. To pass some time, I place my backpack under my head, lean back, and look up at the sky. It's clear today, and even in the shade I have to close my eyes slightly so I'm not blinded by the sun coming in through the dead tree branches.

The few clouds up there are floating slower than usual today. They're the large, puffy white clouds like I used to draw in my notebooks when I was a kid. After a moment, I close my eyes and breathe in deeply. The air is hot and dry, and I would give up everything to have the temperature drop for a few days.

My thoughts are interrupted by a loud noise coming from the house Garven is in. I stare at it for a moment, with faded navy-blue siding on the front that's a deeper and darker hue on the side that doesn't face the sun. He pops his head out of a missing window on the second story and yells out:

"I'm good! Everything's okay!" Toward me.

I check my watch and it's been almost 20 minutes, so I carefully wrap my leg and slowly pull my pant leg down. I then lift myself off the ground, toss my pack onto my back, and limp slowly over to the brick house in the middle.

As I approach, something through the front window catches my eye. It looked like the curtains inside moved. That wouldn't be abnormal for the other houses since all the windows were broken or missing in them, but this one has some windows still intact and some boarded up.

I make sure to put my knife into my front pocket. Although it's probably nothing, you can never be too careful.

I take two steps up to the covered porch and look at the front door. It's large, maybe three feet wide with small windows in a half circle shape at the top. At one point it was probably white or a light color, but now it's dusty and dirty. I walk up to it and run my fingers over it. Then I trace the words "Fin Was Here" in the dirt and laugh to myself.

Before I try to open the door, I look through the large window in front but can't see much. Curtains are obstructing the view, and the layer of dust and dirt doesn't help either, so I take a few steps back to the door.

I try the handle, and it doesn't budge. Most of the houses we've tried over the past few weeks open right up if the door is even shut at all. I try once again to turn the handle while putting a shoulder into the door. Sometimes the wood is so rotted that the door breaks open anyways, but not this time.

Since the door won't open, and I won't be able to easily crawl through the boarded-up windows, I decide to grab my knife and force my way in.

At first, I brace my shoulder into the door, pushing as hard as my leg allows. Then, I take the blade of my knife and push it through the small gap in the door. I wiggle it around to try and unclick the handle lock. If there's a working deadbolt, I'll be all out of luck.

Click.

I hear what I'm pretty sure is the handle unlock, so I turn it. Much to my delight, it opens. This is one of the first times I've felt useful in days and I'm excited to tell Esha and Garven when we meet back up.

I take a few steps in and notice three things immediately. One, it's really dark inside. The only light in the entire first floor is from the now opened door. Two, from what I can see, this place is set up like someone still lives here. It's very neat and organized. Whoever was here last must have left in a hurry, and recently. Third, there is no smell. Usually, in the houses we've been through, there is some sort of rotting food or garbage left baking in the 90-degree weather— but in this house? Nothing.

To take care of the darkness, I take a few steps over to the big bay window and open up the dark red, floor-length curtains. Much like the blue house's siding, the color facing toward the outside is a pale, faded red, while the side facing the living room is a vibrant, velvet red.

As I move them, dust fills the air in the room, noticeable now that the room is lighter, and I sneeze three times. Whenever I sneeze, it's always three times. There are a few other windows around with curtains, so I walk around to open them all. Some of them have boards over the broken remains, but to my surprise, several other windows in the back of the house are still intact. So I open them, and it illuminates most of the first floor.

Once I can see the entire area, I am amazed by how pristine it is. All of this furniture must be well over 100 years old. In the kitchen, there are four chairs around a four-foot circular table, and everything is made from real wood. I knock twice on the table as I pass it because my dad always said it was good luck to knock twice on wooden objects. I asked him why once, and all he could do was shrug his shoulders and say,

"I dunno, tradition I guess?"

As I walk back into the living room, I scan to see if there's anything valuable. When searching homes, I like to go room by room and make a mental checklist so I can stay organized. I look over to the couch and see it's covered in a few blankets. I lift them up and am immediately flooded with emotions.

It's the exact same green plaid couch my parents had, although this one is in much better shape. I can't help but take a seat. The foam on the inside still has a nice form to it; it's comfortable, yet firm. It's the most comfortable thing I've sat on since we left my parents' apartment. I spend a moment sitting there, in the room lit only by sunlight, and enjoy a moment of peace.

I continue to scan the room in silence while sitting on the couch. There's not much here we can take except maybe the blankets. It's surprisingly devoid of stuff. This couch, the table in the kitchen, one other chair, and that's it.

Right as I am about to get up, I hear a loud crash from above me. It sounded like a stack of pots and pans falling onto a wooden floor, followed immediately by a quiet, frantic voice.

"Crap!" They yell in a whispered hush. "Damnit, Ziggy, how many times have I told you to be careful?"

They're right above me. Even though it was barely audible, the voice sounded young. A second voice then says,

"I'm sorry, Petra! Maybe they didn't hear us."

"Shh! Shut up! You're talking too loudly!" The first voice says back.

I scan around the room for a moment to look for the stairs. I know it's not the smartest thing to do but I have the urge to let the people in this house know I'm not a threat. They sounded so young, maybe they could use our help. Then again, maybe they'd ransom me for anything Esha and Garven have left.

It's just that we never want to steal things from people who are still here. That's what the Raiders do, and we're not them.

After looking, I don't see any stairs, which is strange because, by all accounts, this is a single-family house. I walk quietly around the entire downstairs, opening doors, closets, and even cupboards, checking every nook and cranny and I find nothing. Maybe you have to get upstairs from the outside?

Against my better judgment, I yell out to the others in the house.

"Hello, hi? Uh, my name is Fin, and I am not here to hurt you, and I don't want to steal anything from your house."

Well, that was about as clunky an introduction as I could have come up with.

"I heard you upstairs. Petra and Ziggy, I think it was? If you want me just to leave, you can say so or just tap on the floor."

There is silence for a moment, and then I can hear them whispering to each other, this time more quietly than the last time they spoke, so it's tougher to make out what they're saying.

"How do we know you're telling the truth?" A voice finally yells down.

"Shut up!" The second voice says back to the first.

"My friends and I are walking from Cleveland to Buffalo, and we were just going through houses to see if there was anything useful. Sorry to bother you, I can leave now," I say to them.

I start to walk toward the front door when suddenly a panel built into the ceiling drops down and out pops the head of a young girl, maybe 13 or 14.

"Hi, Fin, I'm Petra."

The design in the ceiling is brilliant. When you're looking at it closed, it just looks like a big old plaster chandelier or light covering on the ceiling; the big circular kind you see in all these old homes. It's actually a hidden door. Somehow, they managed to put a hinge on it. The opening is no bigger than two feet and when pressed against the ceiling, it just looks like an out of place old decoration. Even though the location is odd, between the living room and kitchen, you wouldn't even think twice about it.

"Who are these friends of yours, are they here?" Petra then asks.

"Yes," I respond. "I have two friends, Garven and Esha, they're currently looking through the houses next to this one."

Petra snorts, and then says,

"Well, they're not going to find anything over there."

She then looks at me for a moment and lifts her head back up to the second floor so I can no longer see it. I wait for several seconds while nothing happens. Did telling them I'm with friends scare them away?

After another moment, a rope drops down from the opening.

"You really shouldn't go down there, what if they're lying to you?" The voice asks. I'm sure that must be Ziggy.

"Fin looks nice." Petra responds.

With that, I see two feet dangle through the hole in the ceiling. They stop on the first knot of the rope, and then slowly lower down to the next. Once she was about halfway down, she hops off and lands on the living room floor with a thud.

Petra looks a lot like I did when I was her age, maybe 5 years ago. Although her hair is blonde, it is wild and unkempt. It looks more like a lion's mane than a human head of hair. She's rail thin and maybe 5'3". She's wearing a jean jacket and green cargo pants cut off around the knees.

"You comin' or what, Zig?" She yells up through the opening.

I hear a sigh clear through the opening, and then two more feet drop through the opening, following the same pattern. As soon as he reaches halfway down, he jumps the rest of the way and lands hard.

A look of surprise must have come over my face, because Petra said,

"Weren't expecting that, huh?" And started giggling.

Ziggy looks exactly like Petra. They're twins for sure. Ziggy looks around suspiciously and then notices the door open. He walks quickly over to it and checks the handle.

"Did you break the lock?" He asks.

"I don't think so. I usually can get it to open without it breaking," I respond.

He tests the handle by turning it back and forth several times, then closes and locks it. As he turns the handle again, it stops.

"Thank God. You would think these things are everywhere, but most of them are cheap. Not like this one, this one I scavenged myself," Ziggy says, looking proud of himself.

I think to myself that it couldn't be that nice, with how easily I broke in, but decide not to say anything.

"So, these friends of yours, are they going to be cool?" Petra asks.

"Yeah, they're really nice. Well, Esha is really nice, Garven can be a bit grumpy," I smile while saying this to let them know I'm mostly kidding.

"So, what are you two doing here? Does anyone else live here? You both look so young," I ask.

They both look at each other. It's eerie, honestly. They both have similar bright blonde, wild hair. Ziggy is wearing a lightweight green jacket and jeans cut off at the knees. I hadn't noticed this before, but they're wearing the exact same thing, but opposite. He's also around 5'3" and really thin.

After another moment, Petra speaks,

"We're in this house alone, but there's some others in the neighborhood. I feel bad for your friends looking through the other houses, we picked those clean years ago already."

"Maybe in a minute I can yell out to them and let them know?" I ask.

"Maybe. We have some more questions first," Ziggy responds.

"What are you doing here? You said you didn't want to steal anything, but why else would you be breaking into houses?" Asks Ziggy.

"That's a good question. We do want to find supplies since we're traveling a long way, but we never want to take them from people who are," I pause for a moment, trying to find the correct words, "still here."

As Petra is about to ask me a question, movement through the living room window catches my eye. It's the top of Garven and Esha's heads trying to discreetly peer through the window.

"So sorry to interrupt you, Petra, but I think my friends are here and I don't want them breaking your door down to save me. They might be a little protective," I say.

With that, I walk back over to the front door, as Ziggy gets closer to his sister and grabs her hand. He's fiddling with something in his pocket, and he looks nervous.

"Okay, but don't try anything funny, alright?" He demands.

I smile at the both of them with the warmest smile I can manage and say,

"I promise."

I unlock the handle and open the front door. Garven and Esha both stand up and start walking toward me. Before I can get a word out, Garven says,

"Man, there was nothing in my house. I didn't find a single usable thing."

Esha continues "Yeah, I didn't find sh—"

I cut her off quickly and said,

"Hey guys, there's some people in here I'd like you to meet."

THE FIRST DREAM

Sometimes I have the most beautiful dreams. Like last night, I was lying in a field of wildflowers and lavender. They were nearly as tall as I was when sitting up. The air smelled so fresh and clean.

I close my eyes, and a light rain begins to fall. At first, I could feel each individual drop on my face. Then, they become too numerous to count.

As I lay in the field, a calm washes over me. There's not a single sound besides the rain bouncing off the flowers around me. I am at peace.

The Earth is at peace.

CHAPTER 7: DISCOVERY

Tomorrow, 80,000 people are scheduled to land on B.52.C, and tension has filled the ship. At any moment now, Auryn and the rest of the people on board will receive the final results of the short-range sensors they've deployed over the last week while stationed outside the planet's orbit.

The readings from the long-range sensors back on Earth all pointed toward this being a planet that could likely support a colony, but no one could be absolutely certain until they arrived after 15 months of travel.

What would happen to all the people aboard the Amelia Erhardt if it turns out the air has too much Benzene, or any other of a long list of toxic chemicals in large doses? That's not something that Auryn, or any of the other passengers, want to give much thought to at this moment.

To pass the time, Auryn walks into one of the ship's many dining halls, which looks exactly like old sci-fi movies and books had described it: Large, bright, and almost too clean. Every night at midnight, a mist of cleaning spray comes down from the ceiling to disinfect the area and the morning prep crew then comes in at 4am to wipe it down. Because of this, the halls always have a slight disinfectant smell, which Auryn finds really unpleasant.

One of the things Auryn does love, though, is that every meal she gets from the hall comes with a side of fruit or vegetables. She's not sure why they taste so much better on the ship than they did on Earth, but they do. Fruits have more sweetness, and vegetables have more crunch to their texture.

While enjoying her meal at a small two-person table next to a window, a familiar face joins her. Her name is Mina, and she's one of the Engineers on the ship. As they talk, Auryn mentions how good the fruits are.

"Oh! That's because of the vitamin mixture they created!" Mina says excitedly. "On the ship, they're able to add more potassium and phosphorus into the small growing pods, so the fruits are much higher quality than we had been getting on Earth."

Auryn liked that bit of knowledge. She's going to use it the next time her parents comment on how good the fruit is.

After they both finish eating, Auryn says her goodbyes and wanders back toward her living quarters. In the quarters, there's a large central room with three bedrooms branching off. Auryn and Forbin's rooms are both tiny, maybe 6 feet wide by 8 feet long, with a bed and small desk. It's cramped, but she likes having a space of her own. Once the dome and the living quarters are built on the colony, they'll have more room available to them.

That, of course, is the best-case scenario. If the short-range sensors come back and say that yes, they can land and yes, they can live in the planet's atmosphere.

If they come back and it's determined that they can't land, there is a backup plan: Another planet six months away. Auryn can't bear the thought of six more months on this vessel right now. She needs to land, to put her feet on the ground, to build something.

She is going to be partnered with her father, Arthur, who is great at both fixing and building things, for the first four weeks after landing. Her mom, Alia, has been working nonstop on the ship making sure everything runs as smoothly as possible from a software and systems standpoint. She's one of the few people who didn't get to take a cryosleep, so she'll get to take a five-week break when they land. Knowing her mom, it's going to drive her absolutely crazy not pitching in for that long.

Arthur and Auryn will be boots and suits on the ground as soon as they land, building the first dome on another planet. Unless, of course, the first ship that left had succeeded. They are in the first team of 1200 people scheduled to complete the dome in seven days.

It's a huge undertaking. About 15% of the entire ship's cargo is materials brought from Earth. Magnesium-mixed beams, plexiglass panels, wiring for electronics, the list goes on. There are only two large machines available to bring everything out, so the first two days will be a whirlwind of getting materials out, sorting them, and then building. After the first level of the dome is built, they then need to use the same machines to help complete the structure.

It's a delicate and ambitious project. The initial long-range sensors indicated that the air would be breathable, but with a slightly different mixture than Earth's. Those slight differences in the atmosphere would mean that everyone is expected to get tired more quickly. In reality, no one can really be sure how everyone will be impacted.

After the dome is completed, Team 2 and Team 3 will start building living quarters off the main area. In the first eight weeks, they're hoping that everyone will be able to move out of the cramped quarters on the ship and into slightly more spacious living arrangements on the colony.

Once the main living areas of the new colony are built, a large majority of the people there will be helping to build what everyone is excited for: A colony. Complete with greenhouses, farms, medical offices, entertainment areas, and more. Food and medical projects will be in Phase 1, up and running before the ship takes off, since the ship is the only current way to grow food.

Shortly after Auryn leaves the colony, entertainment and leisure activities will be built for the population. Lots of ideas have been floated around, but they're going to concentrate first on parks and walking trails in Phase 2.

For those first four weeks, Auryn will be working on the colony with her dad Authur. She hasn't told her dad yet, but after that she has already been approved to work back on the ship.

She will be on that ship when it leaves, too. She just hasn't told her mom or dad yet. Auryn figures she doesn't have to until they know whether or not they're actually landing. She hates keeping this secret from them, and hates even more keeping it from Forbin, but why cause unnecessary stress when they're not even sure they'll be landing here?

She thinks endlessly about the conversation she's going to have to have. At night, after she tells the ship's system to lower her bedroom lights and activate sleep mode, she stays awake and stares at the gray, perfectly smooth ceiling above her. On especially difficult nights, she'll lay on her side and face the desk. Taped to the wall over her desk is a drawn portrait of her and Fin together. They knew someone on Earth that was a talented artist and asked if they could pay for a portrait.

The artist, Noor, heard that Auryn and Fin were going to be separated and did it for them for free. Fin let Auryn bring the piece with her on the ship. The memory brings a smile to Auryn's face as she lay in the near dark.

"I'm not gonna let you forget about me that easily," Fin had said through tears. "You're gonna have to stare at that every day now, you hear me?"

She does. Almost every morning when she wakes up, and an awful lot of nights before bed, Auryn stares at that drawing. It's what gives her the strength to get up and keep moving on days where it feels like all is lost. It's what is going to give her the strength to talk to her parents about making the return trip back to Earth.

Eventually.

CHAPTER 8: ZIGGY

Esha and Garven walk through the door while Ziggy and Petra immediately grab the rope. There's about 15 feet between the door and them, and I bet at least one of them could get up with it quick enough to escape if they felt threatened in any way.

Thankfully, Garven and Esha stay right next to the door and introduce themselves politely.

"Hey, uh, kids. I'm Garven, this is Esha, and we're friends of Finley's."

"Yeah, we know. Finley told us you were coming over. Besides, we heard you yelling from a couple houses down before Finley even got here," responds Ziggy.

"Is that why you were upstairs already when I came in?" I asked.

Petra smiled a big grin and nodded.

"I was, at least. Ziggy stayed down here for a little bit looking out the window. Pretty much anytime we hear someone who doesn't sound like one of our friends, we go upstairs. I mean, that's where all our stuff is anyway. So, it's more fun up there," says Petra.

Garven and Esha both look at the rope hanging down from the hole in the ceiling with some confusion in their faces.

"There's no staircase, that rope is the only way to get up there. Pretty cool, right?" I say to the two of them.

Esha excitedly takes a couple steps toward the rope. She wants to look up and see how it all works, but Ziggy takes a couple steps back, rope in hand.

"I'm so sorry," Esha says. "It's just really cool, and I wanted to see how it works."

"Maybe we'll let you, maybe we won't," says Ziggy.

After a few more minutes of polite conversation, the tension in the room softens. We talk about the hike from Cleveland, what it was like, and why we're headed to Buffalo. We even tell them a little bit about our encounter with the Raiders, while leaving out some of the gorier details.

"Wow, that's really scary," Petra says.

"Yeah, they still come around here sometimes, but since the houses are already picked through, they mostly leave us alone..." Ziggy says, "mostly."

We talk some more and they tell us their parents passed away three years ago, when they were just 11. They slowly learned how to take care of themselves with the help of some other neighborhood kids. They said there's about 15 of them, between the ages of 10 and 19, and they all help one another out.

"Akilah, she's the oldest, she is the one who showed us how to close up our staircase so no one could go upstairs but us," says Petra.

Garven finally closes the door behind him and Esha, and the two of them sit on the green couch.

"Isn't this the couch your parents owned, Fin?" Esha asks, taken aback.

I smile and confirm that it was. It's strange sometimes, the things you remember.

Petra and I grab some of the wooden chairs from the kitchen so we can all sit in the living room together. The midday sun is heating the house up quickly, and I take my jacket off to try and stay cool.

Ziggy and Petra are nearly tripping over themselves to ask us questions. I can barely get halfway through an answer before the other one starts asking a new question. They haven't left the greater neighborhood area in the last three years, and they have all sorts of questions about Cleveland, and what we think it will be like in Buffalo. How we feed ourselves and get fresh water.

After about 15 minutes of answering questions, there's

a sudden and surprising knock on the door. It's loud and purposeful. Ziggy stands up and says,

"I'll be right back."

He is about to grab the rope when the voice on the other side of the door yells,

"Open up right now, Ziggy and Petra, or I'll break the door down!"

By the time the sentence has been said, Esha is standing up, with her hand grabbing for her large machete on her thigh. Before she can pull it out of her weathered brown scabbard, Petra squeals in delight,

"It's Akilah! I was hoping she would come!"

Ziggy yells back, "Hold your horses, Aki, I'll be right there!"

Ziggy goes to the door and opens it. Akilah takes a quick, purposeful step in and then scans the room. She immediately sees us, three strangers, in the house. She is about my height and muscular, the black tank top she is wearing shows off the type of toned biceps, triceps, and shoulders that would take me a lifetime to build.

She looks directly at me, and I can't help but to stare back at her. Her bright, gray-green eyes are piercing.

"Who are you?" she asks, while grabbing at something on her waist.

"Whoa, Aki! It's okay, they're new friends," Petra says, as she leaps off the chair toward her. Petra wraps her arms around Akilah, but she never once takes her eyes off of us or her hand off her waist.

She and Esha stare at each other. For a moment, an uncomfortable and intense silence fills the room.

"I'm Esha, this is Fin and Garven. We were looking through the neighborhood for supplies and ran into these two. That's all."

Akilah gives her a quick scan with her eyes and relaxes her shoulders a bit. She then looks at Garven, and then me, and deems Esha's explanation good enough. She removes her hand from her waist and takes a few steps into the living room.

"Sorry to come in here like this, I'm just protective over everyone in the neighborhood. I'm Akilah, it's nice to meet the three of you."

We all shake hands and greet one another. While we do that, Ziggy grabs another chair from the kitchen, the last one they have, and brings it into the living room.

"We were just asking them *so many* questions," Ziggy tells Akilah.

"It's true, we're happy to answer any questions you might have for us too, Akilah," I say to her.

"I think I'm good for now, but I bet you have some for me," she laughs as she says this, and I give a chuckle as well.

"As a matter of fact, I do," I say back.

Over the next half hour, I ask them lots of questions: How they've survived this long, is there's anyone older than Akilah around, and where do they get their food and water from. The three of them let us know that there is a still-flowing stream not too far from here, which is more than enough for the 15 of them to live off of.

Food, on the other hand, Akilah seemed to be worried about.

"It's been so long since anyone really lived here besides us," she started. "So now, we have to keep making bigger and bigger circles, farther out from the neighborhood, to find houses with anything left in them. It's become difficult and we've had to hide many times from the Raiders coming through, but we really like it here and don't want to have to move away."

"Have you tried growing your food? Looks like there's plenty of space for it," Esha says.

Akilah, Petra, and Ziggy all look at one another. Immediately they smile and then burst out laughing.

"We tried. Believe us, we tried. But none of us have any idea what we're doing, so it never works," Petra answers.

"What if I showed you how?" Esha responds.

All three of them look at one another again, and a sense of excitement comes over the room.

"You would do that? For complete strangers?" Akilah asks.

Garven looks in my direction, scrunches his forehead, and purses his lips. I can tell that he's annoyed that we're spending time here and not already back on our hike to Buffalo.

"Can you show them everything they need to know this afternoon, Esha? We really have to get back on the road," he asks.

"Absolutely. Grab everyone you want to learn and meet me across the street in 20 minutes. Does that sound good?" Esha asks the three of them.

Ziggy and Akilah practically race for the door, while Petra starts climbing the rope to the second floor. I was right, she can climb that rope faster than I could open a door. Once upstairs, she yells down,

"Wait for me!"

In another moment, she is hurtling herself through the hole in the ceiling and lands on the floor below with the loudest thud yet. She gets to her feet and sprints toward the door. We follow close behind, only so they see that we shut and lock the door behind us.

By the time we're on the porch, Ziggy is three houses down heading east and Akilah is four houses down heading west. Petra turns to us and yells,

"Twenty minutes!!!" And then runs directly across the street, through a couple open yards, and disappears.

Garven sighs deeply.

"They're kids, Garven. If they don't know how to grow their own food, they're never going to make it. I've picked up plenty of seeds," Esha says.

"Akilah is older than you are!" He responds.

We both look at him with disapproving faces.

"Trust me, I want to get to Buffalo just as bad as you, maybe worse," I say as I point to my leg. "But we gotta help them."

"Fine. A few hours and then we're back on the road," he responds.

"Deal," says Esha, unable to hide the near ear to ear smile on her face.

THE SECOND DREAM

I can see him clear as day in my dream. He is beautiful: Brown, wavy hair, backlit by the sun. A perfect silhouette. He has an easy smile and an infectious laugh.

For reasons unknown to me in the dream, he is carrying a bow and arrow. He appears larger than life standing on top of a building. He could be 20 or 200 feet in the air. As I get closer, he climbs down from a building to greet me. I hadn't noticed before, but Garven and Esha are there too. The sun is shining and it's a beautiful morning, but we are all exhausted.

Nothing else in the dream feels familiar. The buildings aren't ones that I recognize. The street is not one I've walked down before.

I am smitten with him almost immediately. Blushing at some of the first words he mentions. I imagine him picking me up and carrying me with such ease. Who is this man? I've never seen him before in my life.

Suddenly, a woman approaches. There were no footsteps, it was like she floated into the area.

Before it ends, I scan the area one last time and notice, across the street, someone else watching every one of our moves. I want to tell the beautiful, brown-haired man to be careful, but before I do, I jolt awake.

Here, in this unfamiliar house, I try to slow my breathing.

"Another one?" Esha whispers.

"Yeah, another one," I reply, before I drift off back to sleep.

CHAPTER 9: ANGOLA

My eyes open after a long night of sleep, my third night in a row. Garven and Esha took four hour shifts so that I could get a full night of rest and fight off this infection. It was a little easier after we all slept through the entire night three nights ago. My night was filled with vivid dreams, and I know why.

"I think I might have a fever," I say as I open my tent flap. It's especially bright out today, and the breeze is actually pleasant. I take a step out and wince as I put pressure on my leg.

Esha stops making breakfast and looks over toward me, then down at my leg. Garven is off somewhere, probably gathering wood to keep our small fire going. We're going to make some mushroom coffee this morning for a little bit of extra energy. It's one of the few "luxuries" we have on this trip, and we're trying to save some in case we need to barter while in Buffalo.

"Yeah, that makes sense," Esha says. "Usually when you get an infection like yours, you'll start to get a fever. It'll last a few days, so you're probably going to have a rough go of it until we get to where we're going. From everything Garven has said though, they'll have some antibiotics in Buffalo, and we'll get you all healed up. Maybe just with a cool new scar."

She chuckled, maybe to break the tension, maybe because she really thought that was funny, it's hard to tell.

"That also checks out since you were so irritable the past few days," she says.

"I was super nice to those kids, wasn't I?" I ask.

"You were alright," she responded.

It was four days ago when we ran into Petra, Ziggy, and Akilah. Once they came back with all their friends, Esha spent the rest of that afternoon and evening showing them how to plant vegetables and fruits. She showed them the entire process of removing seeds from existing foods, how to plant, how deep into the soil to dig, and how often to water the plants. She even took an empty page out of my notepad, after much pleading with me, and wrote down instructions for each kind.

She showed them the best areas to plant, both inside and outside their homes. It was a rewarding and, quite frankly, exhausting day. By the time the sun was setting over the backs of the houses, we couldn't even get a word out of Garven because he was so grumpy.

By the evening time, it was too late to start walking

toward Buffalo, and Petra and Ziggy offered to let us stay in their house for the night.

You would think being able to lock the door would allow the three of us to fall asleep much more quickly than out in the woods, but it took us several hours. I could tell I wasn't the only one awake because Garven wasn't snoring, a sure sign he hadn't passed out. Esha was also fiddling with something that would make a clicking noise occasionally. Finally, after 45 minutes of lying there and staring at the ceiling, I said,

"Why is this so hard? Shouldn't we all be asleep right now?"

"It's almost too comfortable," Esha responded.

"Maybe you two feel guilty about wasting a day of walking when we could be that much closer to Buffalo?" Garven says.

"Nah, that's definitely not it," Esha snaps back immediately, I could feel her eyes roll through the darkness.

When she says it, I burst out laughing. I don't know what came over me, but it was uncontrollable. Within seconds I had tears streaming down my face. They say laughter is contagious and it must be true, because soon Esha started laughing a hysterical laugh. It was louder than I've ever heard her laugh in my life.

After Esha lost it, I looked over in Garven's direction and saw him with a blanket covering his face. His chest was convulsing a little, and he was doing his best to stifle his laugh. It didn't last long though, because a few seconds later he was belly laughing along with the two of us.

There is nothing like the laughter of three delirious travelers to make people uncomfortable, and after two or three minutes of uncontrollable fits, the ceiling door swung open.

"What the heck is going on down here?" Ziggy asks.

Something about his face popping out of nowhere, directly above the three of us, made the entire situation even more hilarious. I started losing it all over again, and then Petra shoved her head through the hole, and we were looking at two wild haired kids, upside down, through a hole in the ceiling.

It was over for the three of us. Tears streaming down all our faces, Esha was having a hard time catching her breath, and Garven's laugh was so boisterous it might have woken the neighborhood, if there still was one.

Petra and Ziggy looked at each other, confused, and then lifted themselves back up to the second floor and closed the door.

It's my favorite memory of anything that's happened since Auryn left the planet. As I fade out from thinking about it, I realize Esha is talking,

"Thankfully, in the late 2090s, the world started moving on from antibiotics that needed to be refrigerated because the power grids were so unreliable. Even though hospitals had their own solar farms that powered them, so much of that power had to be dedicated to heavy machinery and lifesaving equipment, so switching over to room stable antibiotics was the only way to go."

"How do you know so much about all of these?" I ask, hoping she didn't already cover that while I was daydreaming.

"Well," Esha started, and then there was a long pause. In the distance I could hear Garven breaking off twigs from dead trees as he was getting closer to the site.

"After what happened to my parents, I knew I was going to have to take care of myself. I didn't know if your family would be leaving on the ships, and even if not, your mom and dad were pretty sick. So, I started reading through every book your mom had about herbal medicine. Every night before I went to bed, I hand-cranked those small flashlights your parents had and laid on the couch reading as much as I could. I knew that if I was going to make it, I had to be useful."

Useful is an understatement. She's saving my life right now. The least I can do is make it through this pain and hike the rest of the way to Buffalo. After that, I'm vowing to pull my own weight.

I take a few more steps and sit down on a long dead log that Garven and Esha pulled over last night. I roll my pantleg up to take a look at the bandage. While it's partially soaked through, it's not nearly as gross as I was expecting.

"Looks like the salve is helping to stop the spread of the infection," Esha says.

She turns her attention back toward breakfast and places the last couple of sticks sitting next to her onto the small fire. It briefly comes to life with flames and then settles back into a low burn. If Garven doesn't return with more sticks and twigs soon, we might be drinking cold coffee.

I hear a few more twigs being snapped off and look in that direction. I see Garven with one of his arms full of dried wood, making his way back to camp. He sits down and starts breaking everything he brought back into smaller, easier to burn segments. They're easy to catch on fire and they don't create a lot of smoke that would blow our cover when they're as dry as they are. After he tosses them next to Esha, he sits down and lets out a big sigh.

"It's going to be a long day today, Fin. We need to get to Buffalo to get your leg all fixed up. Make sure you have plenty of coffee and plenty of breakfast. If you need a bite or two of mine as extra, just let me know; you need your strength more than me."

My first inclination is to argue with him, but he's right. I'm going to need all the help I can get over the next few days, and the extra calories will definitely help.

After we eat, Garven puts some dirt on the fire and pulls the pan away from the heat to cool off. In another 20 minutes, it'll be at a temperature where we can pack it up and get on our way. It's been really nice sitting around after a full night of sleep, with a full stomach and some delicious morning coffee. But I know the two of them are exhausted from getting even less sleep than normal.

Before we begin the process of packing everything up, Esha slathers on another layer of plant paste for my leg. She lets me know that we don't have to change the wrapping since it's still pretty clean from yesterday. Once she coats the wound, I let my leg air out for a few minutes and then roll my pantleg down.

I stand up to start packing up my tent and supplies, and Garven and Esha both offer to pack all my gear up for me. It's nice of them to offer, but I can't let them do any more for me. They have their own gear to pack up, and I can handle this.

First, I remove the stakes from the ground. I found a useful tool in one of the warehouses for hammering in the stakes and removing them. It's a miniature crowbar, no longer than 10 inches. Once all six stakes are out, I combine them with the handle of the crowbar, slip them into a covering with a carabiner, and clip them to the side of my bag tightly. Sometimes on walks, they jingle in rhythm to my footsteps, and I enjoy a little bit of music along the way.

Next, I remove the flexible tent poles from the tent. They slide out easily at this point because the bottom openings have been stretched out. I worry how much longer the tent is going to hold out, which is why I try to sleep without it as often as nature allows. The tent itself has some small patches and stitches in it, but it's still waterproof for the occasional rainstorm and it still keeps most of the dust out.

The original color of the tent was a mixture of forest and lime green, and it was far too bright. Before we left

Cleveland, we set it up on the roof of our building and let the bright sun fade the coloring. It was Esha's idea, and it was brilliant because it would have stuck out mightily in the dead woods along the Lake Erie shoreline.

Once done, I take a seat on the log again and wait for the other two to finish up. Garven rinses out the cook pot and straps it to his bag. Once everyone is packed, I stand up and swing my backpack onto my back. After taking a few steps, only one thought is flooding my mind:

Geez my leg hurts a lot.

I try not to wince with every step I take, but my face betrays me. Somehow it feels like the flower salve Esha reapplied this morning is making it worse, but she assures me that's not the case.

Once again, every step is like a dull knife being stabbed into my leg. Even though we often walk in silence as a group, as we reach the interstate, I have to do something to take my mind off this constant pain.

"Hey, Garven?"

"Yes, Fin?"

"How much longer do you think we have until we reach your friends?"

"Well, I checked the map after I was done eating breakfast, and I think we're near a place called 'Dunkirk' in the old state of New York."

"That means we have to be getting close, right?" Esha chimes in.

"Yeah, I'm guessing another couple days, depending on how well Fin's leg holds up. We gotta pass through some towns like Silver Creek, Angola, and Lackawanna."

"Oh, my leg will hold up just fine, Garven. Don't you worry," I say, while trying to hold back laughter.

"And if it doesn't, I'll just have Esha hold me down while you cut it off, and then I'll make the both of you carry me all the way to Buffalo."

Garven stops, smiles at me, and lets out a hearty belly laugh.

"Look, Fin. I know I'm talking a lot about getting to Buffalo and needing to struggle through to make it. But your health comes first, so if you need a little bit of extra rest, just let us know. It's fine. I can just add it to the things you've done on this trip that have annoyed me."

Esha and I share a look, something between being shocked and being impressed. This is a side of Garven that seems to be coming out more as we all travel as a group.

"Shut up, the both of you, or I will leave you here to fend for yourselves," Garven huffs.

"Ha! No way, you were JUST saying how much you love us and that you could never ever leave us behind!" I reply.

"That's not even close to what I said! I said add it to the never-ending pile of things that you've done to annoy me! God, I can't stand either of you!" He says.

Esha and I share a look again and immediately burst out laughing. Garven turns away from both of us and starts walking again, while mumbling to himself. I finally stop laughing and catch my breath. One of my favorite past-times is annoying Garven. I don't know if it's because he's like an older brother to me, or just because he is easily annoyed, but at least once a day I try to get him going about something.

Esha and I start walking again. One step in and I'm immediately reminded of how painful this is going to be.

Soon enough, we'll be in Buffalo. From everything Garven had told us, they've set up a nice little society of those left behind to fend for themselves. Better medicine, some crops, and protection from the Raiders. That's all I'm going to be able to concentrate on for the next few days.

That, and this damn leg.

CHAPTER 10: SHAMROCK

I'll be honest, the last few days kind of sucked. My limp continued to get worse. While it seems like Esha's salves have kept my infection from getting worse, it's getting harder to keep going each day. The past few nights I've had terrible sleep, and that really slowed us down. We probably could have gotten to Buffalo yesterday if I had been able to stay the course.

Garven and Esha have both been so understanding. Garven even mentioned last night that approaching the encampment in Buffalo while it's dark out wouldn't have been the best idea. We've talked often the last few days about Buffalo. We've heard along the trail that more Raiders are heading in this direction, so we assume they're going to be on edge.

Surprisingly, this morning we all woke up in a great mood— even me. Garven said we made it into Lackawanna last night, so it's about an hour walk into Buffalo, and then we have to find the encampment. Lackawanna reminds me a lot of the shoreline outside of Cleveland. Huge buildings in various states of disrepair.

Part of the building we stayed in the previous night was burned at some point in the past. Even all these years later, you can see black char marks on the inside and outside of all the walls. The building itself must be a half mile long and a quarter mile wide, with a third of the roof missing. Since the weather was calm last night, we rolled out our mats and kept our tents packed away. Looking out through the huge hole in the roof brought me back to living in Cleveland, where Auryn and I would spend our nights looking up at the stars. The sky was pitch black and filled with stars far and near.

This morning, as we sit on our mats and eat some ration bars, we start wondering what to expect as we approach the city center.

"Last message I received was 'come to City Hall, that's where we're starting over again' from Luna," Garven says.

I have to admit, besides the excitement of getting my leg fixed and having a safe place to stay for a bit, I'm also really nervous. These messages were from two years ago. What if the Raiders had overtaken the area since then? What if the person Garven was friends with was lying, or the city has been taken over by new leaders? It's been so long since he's had any contact with the people from here, anything could have happened.

Any number of things would mean that we no longer have a place to stay, and my leg might not get the antibiotics that it needs. Esha is starting to run out of her herbal medication and if we have to keep marching to Toronto, I'm honestly not sure I can make it.

I brought that point up two days ago with Garven and Esha. We were all in our tents, which we had all tied and staked together so that the openings formed a small triangle between them. It wasn't an overly windy night, so before we all zipped up we were talking about Buffalo and Toronto.

"Garven, what if we get to Buffalo and your friends aren't there? Or if we get there and there's nothing left? You haven't been able to communicate with them for two years, are you really sure they're there?" I asked.

"Am I 100% sure they are still there?" He says back to me, "No, of course not. How could I be? But these people were my friends, and everything they described to me seemed very well planned out. So, I have full confidence that when we get there, they'll be able to help us."

"Plus, at this point, what else are we going to do? We're almost there," chimed in Esha.

"Yeah, I guess I'm just worried about what will happen to my leg if there aren't friendly people, or antibiotics, in Buffalo," I say.

"I get that you're worried, I really do," Garven says, his voice slowly growing more tired, "but I really do believe that in just a couple days, we'll reach the city, meet some friendly faces, and get you all patched up."

"Thanks, Garven," I respond.

"Goodnight, Fin. You Too, Esha."

In the next minute, I could hear Garven start to snore, like he always does. I pulled myself off my sleep mat, took a painful step outside, and closed up his tent for him.

This morning, it's a quick pack up after eating. As we walk along a road called "Route 5", there are small dips and hills but for the first mile or two, it's a pretty easy walk. As usual, we mostly keep our heads down while walking, since the sun shining off the roadways is nearly blinding.

Once we're closer to the city, Garven pauses and looks at his map. I'm happy to stop and rest for a moment so I don't ask any questions, but Esha asks,

"What's up, Garven?"

"Well, on this map it shows that we can follow this road right into the city, but, uh, I'm not sure about walking up that," he says.

"Walking up what?" Esha begins to ask, but before she finishes her sentence, she pauses. I look up to see what they're talking about, squint my eyes hard, and wonder how I ever missed it in the first place.

There is a bridge, maybe a mile in front of us. It's the tallest bridge I've ever seen in my life. The fact that it's still standing is confounding.

"On the map it's called 'The Skyway,' but I didn't think it would be anything like this," says Garven.

"Skyway" is definitely the right name for this. The top is well over 100 feet tall, and parts of it are entirely missing.

It looks like originally there were 2 lanes heading in each direction. It's so tall that it towers over some silos to the east of it. Huge buildings look tiny around it.

"There is nothing I want to do less than climb that bridge," I finally chime in.

"I don't know, looking at the map it looks like the fastest way," says Esha.

We both look at Garven since he's the deciding vote. He scratches his head and takes a deep sigh.

"Let me see if I can find a different route that won't take too much longer, because that bridge does, uh, not look safe," he says.

Esha rolls her eyes, knowing she's been outvoted. After two or three more minutes, Garven says,

"Here we go, if we split off up ahead on this exit, Ohio Street, we can cross a smaller bridge and then head into the city center. It'll be an extra mile or so, but as long as Finley's leg will hold up, I'm fine with that."

"My leg will be fine as long as we're not trying to make it to the top of that thing," I say while pointing at the bridge ahead.

A couple hundred feet ahead, we veer off on the Ohio Street exit. We pass over an old metal grated bridge where it looks like a large river flowed below it. Now it's nothing more than a narrow creek, but as my eyes follow it down, it does look like it feeds into the lake. I'd give anything to run down below and jump in. To lay in the current and ride it out into Lake Erie. Let the water wash away my troubles.

My entire body is covered in a light layer of dirt, except my wound, which gets cleaned off every day, and my face, which I dunk directly into every water source we find, after filling our packs of course. Otherwise, I feel like I haven't been truly, actually, clean in months. I would trade all the mushroom coffee in the world for a long, room temperature shower right now.

As I walk along and daydream about swimming in the lake, I notice a sign that's covered with dirt and plant life. I peel off from Esha and Garven and walk over to the sign. Once close, I pull back the plants, take my sleeve, and rub it in circles to get as much of the dirt off as possible. I take a few steps back to read it.

THE OLD FIRST WARD

Gateway to Buffalo

Home of the Shamrock Run

"What's a Shamrock Run?" I yell over to Garven and Esha.

"What the hell are you doin', Fin?" Garven yells back.

"There's a cool old sign here, I just wanted to see what it said. There was something called a 'Shamrock Run' here and I was just asking if either of you knew what that is."

"No idea. Also, could you hurry up, they said City Hall is close to the tallest building in the city, and we can see that building from here. We've gotta almost be there," says Garven.

"Alright, alright. I'm coming," I say.

I grimace as I half jog back to them. Once I catch up, they become tense. At first, I worry if it's because I upset them by veering off for a moment. They then motion to me to get in tight with them.

"What are we doing? What's going on?" I ask.

Esha fills me in.

"There's a building up ahead, two blocks away, and someone is stationed on the roof. They've been watching us for the last block. We just noticed them talking to someone on what looks like a radio or something."

We slow down as we approach the building. About 30 feet away from it, we come to a complete stop. Garven and Esha put their hands up in the air slowly, so I do the same. We wait for any movement or response from the person on the roof. Are they with the community here? Are they Raiders? I can feel my heart start to race.

"What brings you to these parts?" The unfamiliar voice yells down.

Garven looks at Esha, unsure how much he really wants to share at this point.

"My name is Garven, and we have some friends here that told us to come. They said it was a safe place."

"Oh yeah? Who are these friends of yours?" The voice says.

I don't know how I missed it before, but I am now very aware of the bow and arrow pointed directly at us. I look up at the face behind it, and the bottom half is covered by fabric. It's red, with some black print on it, which means he's probably not a Raider. The rest of his head is covered by a hood that comes out a little past his hairline, helping to shade his eyes from the sun.

While staring at him, I notice him looking back at me. We lock eyes and he winks at me. It startles me, not because I'm afraid, but because his dark brown eyes are beautiful.

"Their names are Luna and Harlian. They got a message through to me a while back, and we've finally made the trek," Garven responds.

"How the hell do you know Luna and Harlian if you're from," he pauses for a moment, "actually, you didn't say where you were from."

I can sense Garven getting annoyed. He hates

answering this many questions. But when you're the one with the weapon pointed at you, you don't have much choice.

"We're from Cleveland and have been walking for several weeks. My friend here is pretty hurt, so we're hoping to get them some medical attention. Back before everything went to hell, or I guess, during the last stages of everything going to hell, we used the AltWeb to play some online games together."

Garven has talked several times on the trip about how much he misses the AltWeb.

"It was slow as hell and all just text, but it was a pretty fun time," he said last time it was brought up.

"Jesus," I hear the voice say, "you were all a bunch of nerds before all this."

With this, the voice on the roof laughs loudly. He then lowers his bow as he scans the area one last time. After a few seconds, he puts one finger up, asking us to hold on a second.

I can hear the walkie-talkie click on.

"Yeah, everything's okay over here. Seems like we might have some friends of Luna and Harlian here, if you can let them know."

He then yells out to us again, "Hey, what's your name?"

"My name is Garven, but they'll probably remember

my game tag better, which was," he pauses for a moment, "Broken Apocalypse 420."

Esha and I make eye contact and try to hold in our laughs, but it's no use. Esha raises her eyebrows and looks at Garven, who refuses to look back.

"Just making sure you are who you say you are. We've had some occasional problems with the Raiders recently, so I'm going to need you to stay right where you are for a few minutes," the voice on the roof replies.

"So," Esha says, "Broken Apocalypse 420, huh?"

"Now is not the time, Esha, you can make fun of me later," Garven whispers back.

"Oh, don't worry, I will," she responds while still laughing.

After a minute, the man uses a ladder on the side of the building to climb down toward us. The bow is strapped to his back, but that's not the only weapon he's carrying. There's a machete on his front left side and what looks like an antique pistol on the other. Do they somehow still have gunpowder here? How's that possible? Even most of the Raiders don't have working firearms like that.

He catches me staring at the gun.

"Yes, it's real, and yes, it works," he says.

With that, he takes off his scarf and hood.

"Whoa," I hear Esha whisper. A look of embarrassment comes over her face, as if she surprised herself by saying anything out loud.

Whoa, indeed. The mysterious man on the roof is beautiful. I'm not sure if it's because I haven't seen many people the last few months, so I have little to compare him to, but this man is gorgeous.

Garven looks at both of us and shakes his head, he then takes a few steps forward and shakes the man's hand.

"Nice to meet you. As mentioned, I'm Garven, this is Esha, and this is Fin. It's been a long couple weeks, and it's nice to see a friendly face for once."

"It's really great to meet all of you too. Sorry about the circumstances, with me pointing a weapon at you and all. We try to keep pretty tight security around the perimeters of the city and get messages back quickly if anything feels off."

"We get it. Better safe than sorry," replies Esha.

"Exactly. The sooner we can mobilize everyone at the Hall, the better," he replies.

"By the way, I'm Kian. I'm glad I was the first to meet you, I'm a little more easygoing than some of the other lookouts. I'm not usually out here, but our normal lookout needed a day off and I was happy to do it. Since I was first to make contact with you, I'm going to walk you to City Hall, we just have to wait a bit for the next closest lookout to shift here, should only be a few minutes."

I can't stop staring at him. Every word he says is enthralling. He runs his hand through his wavy brown hair, which goes down to the bottom of his ears. His light brown eyes feel like they're staring right through me. He must be at least 6'2", standing a clear four inches taller than I am. My heart begins to race a little, and I think my hands are sweaty. Do I have a crush on a stranger? What is wrong with me? We met this guy five minutes ago and he was pointing a weapon at us.

"So, how far away is City Hall, and does that walkie-talkie have a range that works all the way there?" Esha asks. She's always searching for new information. I envy that.

"On really clear days it gets pretty close, so almost never," he laughs to himself. "We have something of a relay system set up. There are lookouts all over the place that make sure the message gets back there. So, even if something were to happen to me, or any of the lookouts, the Hall would still get word pretty fast."

After talking for a few more minutes, another person comes around the corner. In one smooth motion Kian has the bow off his back, stretched out, and ready to fire.

"If I wanted to get the jump on you, you'd already be dead, Kian."

I like whoever she is already.

"Garven, Esha, Fin, this is Annora. Annora, these are

friends of Luna and Harlian. Apparently, Garven used to play online games with them."

Annora is stunning as well. Is there something in the water here? She's about my height, but as physically strong looking as Esha. Sculpted arm muscles that leave me no doubt she could beat me in any sort of hand-to-hand combat. She's wearing a black tank top and hood, her chestnut-colored skin glistening in the bright late morning sun.

"Did everyone in this place used to be a giant nerd?" Annora responded while shaking her head.

"That's what I said!" Kian responded loudly.

They give each other a hug. They seem close, although it's none of my business. They extend a couple more pleasantries with us before I notice a subtle movement across the street on another building top. Someone dressed a lot like Kian has been watching us, who knows for how long. I quietly try to get Kian and Annora's attention.

"Hey, Kian, Annora," I whisper, "there's someone across the street on top of a building, and I think that they're watching us."

"Oh, they are absolutely watching us," Kian replies. While saying it, he chuckles for a moment.

"As I mentioned before, there are a lot of us around, so if something happens to one of us, we can all still communicate. That's a pretty good eye there though, catching

Eno over there. I'm going to have to let him know later that he was spotted. He's gonna hate that."

"Oh, he's going to hate that so, so much," Annora adds while smirking.

Kian smiles at Annora and they both laugh together. Seeing that smile, and how effortless and joyous his laugh is, makes me want to remember all the funniest jokes I've ever heard, but unfortunately my mind is blank. Instead, I'll just have to look forward to our walk toward City Hall.

As we say bye to Annora and head toward the City Hall, I am quickly reminded that I no longer look forward to any walk because my leg is aching, and I am in desperate need of healing for a few days.

Kian turns around and notices my limp.

"If you want, I can try to carry you for a bit. Looks like the hike from Cleveland has taken a toll on you."

My face turns beat red at the thought. I manage to get out a nervous, "No, ha-ha, that's okay. I've walked the 200 miles here; I can manage the next couple minutes."

"Well, if you need an arm for support, I'm here for you." With that, he smiles warmly at me and continues. "What's up with your leg anyways?"

I am about to tell Kian all about our adventure, hiding and running from the Raiders but before I can open my mouth to respond, Esha says, "It's a long story, and we all need some rest before we get into those details."

"That's fair. Sounds like you all have had a long couple of weeks," Kian says.

CHAPTER 11: NEWS

"76% Nitrogen, 22% Oxygen, 2% other. The atmosphere on the new planet is livable," the captain says over the loudspeaker.

A cheer erupts across the entire ship. People who barely know each other are hugging and crying in the hallways of every deck. Auryn jumps off the seat she was sitting on in the Dining Hall 2 and nearly hits the low hanging overhead light when she lifts her arms into the air. She high fives several people in her immediate area.

As she begins to walk toward her family quarters, the captain continues over the loudspeakers with a short speech, which he ends by saying,

"Today is truly a day to *celebrate*."

With that, the speaker system suddenly plays the 1980s song "Celebration" by Kool & the Gang. Usually, she would think that this song choice was a little too on the nose, but today? Nothing can get her down today.

As she exits the dining hall, she turns left, down the

soft gray, well-lit hallways. She could probably make it from here to her room with her eyes closed at this point, she's walked this same path so many times. As she walks, she reaches her hand out and touches the wall; there are several small parallel bumps that run along all the hallways in the ship. She loves to run her hand up and down as she walks along, creating her own soft melody.

Today she moves her hand in the same timing as the song and tries to pace her walk so that when she reaches doorways and has to take her hand off, it's at a natural part of the song. It's silly, she knows, but it gives her a little bit of happiness.

As she reaches the elevator and presses the button, the song ends and then immediately begins again. A smile comes over her face; she turns around and looks back down the hallway she had just walked through, as she sees a couple she knows embracing in the corridor.

The elevator doors finally open and standing in the elevator is Mina. Auryn takes a few steps into the elevator, and as she does, Mina wraps her in a huge hug and picks her up off the ground.

After a couple of shakes, she puts her back down.

"So sorry! I'm just caught up in the excitement!" Mina says.

"Ha-ha! I get it, me too!" Replies Auryn.

Auryn is really impressed. Mina is just 5'3", and a full 6 inches shorter than her.

They chat for a few seconds about being able to land on the planet, and then the elevator doors open to Mina's floor.

"Here's my stop," she says.

"Of course! Don't let me keep you. Maybe I'll see you in the commissary before we all get off this blasted thing?" Auryn replies.

"I'd like that very much, consider it a date!" Mina says, she then exits the elevator and turns down the hallway to the left.

"Wait, what?" Auryn says out loud after the doors have already closed.

Auryn feels a little bit guilty about not talking longer with her. Mina has no family on the ships and although Auryn wouldn't consider them particularly close, she might be one of her closest friends on board.

Auryn takes out her personal communication device, finds Mina's number, and texts her,

"Meet me in the Dining Hall 2 in an hour. Let's Celebrate!"

After hitting send, a smile creeps across her face. She then waits until the elevator reaches her floor. Once it does, she exits and walks down the hallway toward her family's quarters. Excitedly, she grabs her badge and swipes it over the keypad area.

As the door swishes open, her parents and younger brother turn to her and she races toward them. Auryn gets engulfed in a giant hug. All the stress and pressure from the last day of waiting for the scans, and the last 15 months of travel, have been released. Now everyone can move forward with their lives.

CHAPTER 12: APPROACH

As the four of us approach the main entrance to Niagara Square and City Hall, we slow to a stop. Kian tells us to wait a moment as he goes ahead. Over the last half an hour, we've passed countless beautiful buildings, several still in great condition. Kian seems to know a lot about the history of the buildings, and the city itself.

"That used to be the largest space ever for like, businesses and shopping, can you imagine that?" He says, while pointing at a building called "Ellicott Square."

"We actually just started moving people into living there as well. As the population here grows, mostly from people coming from Cleveland, we've been working hard to make sure there are nice places to live for everyone."

A few blocks later, he sees me staring at a gorgeous building. It is a reddish-brown color and everything on the front has ornamental carvings. It must be 12 or 13 floors. The whole building is precise and symmetrical, and almost none of the windows are broken.

"That's the old 'Guaranty Building,' one of the first

ever skyscrapers built," he says. "It's my second favorite building in the city."

His eyes light up and his smile widens as telling me all about the history of all the buildings around. After a few more minutes, I ask him how he knew all this information about these buildings that were built hundreds of years ago.

"Well, my mother wanted to be an architect when she grew up; but unfortunately things went south so quickly that no one was building any new buildings, so she just studied everything she could about the existing ones."

He continues, "Some kids got bedtime stories about cats wearing hats, I got bedtime stories about architects like Louis Sullivan and Louise Blanchard Bethune."

"Is your mom here in Buffalo now?" I ask. I knew it was a mistake as soon as I asked about it. We've all learned over the last few years not to ask about family because most people here don't have any left, for one reason or another.

Kian looks down toward his feet for a moment, his smile vanishes quickly. He sighs deeply and says,

"My parents had seats for the third ship. They won two lottery tickets. They begged and pleaded to get a third ticket, but I told them I didn't want to leave anyways. I saw what could happen down here if we all just stuck together."

So, his parents left him, just like Garven's.

I'm about to ask him another question, but he lets us know he needs to go talk to the guard and that we should stay here for a moment. I look around and am amazed by what I see. A couple hundred feet ahead is a huge building, 30 stories tall, with hundreds of windows facing us. The exterior is a brownish tan color and the building shape looks as if a closed hand had just a middle finger up, with the center being significantly taller than the rest. It also has a dome on the top, which makes it look even more like a finger. As I stand there, it feels a little like I'm getting a fever again, maybe from my infection? I can't tell, but it's making me anxious.

To the left is a building that's nearly the complete opposite. It's maybe 10 stories and has no visible windows. It's basically a tall, windowless gray rectangle. Whoever decided to build these next to one another must have had a sense of humor.

Rounding out the opposite side of this large square that we're in is yet another different-looking building. It's like a sliced-in half cylinder sitting on top of a regular old block building. It's also around ten stories tall, but there's no wall on the side facing me. If I had to guess, it used to be all windows. There were a few buildings like that left in Cleveland too. I can see a few people on the top floor with binoculars, and what I think is a telescope. It must be a lookout point.

The longer we wait here, the more I can feel my anxiety slowly bubbling up to the surface. Maybe it's the exhaustion finally catching up to me, maybe it's the idea that we have to start all over again here with meeting new people and figuring things out. For as smoothly as the last few hours have gone, I can't help but have a worried feeling in the pit of my stomach. It could be having a bow pointed at my face; it could be a lot of things.

As Kian talks to the guards stationed ahead, so many thoughts are running through my head. Is this really it? Are we in a safe place, or is this a trap? Am I going to get medical attention, or am I going to be traded off to the Raiders for some rations? The guard is heavily armed. I am suddenly feeling more overwhelmed than I can handle, more overwhelmed than I have felt in months. That's the thing about panic attacks: They can be triggered by both bad stress and good stress, and I'm getting plenty of both right now.

I'm starting to sweat, which is never a good sign. Esha looks over and, having experienced my panic attacks many times before, asks,

"Fin, you alright? Are you having an attack? I know it's hard but try to remember to ground yourself. Deep breaths, focus on a singular spot and keep your eyes open. Garven, do we have anything cold or cool to help Fin?"

"I mean, I don't think so, it's hot as heck, but maybe once we get inside they'll have something?" He answers.

It's too late for that. I start getting tunnel vision, and their voices start to sound muffled. I can't concentrate on looking at any one thing for more than a second. I try closing my eyes hard to wipe away the blurriness, but it's no use. My stomach starts feeling nauseous; having been through this so many times, it's a slim chance that I'll actually throw up but it's just one of the many things in my body betraying me.

Garven asks if I can hold it together until we make it through the gates, which he should know by now isn't very helpful at all. Esha comes to my side and helps slowly lower me to the ground. There have been times over the past few years that I've had panic so bad that I've blacked out, so she knows to help get me to the ground as quickly as possible so I don't fall.

I hear the two of them talking for a few seconds, but I'm starting to have a tough time responding. I know my pupils are dilated from Esha telling me during previous episodes. Last time this happened she said my blue eyes were nearly entirely black, and it scared the daylight out of her. I've tried to describe this sensation to people before by saying that the blood pumping through my body is too loud. Understandably, most people have no idea what this means.

I look up and, through my cloudy vision, suddenly see Kian standing there. At least I think it's Kian, it's hard to tell. It's also difficult to make out what he's saying, but I think he's asking if I'm alright. Esha tells him that she thinks the fever and infection are getting to me or maybe heat stroke, which is a lie, but one that I really appreciate.

Then it happens, Kian lifts me off the ground and starts carrying me like a newborn child into Niagara Square. I'm pretty sure he's yelling for medical attention, which is so embarrassing. If I had any blood flowing to my face right now, my cheeks would be the brightest red imaginable.

How is he so strong? He looked strong when we met him, but I didn't think he could pick me up like it was nothing. After a moment of carrying me, we are now out of the sun and heading into the shade of the giant building that's shaped like a hand.

I can hear Esha telling him that I don't want to be carried, but he replies that it's the quickest way to get help. I want to die, but not from the panic attack: From the embarrassment of this. While it's happening, my vision keeps alternating between black and fuzzy. I'm doing everything I can, which isn't much, to stay conscious.

We get through a doorway and into the building, it must be at least 15 degrees cooler than it is outside. I ask to be lowered to the ground; Kian mumbles something back to me, but I tell him I'll feel better if he can just put me on the ground. He looks over to Esha and she nods her head.

Once I feel the cold floor, I start to feel just a little better. That's progress, and part of the process of lowering my panic. I roll up my sleeves and place my arms and hands directly on the cool, hard floor. My tunnel vision slowly expands, so I can see things on the edge of my vision once more. The pattern on the floor is something I've never seen before; the square marble tiles are huge and beautiful. I didn't think buildings like this were left anymore. Where the heck am I?

I don't have much time to think about it while my mind is racing. I lower myself fully onto my stomach and rest my forehead on the cold floor. It feels great and terrible all at the same time. My hearing starts to come back, and I notice a new voice.

"Did they pass out? Have they been conscious the entire time?" The new voice says.

"No, they didn't pass out, they've been conscious but in and out of being able to communicate," replies Kian.

"Why the hell did you put them on the floor?" Asks the voice. I'm starting to assume this is their doctor by the way she speaks.

"Because I feel better if I can touch something cold. It grounds me a bit," I manage to respond.

As I weakly push myself off the ground, everyone turns to look at me. I get to one knee and pause for a moment, afraid that moving too quickly will make me faint. The new person is definitely a medical professional. She wears a red t-patch on her pocket. I try to introduce myself, but I still feel my blood pumping and my fight or flight kicking in, so instead I take a couple of deep breaths.

"This doesn't seem like heat stroke, or a fever, to me," the doctor says, "but you already know that already, don't you, stranger?"

"Oh yes, sorry doctor. This is Fin, and that's Esha and Garven. They just got here from Cleveland," Kian says.

"More people from Cleveland, huh? Quite the trek you've all made here. I'm Radia, people call me Rai for short, one of the doctors we have here at the Hall. If you're okay with walking, Fin, I'd love to take you to my office room to check you out a little further. You can grab my arm if you need to."

I nod my head slowly as I continue to come down from my panic. My racing heart is slowing, and my blood doesn't feel as loud. My vision is returning as well, and I notice how clean everything is in this building. My panic is subsiding, only to be replaced by the embarrassment I've felt over the past 5 minutes.

"I'd love to walk Fin to your office, if that's alright Doctor Rai?" Kian asks.

"I think it's probably better if I take Fin, Kian. It's been a long day and the less strangers around the better."

"Do you feel comfortable going with her, Fin? I can come if you want me to," Esha asks.

"I think I'll be alright," I say, "I appreciate it, though. If you want to have a look around or get some rest, I'll be fine."

I give her a weak smile and nod my head, letting her know I mean it.

With that, I start walking with Dr. Rai down the hallway. She's a little shorter than I am, and I hold onto her arm as she smiles warmly at me. Her dark brown eyes feel comforting, and her brown, shoulder length hair has a shimmer and sheen from the indoor lighting. It strikes me as strange that there is indoor lighting in such a huge space, and I wonder what their power source is.

Kian yells out to me that he's going to take Garven and Esha and show them around the place. I wave my hand up to let them know I heard what he said.

Forty feet down the hall, we enter the doctor's office and I immediately notice how nice it is. It's clean and orderly with nice wood furniture, the kind we would have burned to stay warm back in Cleveland. The room also had several doors that head off in different directions. Dr. Rai notices me looking around.

"We're pretty sure this used to be the mayor's office," she says, while having me take a seat.

"The community decided that health and safety were going to be the two most important pillars of rebuilding, so with that we converted the nicest room in the building into a doctor's office."

As she's talking, she's grabbing some supplies from the thick wooden built-in shelves to the left of us. She gets her stethoscope, a blood pressure gauge, and a tongue depressor.

"Rebuilding is such a different term than I'm used to," I say.

"What are you used to saying?" Rai asks, with some amusement on her face.

"Surviving," I answer.

With that, her smile disappears and she looks me directly in the eyes.

"For as long as you're here, Fin, you can concentrate on feeling better. You don't have to live day to day anymore. I can promise you that."

As she says those words, I feel tears start welling up in the corner of my eyes. I close them tight and then look up toward the ceiling in order to try and keep composed, but it quickly escalates into a full-scale cry. I have not been able to relax, to take a single unlabored breath, in so long that the mere idea of having a safe space has made me emotional.

She stands up and puts a hand on my shoulder. For a moment we both say nothing. I wipe my face off with a small towel she hands me, take a deep breath, and laugh. Dr. Rai chuckles a little too.

"Jeez, that's so embarrassing," I say, while laughing again.

"Nothing to be embarrassed about here, Fin. It seems like it's been a hard road for you," she says, using my name again.

I tell her it has been, without giving her too many details. She then asks,

"So first off, obviously what happened outside was not heat stroke or infection. How long have you been having panic attacks?"

"Five or six years now. But I ran out of medication finally about a year ago, so it's been especially tough since then. I had really been using it sparingly for a while because I used it so much when my mom and dad passed. I told myself I would only use it when I was having the worst of the attacks, and I did, but there was only so long I could hold on," I say.

"Well, I have some good news for you," Dr. Rai says. "We have a small supply here, so what I can do is give you one right now, to help you through this new transition, and I can give you one to keep on you in case of emergency. If at any point you need to replenish and get another, you can come in and we can have a talk."

To say I'm shocked would be an understatement. I had no idea there was any anti-anxiety medication left. I've just assumed for the past year that life was going to be difficult for however long I survive, and sometimes I was just going to shut down.

"Wait, you have anti-anxiety medication? How? How is that even possible?" I manage to say through a stutter, before continuing,

"It's been like a decade or more since any was produced. I lucked out in getting mine from an old supply in someone's apartment that left them behind."

Dr. Rai smiles, understanding the shock in my voice.

"Well, we lucked out, really. The main maker of the medication was headquartered not too far from here throughout the late 21st century, so when we searched the building there was a lot just left here. They aren't nearly as potent anymore, but they work. They also left all their patents and instructions, so we're working on producing a very, very small amount here as well along with other stuff like pain relievers and antibiotics."

"Speaking of antibiotics," I say to her.

I slowly roll up my pant leg for her to take a look at my infection. As it gets to the point of the wound, I wince. Once it's visible, I look away, so I don't make myself sick. It's especially bad looking today.

"Oh, wow. That's pretty gross. How long has this been going on?" Dr. Rai asks.

"Around a week, week and a half," I respond.

Do doctors usually use the word "gross"? Not any that I've ever known, which to be fair isn't that many.

"You know, for it being that long, it's actually not as bad as it could be. It usually spreads way farther than this. You put anything on it?" She asks.

"Yeah, Esha ground up some chamomile and calendula and applied them regularly. She said they should help slow the spread of the infection. Hurts like hell when she puts it on each day."

"Well of course it does," Dr. Rai laughs. "This is one of the uglier infections I've seen recently. If she hadn't done that you might have lost your leg. How on earth did she know to put those on? Was she studying that type of thing before everyone left?"

As she was talking to me, she was pressing on different parts of my exposed leg. The only time it really hurt was when it was close to the wound. I wince as she's an inch away.

"She's a pretty private person, I'm not sure she would love me telling everyone her business," I say through a low, nervous chuckle.

"That's fair," she says matter of factly. "Back to you, how did the injury initially occur?"

This is the first time I've noticed her slip back into her "Doctor Voice" since I was on the ground and she was talking to Kian. They all have it, every doctor I've ever met. This combination of stern but warm, reassuring but warning you not to lie to them. I always wondered if they passed the voice down when teaching future doctors.

"Do you want the whole story, or the abbreviated one where I just tell you what caused it?"

"Patient's choice, Fin," she replies. Another common Doctor tactic is re-using your name over and over, and it annoys me.

I decide against telling Dr. Rai the full story. She seems nice enough, but I'm not entirely sure what Esha and

Garven would want to share. We're all new here and I don't really want to mention anything about the Raiders.

"We were searching through an abandoned warehouse a little bit outside of Cleveland. I tried fitting through a small gap to another room and I didn't notice some rebar sticking out of the collapsed wall. Like an idiot, I went through and caught my leg. It hurt right away but I didn't want to be a burden on the group, so I didn't tell them for a few days. After that, Esha has been patching me up as we went along."

"Find anything good?" Rai asks, and she can see the confusion on my face. "In the warehouse you searched, did you end up finding anything worth nearly losing your leg over in that room?"

"Oh," I respond, and laugh nervously, "no, not really. There were some crates in there, but when I got to them, they were all empty."

Maybe I'm better at lying than I give myself credit for. I better make sure I see Esha and Garven before the doctor does, so we can keep our stories straight.

"Well, I for one am glad that Esha was there this whole time. I'll have a talk with Luna, she's one of the people elected to be in charge here, so Esha can have a tour of our greenhouses when she feels like it. Someone with that green of a thumb could really come in handy around here."

"Oh, Luna is one of Garven's friends. She's the reason we came here in the first place," I respond.

"Well then your friend Garven knows a very important person here in Buffalo," Dr. Rai says. She continues. "Take this, it's probably similar, if not the same as what you were taking before for your anxiety. After what you've been through, you might sleep for a long while. So, why don't you lay down in the room next door? I can shut the door behind me on the way out if that would make you feel more comfortable. First, though, let me clean up that wound and give you a quick shot of antibiotics to start healing that leg."

She goes over to a wall across from me and swings open a panel. Inside, it has all sorts of vials and tubes filled with different medicines. She grabs one, and a syringe, and brings it over toward me.

"Do you mind if I take a look at the medication first, doc? I get pretty nervous with new stuff," I ask.

"Of course I don't mind, Fin," she smiles warmly while saying it. "If you have any questions at all, I'm happy to answer them for you."

I take a look at the bottle and carefully read the handwritten words on the label. It's all completely meaningless to me, but it makes me feel better checking it out. While I'm pretending to acknowledge the writing, she has a clean cloth with some liquid on it and wipes the area around my wound. She then applies more liquid to the other side of the cloth and wipes over my wound. I once again wince and make an audible gasping noise. That really stings.

"Any questions before I get to it?" Dr. Rai asks.

"How long until this starts to work?" I reply.

"You'll actually notice yourself feeling a little better in 2-3 days, but to get an infection totally gone we'll have you in here once a day for a week."

She fills the syringe and taps the side of it. I prepare myself for it to hurt, but, honestly, I barely felt it. I don't know why but I thought she was going to have to stick the needle right in the infected spot, but she only stuck it into my lower thigh.

"After you wake up, you're going to need a full shower. We have to keep all of you clean in order for the wound to really start healing. When you wake up, I'll make sure someone shows you where all that is," she then says.

I thank her profusely. The idea of a real shower is one of the only things that kept me going the past few days of walking.

"Alright, now that we've started taking care of that, let's get you some rest and have you take that anxiety medication."

She brings me to the next room, and she confirms that I want the door shut behind me. I nod that I would and place the pill on my tongue. Before I take a chug of water, I move the pill in between my teeth and gums.

"Can I keep the rest of the water with me? In case I wake up and I'm thirsty?" I ask Dr. Rai.

"Of course you can. Let me grab you a small snack as well. You're probably starving. Feel free to eat it now, we'll get you a full meal whenever you wake up," she answers.

Dr. Rai walks out of the room and into the one next to it, I quickly take the pill out of my mouth and put it into my jacket pocket. None of it dissolved so I should still be able to read its markings once she's gone.

She enters the room once more and hands me a piece of bread and a couple of vegetables. The bread looks fresh and smells delicious. I hold it up to my nose and take a deep breath. It smells a little bit sweet, but it also has some sourness to it; it also has a strong, but pleasant, yeasty smell.

"Sourdough. It's my favorite. It's not as healthy or filling as most of the bread around here, but we make it as a little treat. Enjoy that, and the nap," Dr. Rai says.

She leaves the room and closes the door behind her. After taking a bite of the bread, I realize how thirsty I am. With my mouth still half full of bread, I take a big swig of water. I have to make a giant, exaggerated chewing motion in order to make a dent and then let out a long, happy sigh. It's been so long since I've had fresh bread that I've forgotten how to eat it like a normal person.

After another bite, I take the pill out of my pocket and read the numbers on it. "X1.0". Alright, so it looks like what she said it is. I feel bad being so untrusting of the people here, but I've heard enough terrible things that I also want to make sure that I actually wake up in a couple hours so I can see Esha and Garven again.

And maybe, if I'm lucky, Kian.

THE THIRD DREAM

I see it clearly. There are four of us walking up to the gates. The passageway leading to them is vast, miles long and at least a hundred feet wide. A concrete wasteland.

The day itself is bright and sunny, blinding even. Without a cloud in the sky and with nothing to block the corridor, the wind whips through with the occasional gust nearly knocking us over.

As we approach, I notice we are running and I am frantic. We are stopped by an unfriendly voice and after a few moments of banter, we are suddenly surrounded by a large group of armed people. In the dream it is stressful, but I don't know who they are or why they're here.

Then, they make us lay down our arms. Once collected, they round all of us up and I turn back to see a face that stares daggers at me.

In the dream, I know who it is. Their face is contorted in a hideous way. Evil screaming at us. In the type of suddenness only dreams can have, we have been captured.

Before the dream can continue, I wake up. In the fleeting moments before the images leave my mind, I try to remember who it was. The face seemed so familiar. It wasn't Garven or Esha but was it somebody that I knew? She felt so familiar.

The feeling gnaws at me for a few more seconds, and then I drift slowly back to sleep.

CHAPTER 13: KIAN

"You all have been on the road for a while now, huh?"

The voice cuts through a dead silence.

"I can tell you're not actually asleep anymore. You keep fiddling with something in your pocket," I recognize the voice as Kian, and my heart rate quickens slightly.

He's right, I've been awake for a little while but haven't wanted to move off of this couch. It's the most comfortable thing I've slept on in a month. Faux leather, three full cushions. Some wear and tear, but that just makes it even more comfortable. I might just lay here forever.

"Dr. Rai asked me to come in and check on you, see how you are doing. You've been sleeping for a solid eight or nine hours now."

"It's just so weird," I say, "being able to sleep in a place where I don't have to worry about the Raiders showing up. Without having to worry about… much."

"I don't know if I'd say it quite like that," replied Kian.

"You still have to get that gross infection treated, and this place isn't entirely Raider-free."

I haven't had a night of peace in I can't even remember how long. Now I'm lying here, in a beautiful and grand old building, with guards stationed outside. Food. Medicine. My leg is being treated and my anxiety is at the lowest point it's been in months.

If this isn't nirvana, it's the closest thing left on Earth.

"Sorry, I didn't mean that to come off as…" Kian starts,

"No, no, I get it. There's no perfect place left on Earth, but this is the closest I've been to it since before the ships left," I say.

"You, Esha, and Garven have had a pretty rough time. Since I've been here a while it just all feels so boring, or safe? I don't know, but I do know that some days it doesn't feel like living, that's for sure," he responds.

Living. Heck, all I've been doing the last few years of my life is surviving. That's all most of us have been doing for years now. A safe, comfortable place to stay for a week or two is a dream come true at this point.

"I hope I reach the point where this all feels boring," I say back to him.

He chuckles a bit, then walks over and sits on the arm of the couch. The only light in the room is coming from the open door, and his body is silhouetted by it.

"So, Luna said you're heading to Toronto? A couple of us here have been thinking about making the trek ourselves. We heard they have a nice little city happening up there, but it's hard to tell the rumors from the truth," he says.

The last thing we need is even more people on this slog. Even though there's power in numbers, more people also means you're easier to spot. More people increases the chance that someone gets injured or two people don't get along. It took Garven long enough to like Esha and me, and he knew us already.

"I'm not sure if I should be telling you this, in fact, I know I'm not supposed to," Kian says, and then gets quiet for a moment.

I let him have his thoughts, nothing anyone says at this point could possibly surprise me. Not after everything we've been through the past two plus years.

"We've managed to find enough parts to build a working solar-powered van."

I was wrong.

A silence fills the space. My brain is trying to wrap around the words that this handsome man just told me. I don't even believe it. I can't believe it. I haven't seen a working car in ages. Old photographs and movies make it seem like they used to be everywhere, but in the last couple of decades they have been pretty much just for government officials and the super-rich. You could only find gasoline for the antique ones on the black market; while electric vehicles were standard through the late part of the 21st century and early into the 22nd, no one was making direct solar-powered cars.

How is this even possible?

His voice cuts through my racing thoughts.

"I was as surprised as anyone that we got it to work. So far on tests, it only goes about between 12 to 15 miles per hour and runs for one, maybe two hours at a time, but that's a lot faster than walking, that's for sure."

My heart rate is through the roof now. A van? Solar-powered? The words are floating around but I'm barely able to comprehend it because of the rush of excitement flowing through me right now. Finally, I force myself to say something.

"How is that even possible?"

Kian turns to face me more directly and puts his foot up on the couch cushion closest to him, briefly brushing against the side of my leg.

"Well, a lot of really smart and talented people in this area didn't go on the ships. The government tried to make them, but they refused and said they wanted to start anew down here. So, we have some mechanics, some engineers, some solar experts, and some electricians. We also have a lot of spare time, so for a small group of people, that's been our main project."

"So, you've seen it? With your eyes? Not just rumors?" I ask.

"I—, uh—" Kian stutter for a second. I sense he feels embarrassed by something. Even with it being a little dark in here, I think he might be blushing.

"I'm one of the engineers that stayed behind. So yeah, I've seen it firsthand."

Friendly, good looking, and smart. I was not prepared for any of this. I'm just trying to get a good night's rest and suddenly, everything feels like it's changed.

"We're thinking about taking it up to Toronto for its first long test, but we need a crew of people because we'll need people to clear road debris on the way up. Maybe in the next few weeks we can talk with Luna and Harlian and see if the three of you can join us. If you'd be interested, of course."

"Hell YES, I'd be interested!"

I realize that I'm yelling, but I can't help it. The words "Hell Yes" echo in the room, and I laugh a laugh I've never heard from myself before. I am giddy with excitement and exhausted from the infection. My body does not know how to handle the flood of different emotions coursing through me right now.

"I mean I can't answer for Garven and Esha, but not having to walk another 100 miles? Please let me in that van," I say after my laughter dies down.

I genuinely cannot believe our luck. Are things actually, finally, looking up for us? We had nothing but trouble the entire way here, and now the first night that we arrive here I find out we might have a *ride* up to Toronto? It feels too good to be true. Why is he even telling me this? We barely know each other.

"It won't exactly be an easy trip if you're even allowed on. It's going to be a lot of us stuffed into a van, driving slowly for a few hours at a time. Lots of battery recharging. Lots of lookouts. Lots of sleep out in the open. So why don't you sleep on it tonight, and we can talk about it more tomorrow."

Sleep on it? How am I supposed to sleep now? I've been dreading the march up to Toronto. Even when I'm at full health I'm not as good at traveling as Esha and Garven are, and I am past worn down at this point. Not having to hike all that way would be a miracle.

"Goodnight, Fin, I'm looking forward to seeing you tomorrow. I have to ask you to promise me something, though," Kian says.

I can feel a warm smile even while I can't see his face. His hair is still silhouetted by the light from the doctor's room next door, and he runs his fingers through it once more.

"Yeah, of course," I respond.

"Please don't tell anyone about this. Not even Garven and Esha. I wasn't supposed to tell you, or anyone, and I feel like a complete idiot for blurting it out to you the first night. Like I'm some sort of gullible idiot who will tell an attractive stranger anything they want to know. It's just seeing the three of you make it from Cleveland, you've obviously made it through some things over the past few weeks. I feel like we need some survivors in the van. People who can overcome things."

"Yeah, of course. My lips are sealed, Kian," I say back, trying to reassure him that I won't be telling anyone.

With that, he walks out of the room and lightly closes the door behind him. I would be annoyed that there is still a sliver of light coming from the doctor's office, but my mind is too flooded at this moment to care.

Did he just say an "attractive stranger"? Did he just drop the greatest news I've heard in forever, a solar-powered van, and flirt with me in the span of a minute?

How am I supposed to sleep now? A roof over my head. Medicine for my leg. A real breakfast in the morning, and maybe a ride up to Toronto? I can't believe I ever gave Garven a hard time on the hike here. For the first time in a long, long time, things are looking up for the three of us.

I lay back down and try to get comfortable again on the couch. It's a strange sensation, falling asleep with no stars above. Tonight, of all nights, I have a thousand thoughts racing through my head. We've been living day to day, hour to hour, for so long that I don't even remember the last time we took a true break. Even at Ziggy and Petra's house we were gone in less than 24 hours.

I'm trying to concentrate on the prospect of a van ride up to Toronto. What does it look like? How many people can it fit? What type of weird coincidence is it that it's going in the same direction we're heading? Is it too much of a coincidence? Should I be more worried that this is all too convenient?

All these thoughts racing through my head, and the one that keeps breaking through is Kian calling me attractive, which I know is stupid. I guess the thought of someone complimenting me for the first time in two years means a little something extra.

I am unable to think about any one thing for more than a few seconds, and all the things I do to try to calm myself aren't available to me here. There are no branches or stars to count. No wind to feel on my face. No settling into the regular rhythm of Garven's snoring. I'm just laying here, looking up at the beautiful ceiling in this room. I can see it a little more clearly now that the room has a small amount of light shining in it.

I think to myself that I should get up and close the door, but honestly I'm just too comfortable on the couch to care.

In moments like this, when I feel excitement, it's hard for my body to tell the difference between that and anxiousness. I can tell myself over and over that I'm not having a panic attack, and that I'm not even feeling particularly anxious, but my body, my physical body, still hasn't figured out a way to tell the difference.

I close my eyes, hard, and try deep breathing exercises before it gets any worse. Almost as quickly as I start, I give up because deep breathing almost never works. I reach my hand out from under the blanket, down toward the floor, and touch the cold marble. That helps. I like concentrating on the chills it sends to my body.

I take off my tan jacket and have my undershirt still on my upper half. The green tank top looks even worse than it did a week ago and is in desperate need of a wash. Thankfully it's late and almost everyone is in their rooms, I assume. Eventually, I remember to reach my hand inside my pocket and grab my chain.

Feeling the cold, fiddling with my chain, and letting my mind wander help. After a few minutes my heart rate starts to slow back down. What a strange life this has become, where excitement can be just as bad as being scared. Today it's been especially bad, a culmination of a long journey, a new beginning, and an unknown future.

I realize that I'm still wearing my boots, an old habit from making sure I can run out of my tent if I need to. I sit up and unlace them slowly. They are black in color but with all the layers of dust, dirt, and grime, it's hard to tell. It's surprising how well they've held up during our journey, considering I found them in a random apartment in Cleveland about a year ago.

I then stand up to place them and my jacket by my backpack, which is across the room. The small bit of light in the room gives me enough vision to avoid smacking my shin into a low table. The cold marble floor feels good through my socks, which are in desperate need of a wash. I remove them too and place all three things against the side of my backpack, then head back over to the couch and lay down.

As I try to drift off to sleep again, I once again look at the beautiful tile mosaics above me. Stunning in both their beauty and in the fact that they've survived the last two-hundred years. I begin to think about what I want out of the next few days while I heal up. It's simple, really.

One, find out more about this place. How long has it been here? How is it so well preserved?

Two, see this solar-powered van and make sure it's real. I have to see it for myself, otherwise Kian could just be playing some cruel trick on a weary traveler. What a horrific joke that would be.

Three, get this leg healed up.

With those thoughts, I begin to count the tiles on the ceiling above me. I reach 300 before I start to feel my eyes get heavy. At 400, long blinks begin and I lose track of where I was. I'm about to start over, but before I do, I drift off.

CHAPTER 14: APPLE

I open my eyes slowly in the morning, trying to figure out if everything Kian told me last night was a dream. I have no idea what time it is as my watch is across the room, next to my boots, socks, and jacket. I immediately fiddle with the chain in my right pocket again, it's something I do to make sure I'm not dreaming anymore.

I use my left hand to try and wipe the exhaustion from my eyes. I feel like I've been sleeping for a week. Suddenly, I'm startled by a voice.

"Finally," Esha says.

She then bites down on something. The food makes a satisfying crunching sound.

"I thought you were never going to wake up," she then says while still chewing.

People talking while eating is one of my biggest pet peeves, and Esha knows that. Is she trying to annoy me? I sit up and rub my eyes a bit. I finally focus and notice what she's eating.

"Is—is that an apple? I stutter, not quite believing my eyes.

Esha grins. She's using one of her knives to slice off one piece at a time. She slices one and tosses it over to me. I cup my hands under it like I'm catching the most valuable thing on Earth. It lands softly in my palms, and I can feel the crispness of the skin immediately.

We eat so much dry food, the fact that there is a real, actual fruit in my hand is unbelievable. After looking at it in disbelief for what feels like an eternity, Esha speaks:

"You gonna to stare at it, or are you gonna to eat it?" She chuckles to herself, obviously amused at how I'm reacting. I take it and bite the piece in half.

I've never actually tasted an apple before, so I wasn't sure what to expect. It's one of those famous fruits that everyone knows about, but by the time I was born all of the orchards had died off and apple trees aren't well suited for small rooftop gardens.

At first it snaps a little between my teeth, I like the texture immediately. Then it's a little sweet, but also a little tart. It also feels like it's hydrating me while I eat it. It's amazing. I feel like I could eat a thousand of them right now.

"How the hell did you get an apple? How do they have apples? I don't understand. Are there any more?" I say as I'm still chewing the first bite, ignoring my own pet peeve.

At this point I have so many questions that I'm not sure where to start.

"Well, to answer in order. I got an apple from Luna this morning, she said it was a welcome gift, and we could each come get one from them. Secondly, I have no idea how they have them, I'm guessing they have some greenhouses and orchards around to be able to feed everyone. Finally, I'm not sure how many more they have, but they definitely have one for at least you. Garven ate his already."

"Did Garven think they were amazing?" I ask.

"I saw him smiling while eating it, but when I asked him about it afterwards, he said it was 'fine.'"

"Ah, so he was lying about it," I say while chuckling.

"Yeah, he was lying about it. Anyways, let's get you some breakfast, get you cleaned up, and then we can bring you back here to the medical area. They're gonna wanna change that bandage and give you a second dose of antibiotics. Sometimes day two can make you a little nauseous if your stomach is empty, so we should make sure you have some food in you first. They have all sorts of stuff to eat, and then afterwards we can get you that apple."

The only time I've ever heard Esha talk this much is when she's going on about plants. Whether it was telling Garven and me about what she found or teaching those kids how to grow their own food.

"It's pretty nice here so far, but make sure you stay on high alert for anything weird. We're not settling down here so try not to form too many attachments. I know you're the sentimental type," she says while making very direct and purposeful eye contact with me.

There's the Esha I know and love.

"So last night, Kian came in to check on me and he told me about—" I pause. I'm torn between telling one of my oldest friends the truth about the electric van or keeping it a secret and gaining Kian's trust.

"Told you about?" Esha asks impatiently.

"He told me about them having, uh, an area to shower and clean up," I say.

"Oh. Yeah. I heard through the grapevine that you'll be getting a full tour today, so I'm sure they'll show you where the showers are on the tour," Esha responds.

"Okay, cool. I'll be out in a second, just need a minute to get dressed and get my stuff on," I respond.

"Alright, see ya out there," with that, Esha turns around and leaves the room, closing the door tight behind her.

I feel bad about not saying anything to her, but this also feels like a test and I'd like things to go well while we're here. I can't believe the start to our new, temporary life here. Kian tells me about the van, they have fresh fruit, and I got a full night of sleep. I haven't been this excited to get up in the morning since I was a kid.

I walk over to my clothes and notice my notebook has fallen out of my bag. Strange, for sure, but not the first time I didn't strap everything in after a long day. Hopefully they have somewhere here where I can wash my clothes. I hate putting on the same dirty clothes day after day. I especially want to wear something clean after taking a shower.

I grab my bag, fling it over my shoulder, and head toward the door. I walk through the area where I had my shot yesterday and see Dr. Rai sitting at her desk. I give her a friendly smile and wave.

"Feeling better after sleeping for the last day?" She says with a warm smile.

"More rested than I've felt in years, Doctor," I say back.

"I'm glad to hear it. Why don't you swing by a little later today and we can get you your second shot?" She asks.

"Sounds perfect, see ya then," I say back, as I make my way toward the hallway.

Once outside the doctor's office, I see Esha standing in the hallway having a conversation with someone I haven't met. The stranger has the brightest, white-blonde hair I've ever seen. It's currently in large, oversized braids. I have to think it would be down to her lower back if not in the braids. It's especially contrasted next to Esha's shorter wolf cut.

As I walk toward them down the hallway, I see it in her hand: The most perfect red apple I've ever seen. I can't help but smile ear to ear as I approach. As I near, she turns to me.

"I hear she ruined the surprise already but, yes, here is your apple."

As she says it, she tosses the apple toward me. My heart skips a beat while it's in the air, but thankfully my hands don't betray me and I catch it. Before I can even say thank you, she continues, "We try to grow enough so everyone here gets one once a month, as something of a treat. I heard from Dr. Rai that Esha is actually quite a horticulturalist herself," she turns back toward Esha and says, "If you want, I could show you around the greenhouses this morning?"

"That would be amazing," Esha replies, "but I was going to show Fin where breakfast and a few other things are."

"Oh, don't worry about that, Kian is coming over to show Fin around. He asked me specifically this morning if he could do it. Let's go take a look at plants, shall we?" Luna responds.

Esha looks over at me to make sure it's okay that she's heading elsewhere. I smile and nod, knowing this might be the best day of her life seeing a bunch of fruits, vegetables, and plants that she's never seen before in their greenhouses. Besides, Kian wants to show me around and who am I to say no to a free chaperone?

The woman turns to me and says,

"I'm Luna, by the way. Garven's friend from way back when. It looks like you're feeling better than when you arrived yesterday. If you need anything, don't hesitate to ask, I help run this place."

Her face looks so familiar. I wonder if I saw it yesterday on the way to the doctor's. All of that is such a blur that it's hard to remember, but I could swear I've seen her before.

As Luna and Esha turn down the hallway, I hear a friendly, familiar voice,

"How's life treating you since yesterday

afternoon?" Garven says with a huge grin on his face.

He wraps me in a big bear hug, lifting me slightly off the ground. It's great to see him, but I know exactly what he's about to say.

"I told you so," he whispers.

Yup, I was right.

"I told you this place would be amazing! They're getting your leg patched up, we don't have to worry about the Raiders for a bit, and I see you got your apple from Luna! Pretty great 24 hours so far, eh?" he says.

He was absolutely right, it was a great 24 hours, and he doesn't even know about the van. It's going to take everything I have not to tell him or Esha about it. I'm definitely a person who likes to give good news and I'm also someone who accidentally spoils surprises so, beyond fighting off this infection, not telling the two of them might be the hardest thing I do here.

"I heard through the grapevine that Mr. Handsome went into your room to check on you last night, what was that about?"

"Who?" I say meekly, trying my best to play coy.

"Oh, come on now, Fin, that dude's attractive as hell. I'm pretty sure they use his jaw line to cut the stones placed around the outside of the building here!" Garven lets out a huge laugh after saying this. He has always been the biggest fan of his own jokes.

I roll my eyes and respond "Yeah, he's alright, if you're into that sort of thing."

"What sort of thing?" Kian says as he turns the corner.

Garven starts laughing harder, makes eye contact, and turns a perfect 180 degrees without saying a word. With that, he walks away. He always has a penchant for making situations as awkward as possible. He finds joy in it, and also in embarrassing me. Kian watches Garven leave with a confused look on his face and then turns to me.

"That was weird."

That was, in fact, very weird, but I do my best to change the subject as quickly as possible.

"So, I hear you volunteered to show me around today. I feel like a pretty important guest right about now."

CHAPTER 15: LANDING

Auryn holds tightly onto a railing in front of the ship's giant view screen. All she can see now are flames engulfing the entire ship. She looks to her left and sees a crewmember expelling today's lunch into a trash bin. The ship jerks hard to the left and the same person falls to the ground. Auryn takes a step to go help but the ship jerks violently back to the right, so she grabs back onto the railing with her second hand.

No one expected entry into the atmosphere to be quite this violent. So far the ship is holding up, but injuries are beginning to add up. If enough injuries happen, it will delay everything on the ground.

An announcement comes over the speaker system,

"I know it's a bumpy ride right now," the second in command of the ship says, "but we're almost through, and it'll be smooth sailing from there. Please make sure to check on each other as soon as you can."

The ship tries once more to throw Auryn from the railings, but she is clutching tight. The crewmember who threw up a few seconds ago isn't so lucky, and he goes sliding into a nearby wall.

As Auryn is trying to formulate a plan to help him, the turbulence stops. She turns toward the screen and now, all it shows is gray. They made it into the atmosphere. She then runs over to her injured shipmate and kneels next to him.

"Are you alright?" She asks.

He looks up at her and then grabs his knee area while wincing.

"I don't think it's anything too bad, but I hurt my knee when I slammed into this wall," he replies.

Auryn puts his arm over her shoulder and on the count of three, helps him up to his feet. He's limping badly, and she offers to help him get to the medical office on this floor.

They take a few steps and then the man stops. Auryn is about to ask him why, but she sees him looking toward the screen. She turns slightly to look in the same direction.

They have a full view of the planet's surface, and it's gorgeous. Wide areas of lush vegetation. Deep greens, like pictures from Earth in the 21st century, but also fiery reds, bright oranges, and more. There are also large swaths of water all over the place. Auryn's never seen land look so beautiful.

After a few more seconds, the man cuts through the silence and says,

"I wish I could stare at it for hours, but I think I should get some medical attention."

Auryn apologizes for getting caught up looking at the screen, and the two of them make their way down the gray, brightly lit hallway toward the medical office. Fifteen steps into their walk, another passenger comes over and grabs the other side of him and the three of them head further down the hallway.

After dropping the man off with the doctor, she walks back down to the view screen. By now, a crowd has formed and are talking amongst themselves. Auryn walks up, and as she's looking at the screen, she hears a friendly, "Hello!"

She scans the area and sees Mina, standing about 10 feet away. She heads over and, as is becoming the routine, Mina gives her a big hug.

"Can you believe we made it?" She says to Auryn.

"I was honestly not sure I'd ever see the day," Auryn replied.

"How'd you survive the entry? That was pretty rough, huh?" Mina then asks.

"I was alright, but I just had to help a guy to medical. Poor guy threw up and was then tossed into a wall. Not a great way to start life on a new planet," Auryn says while stifling her laughter.

"Oh man, that is so rough," Mina replies. She continues,

"I was in the Engineering room on this deck and my work partner, Klay, was almost flung over the railing to the deck below. I grabbed onto his sleeve when he was like, halfway over."

"Wow! Good thing you were there!" Auryn replies.

After some more talk about the rough entry, they both turn to look at the several story tall screen in front of them. The ship then slows down to almost a standstill, and an announcement comes over the system,

"Congratulations everyone, we have made it into B.52C's atmosphere! It was a little rougher than we would have liked, but we've reported no casualties and mostly minor injuries. Over the next several hours we'll be scanning the new planet's surface to find the best location to set up our colony. Please be patient while this is performed, and congratulations to everyone again!"

Soon, the ship will be landing and the hard work will truly begin. Auryn wishes she was in the initial landing party, but that's well above her status. The captain, assistant captains, head engineers, and "honored" guests would be the first to step off the ship. They would be the ones future learners of the colony would know the names of, and the ones whose statues will someday adorn the cities here.

Auryn didn't care about all of that. She wasn't interested in legacy. She just really wanted to get off the damn ship.

CHAPTER 16: HOPE

Kian and I walk through the hallways in this beautiful building. The marble tiles below us are black and gray, but it's the ceiling I can't stop staring at as we walk. It's such an intricate design, the amount of time it must have taken to complete is astounding.

"Art Deco," Kian says.

"Huh?" I ask.

"The building style, it's Art Deco. The ceiling is amazing, isn't it? The tile work is so intricate. Stunning tans and oranges and browns, with little highlights of green and blue. I've been here for years and still find it fascinating," he replies.

He then asks me if Dr. Rai told me about the place, and I mentioned that she said it used to be Buffalo City Hall. He knows all sorts of historical facts about the place, and the city, and will tell me these random things all throughout the next few weeks.

It's endearing, and I would usually love listening to him talk, but I interrupt,

"Hey, Kian, I would love to hear all about this, genuinely I would, but I haven't had a real shower in…" I pause for a moment, "well, I don't really want to admit how long. Any chance you could take me to where the showers are?"

"Oh god, I'm so sorry, Fin! Here I am blabbering on about a building when there is so much for you to do first. I'd be happy to take you to them, they're over by the main greenhouses, let's walk over."

I thank him profusely and apologize for cutting him off.

"Don't even worry about it," he says, "Luna had me grab some new clothes for you so we can show you where to wash your old ones after. There are also some towels in the changing area."

"Does everyone in the city shower in the same area?" I ask, genuinely concerned not out of any prudishness, but because I really don't want to wait in line.

Kian laughs and says,

"No, no, not at all. We actually have this same system set up in all the areas of the city where people are living. We collect the water from the showers to reuse it in the greenhouse. It's why we built them right next to each other. Greenhouses to grow food and medicinal plants, water collection for when we get big storms once a month, and showers that recycle the water back into the greenhouses. Even the soap we make is okay for the plants to absorb."

"Wow, you guys have thought of everything, huh?" I say.

"Well, most of this stuff has been around hundreds of years, if not longer. All we did was make the conscious decision that everyone in the city gets equal access to it all. So, no neighborhoods are left behind," he replies.

I've been here one day, and I love this place already. Esha was right, I'm definitely going to get attached.

As we exit the building into the Niagara Square area, I'm astounded how vibrant it all is. One area has stands for people to pick up food, a mix of fresh vegetables and grains; another area has a small wooden stage, no more than a foot off the ground, with a sign right in front of it. The handwriting says:

"Storytelling Hour: 6 and 8 PM Every Night (Except Mondays. Boo Mondays!)"

"What's that about?" I ask.

"Well, people put in a lot of work around here. Everyone works the greenhouses, tends to the small fields we're able to keep up, fixes building issues, and improves quality of life, all of it. So, at night they want to make sure that people have the opportunity to relax and enjoy some entertainment. Storytelling is one of those options," he responds.

We walk north for two blocks and then turn the corner. There I see a gigantic structure, multiple stories high by several city blocks long. I pause in amazement.

"That," Kian says proudly, "is the greenhouse. Greenhouse 001, to be precise."

"It's gigantic!" I exclaim.

"It has to be," Kian continues, "In this sector alone we feed and provide medicine to around 4,000 people. That's a lot of food every day to hand out."

"After I shower, can I see the inside?" I ask excitedly.

"It's all part of the tour!" Kian answers while laughing.

I head directly toward the large greenhouse doors, but Kian steers me a little to the right, where the showers are.

"First, let's get you showered. You have a busy day today, which means I have a busy day today as well. After the shower I'll show you the greenhouse, then we'll take you over to get your badge so you can pick up food each day on your own. Then, if you would like, we can have some breakfast together. After that you need day two of antibiotics for that gross cut of yours. Plus, I'll show you the clothes washers. Busy day ahead!" Kian says.

We walk the remaining two blocks to the shower area and Kian hands me my new clothes and shows me where the towels are. They have a shelf and hook system for clean and dirty towels. Kian mentions that after my shower, I can hang my dirty towel on the hook. Generally, he says, they want you to use the same towel several times before it is washed, but since I have a lot of grime and dirt on me I should just hang it up after this shower.

He then lets me know that he'll be at the entrance to the greenhouse, or "The Oh One," as they call it, after I'm done.

"Meet me over there when you're done. Since it's your first shower in so long, feel free to take as long as you want, but after this one you only get five to six minutes."

With that, he walks away, and I walk into the shower area. There are large pipes coming down from the top of the building that then spread out into small, individual rooms. I have no idea what to expect, or really how to work them. I just hope that I don't have to ask a complete stranger for help.

I walk along a wide corridor that has small rooms on each side of it. If the door is closed it means someone is inside showering already, so I look for a room with the door open. About halfway down, I get to one that's available.

The small room is surprisingly clean. It has four walls that start about six inches above the ground and stop about a foot taller than me. The pipe comes down and only has an on or off nozzle. There was a small part of me that was hoping maybe the water would be heated, but I'll take anything at this point.

I turn the nozzle on and, unexpectedly, the water is actually warm. Later Kian mentions that the water is heated by the sun outside before flowing down into the pipes, so the temperature is often five to ten degrees warmer than it is outside. It feels amazing. Weeks of dust, dirt, and grime wash off of me. I stand there, close my eyes, and put my head under the shower. I then tilt my head directly toward the water and let it run over my face.

After a minute or two of enjoying the clean water on my face, I lather the soap in my hands and wash my face and my neck. I look down toward the drain and see the water turn from clear to dirty. I'm not even sure I realized how many layers of filth I had accumulated, which makes Kian complimenting me last night seem even more impossible to believe.

This entire time, I had forgotten how sensitive the wound on my leg was. That is until I run the soap over it. I accidentally let out a loud yelp and immediately cover my mouth with my soapy hands. There are other people showering around me who no doubt just heard that.

After a moment, I hear a soft voice say,

"Everything alright over there?"

My cheeks get hot with embarrassment. I'm glad that no one can actually see me at this moment.

"Yes, sorry, I'm fine. Just forgot about an injury of mine. Thank you for checking in!" I reply.

I try to sound thankful, because I am, but I also feel like I have to finish showering as fast as possible, so this nice, kind stranger and I don't get out at the same time. I want nothing more in the world than to be invisible right now.

I finish up quickly and grab my fresh towel, dry off, and put on clean clothes for the first time in a month. Grey jogger pants that go down to my mid-calf, and a lighter gray, super lightweight long sleeve shirt. I roll the sleeves up and put my dirty boots back on.

I walk out of the shower area feeling better than I have in weeks. The sun is bright in my eyes as I look for Kian. I see him by the front of the greenhouse talking to Annora, and someone else I don't recognize.

"Finley, it's so good to see you again. Are you settling in okay?" Annora asks.

"I just had my first shower in forever and I can't even explain how good it felt," I say. "I mean, until I embarrassed myself by screaming."

"I'm sorry, you did what now?" Kian asks, while a smile creeps across his face.

"I may have forgotten about my leg wound, because the shower was so amazing, and I ran the soap over it and it hurt so, so much, so I, uh, I yelped I guess I would call it," I answered.

The three of them look at each other and laugh. I look

at the third person, a man, and he looks vaguely familiar. Kian notices me looking at him.

"Ah, yes, Fin, this is Eno. Eno, this is the person who spotted you on the rooftop," he says.

Eno shakes my hand and gives me a sly smile.

"You know, because of you seeing me, these two are going to give me a hard time about it for months. I'm gonna have to ask for a different lookout location just to get away from Annora for a bit," he says while gently punching her shoulder.

Eno laughs softly while saying this, which gives me the impression he's not too mad about it.

"You spotting him was one of the best things to happen to me in weeks," Annora says.

She then turns to him and says,

"Also, Eno, transfer denied. You're stuck with me on South Park Ave duty for the foreseeable future."

Eno rolls his eyes and laughs.

"I'm never going to forgive you for this, Finley," he says.

"Alright," Kian says, "I'm gonna show Fin around the 'Oh One' now. I'll talk to you both later about what you saw earlier."

That was cryptic, but I'm new here though so it's not like they're going to tell me anything important. Kian motions for me to follow him. He takes a few steps and then opens the doors to the greenhouse.

As I walk in and look around, it's even more gorgeous than I could have imagined. The sheer size of the inside is overwhelming, and it's filled with lush plants everywhere. Right now, there's a mist falling from the sky over almost the entire greenhouse, which must be four blocks long.

"This," I pause, "is amazing. How is all this possible? How is it misting like that, doesn't it draw a ton of power?"

Kian's familiar smile once again appears.

"Actually, I helped design that. It's gravity based and turns on and off with a simple valve system. We implemented it at all our greenhouses, and it made a huge difference in the crop yield the past year."

To be able to help come up with all this while only being 20 is beyond words. I can't even begin to imagine how many engineering books he's read to be trusted this much by the elected officials here.

I start to wander further into the greenhouse. By a row of apple trees, which Kian says aren't practical, but important for morale. By all sorts of leafy greens like kale, bok choy, swiss chard. Vegetables like cucumbers, carrots, celery, peas, radishes, and so many tomatoes. Kian says it's probably too many tomatoes, there's so many they often have to make big batches of soup and binge on it for a few weeks.

As we walk, I notice the vast and complex drainage systems under some of the hanging plants.

"We use some principles of hydroponics and aeroponics here, along with good old dirt and soil," Kian says. "With our aeroponic water system, any of the water that makes it to the bottom of the tube then gets taken, by gravity, to the plants that are growing directly in the soil."

He continues, "Part of the reason we built this here was because this area had already been reduced to rubble and ruin, well, the ground at least. It seems like they were trying to clear out the road for something when all work stopped, so we just came in, added a new layer of topsoil, and built a greenhouse over top of it."

We walk through rows upon rows of edible foods at all stages of growth. It's incredible. Kian then asks me if I want to see the rest, which includes plants and flowers for healing and remedies.

"Absolutely, I do!" I say excitedly.

He motions for me to follow him through another set of plastic doors. Once open, the most amazing scents waft through the air. It's overwhelming in the very best way. We walk by rows of calendula, chamomile, echinacea, gingko, and ginseng. We get to rows and rows of lavender and what I usually just call wildflowers. Muted purples, vibrant oranges, all sorts of different colors as far as the eye can see. He puts his arm around my shoulder, and we start walking between them.

It's a narrow path, and a few steps in I trip over a small bucket that was barely poking out from the flowers. As I fall, Kian tries to catch me but instead just accidentally flips me over on the way down. I land on my back, laughing. Surrounded by wildflowers, I look toward the ceiling, and I can feel the warm mist hitting my face. For a brief moment I lay there, laughing, and all seems right with the world.

Kian, now down on one knee after I also threw him off balance, asks me if I'm alright, and I tell him that I am but that I might need yet another new set of clothes already. I sit up and the flowers are as tall as I am, some even twice as tall. The air is so clean and so fresh. If I could just stay in this moment, I know everything would be alright in the world. I close my eyes for one more moment just to feel the mist on my face.

Kian helps me up, and I try brushing the dirt and mud off of me, with little success. I look at Kian and his knee is entirely coated in mud. He tries brushing it off as well, but it just makes his hand muddy.

"Good thing I still have my shower left for today," he says, playfully rubbing it in that I've already used mine.

We get to our feet and continue walking through the 'Oh One,' and Kian points out numerous other plants. Eventually we reach the end of the greenhouse. I turn back around to marvel at its sheer size, and how much is grown here.

"So, what do you think? Pretty cool right?" He asks.

"It's one of the most amazing things I've ever seen in my life. I can't believe how much food is in here!" I respond.

"Pretty impressive, right? It's become the model for all the other greenhouses across the city. There are, jeez, 18 of them now? Not quite as big as this one. With another couple being built. We've had so many people arrive from Cleveland that we're starting to fall behind on building them. Thankfully all the new people are more than willing to pitch in so hopefully we can catch up soon."

We talk as we make our way out of the greenhouse, and I immediately run into Esha.

"Did you get a tour of the 'Oh One'?" She asks excitedly. "Isn't it so freaking amazing? They have so many things in there that I haven't seen in years, or ever!"

As we catch up, Kian gets a call over his walkie-talkie. Before he picks up, he walks a bit away from us.

Esha continues, "Have you had any real food yet? It looks like you got a shower but you're, uh, a little dirty. What were you and Kian up to in there?" As she says this, she wiggles her eyebrows in an exaggerated way. I immediately start blushing.

"Oh geez, I tripped over a bucket and landed in some wet dirt! Nothing happened!" I protest.

The heat from my face could power a thousand solar panels right now.

"Oh? Why is Kian dirty then too?" She says, continuing. "Look, all I'm saying is that dude isn't going to be available for long, so if you're gonna get to it, get to it. If you don't, I might."

I quickly shush her as Kian walks back toward us.

"Well, sorry to cut this short, but I actually have something I have to take care of. Would you feel comfortable showing Fin how to get breakfast, Esha? I'll be back in a little while, hopefully, to show you around the rest of the place." Kian says.

"Absolutely, I was just going to head that way, anyways. It's no problem at all, Kian," Esha says back.

He hurriedly shuffles off while Esha takes me in the direction of food. I look over my shoulder and see him meeting up with Eno and a few people I don't recognize. As I turn around and continue walking with Esha, I realize how starving I really am. Suddenly the best thought comes to me:

I haven't eaten my apple yet! I swing my backpack around to the front of my body and dig through it for a moment. Finally, I feel it in all its round splendor and pull it out.

After I flip my backpack back onto my back, I take a huge bite.

"You know you owe me a piece, right?" Says Esha.

I go to grab my rusty old knife out of my backpack, before Esha cuts me off.

"I'm KIDDING, Fin! Kidding! Enjoy the apple, you've gotta be starving."

As we cross back through Niagara Square, I finally get a better look at the building I was in overnight, the old Buffalo City Hall. It's difficult to put into words how large and beautiful it is, even with some broken windows and one of the large marble columns crumbling. Esha tells me that the style of the building is "Art Deco", which Kian already mentioned this morning, but I didn't say that to her.

In its shadow is a large, narrow, white marble monument, and surrounding the monument is a large pool carved into stone. Some parts of the monument are coated in the same dust and dirt everything else is, but on the bottom ledge surrounding the pools the white marble shines through in all its beautiful glory. I notice some people sitting on the edge and realize that it must be kept clean in those areas from people leaning up against it.

As we continue walking, Esha mentions to me that our rooms are in City Hall, on the 5th floor. The elevators don't work anymore, and usually people as young as us would have a room on a higher floor, but with my leg injury they didn't want me taking too many stairs at least at first. They also didn't want to split the three of us up, so we're all in one old office that has been split into three sections.

"It's not like the nicest accommodations I've ever seen, but it's nicer than what we're used to, that's for sure," Esha says.

"It's going to be amazing to not have to sleep outside for a few weeks," I say.

"Having food available to us whenever, getting a good night's sleep without having to stand guard. Having medicine, and helpful people around? I mean, are we sure we even want to go to Toronto anymore?"

I chuckle as I say it, but I'm not entirely joking. This place has been a revelation so far.

"We're not traveling to Toronto just for safety, Fin. We're traveling there because people, *your* people, *Garven's* people, might be coming back," Esha replies.

Auryn. I haven't thought about Auryn in almost two days, and my heart sinks. That's the longest I've gone without thinking about her since she left. I am immediately overcome with guilt.

"God, I feel like such a terrible person. I'm so glad I didn't say that around Garven. Please don't mention to him that I did," I say to Esha.

"Don't worry, Fin," she says, "I'm not going to say anything. I know it's hard not to get carried away here. I mean, I saw a real live apple tree."

Esha shows me where the food is, and how to get a "food badge". It's really just a way for them to make sure no one is taking more than they need. There's a regular daily amount everyone gets and then some specialty items, like apples, people get less often.

We sit down as I eat my breakfast, some oats and blueberries. Over the next 20 to 30 minutes, Esha explains that there are some large plant crops growing around the outskirts of the city, closer to the water. She starts talking about how amazing it is to grow warm weather oat plants, and the process behind it, but I start to zone out.

As she talks, I daydream about making a life here in Buffalo. In all likelihood, Auryn is not coming back. We could help and be a part of this community. They're already doing so many amazing things, feeding everyone, getting people healthy, even providing entertainment. We could put down roots here and rebuild our lives.

I look up at Esha, and she's quiet, sitting directly across from me at the wooden picnic table, and staring at me with her golden, honey brown eyes. Sometimes, when the light hits them, I would swear they're nearly translucent.

"Welcome back, you were gone for a few minutes there. Sorry if I was boring you," she says, laughing.

"Oh god, I'm so sorry, Esha. It's just been a long couple of days," I say back.

"You seemed to have no problem being fully locked in when Kian was talking."

With that, she gives a gentle slap to my hand.

"I'm never going to hear the end of this, am I?" I ask.

Right as I'm about to protest, there's a commotion from behind me. I turn to look around and see Kian, Annora, Eno, and a few others quickly walking toward City Hall. I look closer and notice that both Kian and Annora are bleeding, and Annora is bleeding badly. It looks like a wound to her midsection, if the blood is any indication. She has an arm each over Kian and Eno, and they're basically carrying her.

I start to stand up and Esha grabs my hand. I try to pull it away, but she holds on tight.

"You are new here," she says sternly. "You can't just barge into anywhere you please. In a few minutes we'll head to Dr. Rai to get your second antibiotic shot, and you can see what's going on with them."

She was right, of course, but I still don't have to like it. I want to rush in and see what's happening with Annora, and yes, Kian. What was that call over the walkie-talkie about? Kian mentioned last night that they still had to worry about the Raiders, was there a fight? All this uncertainty is killing me. My anxiety begins to spike.

"Everything is going to be okay. They have a great doctor here, and plenty of medicine, and she'll be fine in no time," Esha says. "So will Kian," she adds.

"I know, I know, I just hate not being able to help. Maybe if we went to the doctor's office, we could help. You could help, like you did with my leg."

"Fin, I rubbed some plants on a wound, that's probably not what they're looking for," Esha says.

I sit on the uncomfortable wooden picnic table seat and stew in my emotions for a minute. My heart is beating quickly, and I'm rubbing my hands together repeatedly. I haven't taken another bite of my food, even though 15 minutes ago I was starving.

"How many more minutes do you think we have to wait until I can go get my shot?" I ask Esha.

"At least five," she replies.

CHAPTER 17: MINA

After scanning for a few hours, The Amelia Erhardt found a place to land. After watching her shipmates being thrown around during atmospheric entry, it was a relief how smooth it was during landing.

"Crew and passengers of the ship," the speaker system yells out, "we are happy to announce that the ship is safe on the ground, and the captain and select crew members will be taking the first steps onto B.52.C in a few moments. We encourage everyone to turn on their viewer screens and watch this historic moment!"

Auryn, sitting on a white couch in her quarters with the rest of her family, rolled her eyes at the announcement. Her dad, Arthur, noticed and immediately started laughing.

"You just know they're gonna talk about this in every speech they give for the next 20 years," he says.

They both start laughing even harder. Auryn's youngest brother, Forbin, asks,

"So do we get to leave the ship now?"

He's 11, and Auryn is pretty sure he's already the smartest one in the entire family. This trip had been especially tough for him because he looked up to Garven so much. Many nights, Auryn stayed up to tell him stories about how Garven was back trying to save Earth and, when he's done, he can come here and live with them again.

She can't know if it's true, of course, but it makes both her and Forbin feel a lot better.

Over the next several weeks, Auryn and her dad are on the planet building the dome. Even though the planet is inhabitable without any assistance there are slight differences in the air, which make the crew more tired than normal. To combat this, the initial building crew are all wearing masks that cover their nose and mouth, with a tube that wraps around to a backpack which increases and decreases oxygen levels as needed.

It's a lot of extra weight to lug around, and Auryn would rather be tired from the planet's atmosphere than tired from the backpack.

She is working on the dome for one more week, then she's going to switch to the ship. On a lunch break with her dad, she finally has a conversation about it with him.

"Hey, Dad," she starts.

Arthur looks over while chewing a sandwich he picked up from the ship's commissary.

"I thought I should let you know that starting next week, I won't be working on the dome anymore. I'm actually," she pauses, nervous to tell him, "I'm going to be working back on the ship, to get it ready."

Arthur finishes chewing his bite, and swallows hard.

"That's amazing, Auryn. I'm really proud of you," he says and gives Auryn a smile and nod.

Auryn then returns the smile and throws an arm around his shoulders. She leans in and gives him a hug from the side. He then takes another oversized bite from the sandwich, and they both finish eating their lunch.

"Just make sure whatever you do, you do it to the best of your ability," he says to her as they stand up.

"Those people are counting on you."

Auryn smiles and says she will, but feels guilty, because she plans on being one of "those people", but just hasn't had the heart to tell them yet.

Auryn's relationship with her dad has always been good. They can go long stretches while working without saying a word, and Auryn finds comfort in that. Even back on Earth, she was always helping him tinker with whatever he was trying to salvage. Maybe it was an old window fan that could run off some solar panels. The same panels Auryn helped him fix the year before. They always loved working with their hands and solving problems. Alia, Garven, and

Forbin always liked to solve problems with their mind more than their hands.

Still, not telling her dad has been giving her massive guilt in the last month or so.

So instead, she buries herself in her work over the next four months. Even if she didn't have a task assigned right then, she would pitch in with someone else on a different system. She wanted to be as invaluable as possible for two reasons: The first was so the ship was in the best possible shape for anyone who gets selected for the return trip and secondly, when the selection process came up, the people she helped along the way would hopefully remember her and her contributions.

She spent time in the engine room, on the electrical consoles in the bridge, in tiny spaces and gigantic caverns all over the ship. She learned a little bit about a lot of things and soaked up more information that she had in her entire life up to that point.

One specific Team Lead for the trip back has taken a sheen to Auryn: Mina. They've been working more closely together as the weeks go by. Anytime Mina needed a second pair of hands for a project, Auryn's communicator went off. She was happy to oblige. Sure, it was good for her chances of returning to Earth, but it was also nice spending time with Mina. If she was going to be spending long hours in cramped conditions, why not do it with the company she enjoys?

One night, after a specifically long day of work, Auryn's dad pulled her aside.

"Your mom and Forbin are out and about in the colony. Figure now would be a good time to share this with you."

With that, he went into his room and came out back with a dusty, antique bottle filled with a clear liquid. Authur grabs two highball glasses from the kitchen and sets them down on the table in front of the couches. He motions for Auryn to take a seat and grabs one himself.

"I've kept this around for 25, 30 years maybe at this point. It was your grandpa's before that. It was one of the few things I actually brought along on this ship. On special occasions, your mother and I take a sip and savor it. You're 18, almost 19 now, and I just want to say. I'm damn proud of you," Arthur says.

With that, he pours a small amount of the clear liquid into a glass for each of them. They both raise their glasses toward each other, until they meet and make a *clink* noise.

"They called this vodka. It was made from potatoes, I guess," Aurthur says. "Here's to all the hard work you've put in over the last few months."

Auryn brings the glass up to her mouth and briefly smells the liquid. It smells an awful lot like the cleaning agent she uses to strip grease off of consoles. She then takes the liquid and downs it in one gulp. She can't help but make a face. Her cheeks squeeze up to her eyes, she sticks her tongue out for a moment, and she shakes her hands vigorously side to side.

"Wow, did people actually like this stuff?" Auryn asks.

Arthur looks at her a softly chuckles,

"I highly doubt it."

CHAPTER 18: TENSION

Five minutes felt like five hours. After Annora, Kian, and the group disappeared inside of City Hall with their injuries, Esha made me stay outside. I couldn't make myself sit or eat, so I stood up and paced. I knew if I tried to make a run for it Esha would tackle me, causing a scene. Finally, she said we could head into the doctor's office, and I nearly sprinted there.

After passing through the front doors, a security guard stopped me. She is wearing a light blue, short sleeve button up shirt, black pants, and an annoying look on her face.

"What's your business here?" She asked.

"Oh," I stutter slightly, "I have to get a second antibiotic shot for my leg from Dr. Rai. She told me to come in right at this time."

That wasn't exactly true. She did ask me to come in this afternoon, I just added in the "at this time" part. The guard uses her walkie-talkie to radio the doctor. After a seemingly endless amount of time, but was actually closer to

15 seconds, Dr. Rai answers and lets the guard know that I can come through.

Quickly, I head down the familiar hallway that leads to Dr. Rai's office with Esha trying to keep up. My shoes make a loud echoing noise through the cavernous hallway. As I turn the corner into her office, they squeak loudly. Once I'm a foot or two inside, I can hear Kian talking.

"The weirdest part was I actually dreamed this exact thing happened like a week ago. Then bam, the Raiders show up on that exact street."

I pause for a moment. Did he just say his dream came true? Esha catches up to me and starts talking loudly, which alerts Dr. Rai and Kian to my presence.

"Hello, Finley," the doctor says, "here for your second shot of antibiotics?"

"I am," I say, then pause awkwardly for a moment. "I saw Annora came in looking pretty hurt, is everything okay?"

Dr. Rai spins back on her stool toward Kian and looks at him, he nods to her, and she turns back to me.

"Annora is going to be fine. Unfortunately, our security patrol had a run-in with a group of Raiders. Some people were hurt, like Annora, but everything is alright now. Why don't you take a seat while I finish up with Kian."

I nod and head to a row of chairs about 20 feet away, toward the back of the room. These chairs must be a hundred years old. As I sit, the chair creaks loudly. I look over at Kian and he's getting stitches put into his upper arm. It looks like a pretty deep cut, maybe a knife or an arrow?

Either way, it looks pretty bad.

Suddenly, another door across the way opens and for a brief moment I can see into the room. Annora is lying down on a table, and a different doctor appears to be stitching up her side. There is a lot of blood on the table she's laying on, and her face is contorted. She is wincing in pain. She has a piece of wood or plastic in her mouth that she is biting down on. I lean to my right to try and get a better look, but the door is slammed shut.

Esha, sitting next to me, looks over to me and then grabs my hand and squeezes it tight.

"She's gonna be okay," she whispers to me. She's using the same voice that she uses when I have panic attacks.

"I know," I whisper back, as I lower my eyes to look at the floor and nod.

A moment later, the door swings open again, and the doctor comes out. His gloves and sleeves are covered in blood, and he walks straight over to where we are sitting.

"Do me a favor and open up that cabinet, will you?" The new doctor asks.

Esha gets up and quickly and opens the doors. The

doctor points to a stack of gauze and Esha grabs it for him. He nods and asks her to close the cabinet back up.

"She gonna be alright, Doc?" Kian asks.

He looks over at Kian, nods his head, and says,

"Oh yeah, she'll be alright. No main arteries were hit, so in a couple of days she'll be on her feet again. Might take a couple weeks for her to be back on patrol though."

Kian nods his head and thanks the doctor, then looks over at me and smiles. I sigh in relief that she's going to be okay. After another couple of minutes, Kian stands up and thanks Dr. Rai. He looks over at me and says,

"Don't think you're off the hook for the rest of the tour. Give me a couple of hours and I'll show you the rest."

With that he smiles, puts his thin, dark brown jacket back on over top of his gray T-shirt, and leaves the doctor's office.

"Alright, Fin, give me a couple minutes to clean up and we can get you your second antibiotic. If it's alright with you, I'd like to ask Esha to leave the room. I have a couple of things I'd like to discuss," Dr. Rai says.

Esha looks at me to make sure I'm okay with this. I let her know that I'm feeling fine and I'll meet her outside in a bit. She nods, apprehensively, and exits the doctor's office.

"I'll be right down the hallway if you need me, alright, Fin? Just yell out if you need anything at all," she yells back in my direction.

Dr. Rai spins on her stool toward me and waves me over.

"It's nice having close friends who care about you, isn't it?" She says.

I laugh and say,

"It is nice, maybe a little bit overprotective at times, but nice."

"Alright, have a seat here, we'll reclean that cut and get you your second dose of antibiotics. Fair warning, you might feel a little cruddy after this one. For some reason people tend to take this one the worst."

"Well, I've slept so much the past few days I don't even know when I feel cruddy or not," I respond.

She chuckles and starts wiping down the wound.

"So, when you were coming in I'm guessing you overheard Kian talk about his dreams? You paused for a moment, and I noticed a strange look on your face. Wanna talk about it?" Dr. Rai asks.

So, she did see me there, but for some reason didn't stop Kian? I'm really not sure if I should talk about this with her. The only people who know about my dreams are Esha and Auryn, and one of them isn't even on the planet anymore.

"Look, Fin, if you don't want to talk about it, it's fine. But I want you to know that this is a safe space."

I think about it for a moment and decide why not. It'll be nice to get this off my chest.

"Well, I just thought it was strange that sometimes what he dreams comes true," I say.

"Well of course you think it's strange. It's not every day you hear someone has that ability," Dr. Rai responds.

"Ability?" I ask.

"Well, yeah. Over the past few years we've noticed some people, a very small section of people, have an ability to see the future within their dreams. Usually in small pieces, specific happenings. Last week Kian came to me and said in his dreams he saw the Raiders surprise attack on one of the lookouts, Annora. With that information, we had an extra person with her on patrol and lookout all this week and, wouldn't you know it, he helped save her life today."

I am dumbfounded. I thought my dreams happening later in real life was just a coincidence. Sometimes, I thought I was just making it up in my head or had a severe case of déjà vu. Knowing that there are others, and they use that ability?

"Is there something you want to tell me, Fin?" Dr. Rai says, "You look like you're really mulling something over."

"I've had one or two dreams that came true later. But nothing useful. Nothing that could have saved a life. I've also had plenty of really vivid dreams that never happened, so I don't really know what to believe."

"Yet. Fin," Dr. Rai says.

I'm confused by this and give her a look to let her know I don't understand.

"They haven't happened *yet*."

CHAPTER 19: SURPRISE

After five long months of work, tinkering, calculating, and restocking, The Amelia Erhardt is ready for its return trip to Earth. The announcement was made this morning over the loudspeakers in Central Park and throughout the hallways and quarters in the colony. Even though everyone is welcome to head outside the Central Park Dome area during the daylight, it's still the most popular place to hang out amongst the colonists.

While the planet is livable without any assistance, the slight variation in oxygen levels means you get tired a lot quicker, which means the fully controlled dome more closely mimics the experience of Earth. Plus, with the days being closer to 35 hours instead of 24, everyone's sleep schedules are pretty out of sync, even all these months later.

In the park, the engineers and agriculturalists filled the area with plants and trees and even turf. There was debate on adding real grass in some small areas but, since there's no real value to it, they compromised and chose artificial turf instead.

They designed it off of old pictures of Central Park in

New York City. It's really quite beautiful and the place Auryn spends most of her time when not working or sleeping.

When the familiar beep of an announcement began, Auryn had a feeling today was going to be the day. Her portion of working on the ship ended a few weeks ago, and that meant it wasn't too much longer before the whole thing was ready to go.

She had spoken to the main crew assignment officer, Oren, about the trip back to Earth a few days before her assignment wrapped up. He agreed that she could make the trip back, since he had heard such great things about her from Mina. Auryn also asked him not to say anything to her parents.

"I have no intention of talking with yours or anyone else's parents, Auryn. That is your responsibility," he replied.

At this point, Auryn is 18 and in charge of her own destiny. The one thing he did make her do is take a month off after her ship assignment was done. To have time to decompress and relax. She also has to figure out a way to tell her parents.

"You've spent the last 2 years either on the ship or fixing the ship. Everyone needs a little time to decompress. So, in order for you to return to Earth, you have to take four weeks off to wander around the colony and just relax," Oren said.

During her time off, she was finally able to experience the long afternoons on B.52.C. She would often head to

Central Park, lay in the surprisingly soft turf or sit on a bench, and daydream. Sometimes those dreams were about hopping on the ship and not even telling her parents. She would never do that, of course, but avoiding the inevitable confrontation is something she would love to do.

It's been almost two years since she left Earth. Two long years she's been waiting for this announcement. Her mind wanders for a moment and she thinks of Finley, as she often does. Tears well up in the corners of her eyes and she lets out a long, happy sigh. She can finally go home and, just like she promised, rescue her little penguin from a dying planet Earth.

"People of the colony, we have exciting news," the announcement begins. "The amazing crew of our ship has wrapped up their work, and in four weeks a returning crew piloted by Captain Rossi will be flying the ship back to Earth to rescue the remaining members of our society. Everyone please give a big round of applause for all those who have worked tirelessly over the last six months, both on the ship and on the ground!"

With that, a thunderous round of applause went up not only in Central Park, but all throughout the hallways and corridors of the colony. Auryn sees people high fiving, hugging friends and family, and celebrating all around. There's never been a better or worse time to tell her parents that she's going to be on that ship.

She collects her things and makes her way back toward the family quarters. She gets stopped several times on the way and speaks with friends. Everyone has an extra bounce in their step, knowing that in three years or less, people they know and love could be joining them here. It was truly an amazing day for humanity.

As Auryn approached the quarters she could hear loud voices coming from behind the door, but it didn't sound celebratory, it sounded like they were arguing. She places her ear on the door but can't make out any of the words being said.

She swipes her badge, and as the doors swing open, her parents stop mid-sentence and look over. Her mom with an angry expression on her face, and her dad with an exasperated one.

"What's going on guys, aren't you excited about the announcement?" Auryn asks.

Her parents dart looks at each other, her dad then looks toward the ground. Her mom, Alia, sighs deeply and says,

"Well, I *was* excited about the announcement, until your father ruined it 30 seconds later."

"I just, I didn't just know when to tell you and it felt like it was now or never," her dad said back.

"You promised that once this was all over, once the ship was heading back, once the colony was stable, that we could slow down and enjoy some time together. Both of us have been working nonstop for years!" Her mom replied.

“Someone needs to go pick up Garven! We can’t have the ship go back with no one to greet him!” Arthur says, exasperated.

Auryn is certainly her father’s daughter. From what she can gather through the yelling, he wants to head on the ship back to Earth to pick up Garven and hadn’t told anyone either.

“Well, I have good news and bad news for the both of you,” Auryn interrupted.

They both look at her with an intensity that only parents who are in an argument can produce. Her mom’s lips pursed tightly shut, her dad’s eyes wide with the same exasperated and guilty look on his face from a minute ago. She readies herself to tell them the news she's been avoiding for the last month, if not longer.

“The bad news for Dad is that all the spots on the ship are already spoken for. So, unless you have already asked to be on the ship, at this point it's too late. So, mom, that's the good news for you,” Auryn said.

“What's the bad news for me?” Her mom replied, arms crossed, brows furrowed, lips still pursed.

“I have one of the spots.”

CHAPTER 20: READINESS

It's been a few days since my conversation with Dr. Rai about my dreams. I've finally gathered up the courage to ask Kian about his dreams, and how often they come true. I've never been able to talk to someone else who experienced this.

We're meeting for some breakfast and to have a chat. I've seen him every day since then and I've tried to find out some pieces of information about what happened to him and Annora, but he talks around it a bit. The most I've got from him is,

"She's doing really well, up and moving around."

As I approach the food stands in Niagara Square, I look around for Kian. I can't see him anywhere, which is a little weird, he's always early to everything. I say "Hi" to the morning vendor, Ramson, and grab my breakfast. I take a seat at one of the wood picnic tables and take my first bite. I look up toward City Hall, like I do every morning, and try to notice a new detail that hadn't caught my eyes before.

This morning, it's the intricate upside-down red and

orange triangle pattern right near the very top. It's hard to see when the clouds are out or the sun is behind the building, but this early in the day, the sun is shining bright on the front of the building, illuminating the patterns underneath the layers of dirt.

"Sorry to interrupt, but are you Finley?" A voice I don't recognize says.

I try to chew my bite quickly and answer. Instead, I choke a little bit and cough very loudly.

"I'm so sorry, I didn't mean to ask you with a mouthful of food!" The stranger says.

I laugh and clear my throat, "It's no problem. Yes, I'm Finley, what can I do for you?"

"Kian asked me to meet you here. He asked me to tell you that something came up, and he's really sorry, but he'll hopefully see you for lunch," they say.

"Oh, uh, okay. Did he say why?" I ask.

"He didn't, I'm sorry. Well, I've gotta go, enjoy your breakfast."

With that, the stranger left. I didn't even get their name. It's definitely odd that Kian isn't able to meet with me, but he's always being pulled in different directions here. Sometimes I think it's to the detriment of his own health, but I'm not in charge of what he does.

Unexpectedly, I now have the morning available; I don't have to see Dr. Rai until the early afternoon. Maybe I'll swing by the room and see if Garven and Esha want to hang out. We've all been so busy the past couple of days, I feel like we only see each other right before we pass out at night.

I finish up my meal and say goodbye to Ramson before I head out. I then cross the square and head toward City Hall. I walk up the steps – five to start, then a landing area about 8 feet wide, and then eight more – and go through the gold-toned revolving front doors. By now, the security guard, Devena, knows me and gives me a friendly smile and wave.

"What's on tap for today, Fin?" She says.

"Oh, just getting stood up for breakfast," I say while grinning. "Hoping maybe Garven or Esha are in the room."

"What? So sorry to hear that! Who on earth would stand you up? A fool, that's who!" She snorts from laughter.

Devena is one of my favorite people here in Buffalo. She has an infectious laugh and an amazing smile. I've also come to find out that it was her asking if I was alright in the shower when I yelped the other day. Being able to joke around with her about it has made me feel less embarrassed by the whole thing.

She continues, "Garven and Esha both left pretty early this morning with Eno though, and they haven't been back. I can let ya know if I see them."

"Oh, thanks, I appreciate that, Dev," I say back.

With that, I turn back around and leave through the revolving doors once again. While wandering the city I start to wonder: Kian, Esha, Garven, and Eno are all gone? I wonder if it's related. We've spent such little time together the past few days, maybe they're working on something together.

As I stroll through the streets, I decide to check out the greenhouse again. The last time I checked it out, with Kian, I noticed a small cart of old books near the front door. I have to pass a few more hours before I can get one of my last antibiotic shots. What better way than to breathe in some fresh air and read an old book.

As I enter the doors, there's a hum of activity inside. Lots of people are picking fruits and vegetables, adding nutrition into the soil, and doing other various greenhouse jobs. I flip through the cart and grab a book that looks promising and start looking for somewhere to sit.

I find a nice bench in the floral section of the "Oh One" and grab a seat. Breathing in the smell of lavender, watching the mist float down to the ground on timed intervals, and reading a book. I could only have dreamed of these things just a week or two ago.

When I open the book, I notice a couple of early pages missing. I sigh and hope I'll still be able to understand what's going on. Flipping through the book reminds me of my parents. I look around and, after seeing no one nearby, I hold it up to my face and take a big breath in.

How do all old books have that same smell? I take it away from my face and run my fingers along the edge of the page, then I turn a few pages quickly just to hear and feel how it is in my hand. Part of me really wants to bend the spine, to see if it has any cracking sound left to it. My dad always hated it when I did that to his books.

Mom would always say "Books are meant to be lived in, dear", while he would huff and puff about it. I don't think I ever saw my dad actually mad at mom or me, but he would definitely be annoyed.

I get lost in the book for a little while. Could have been twenty minutes, or an hour, I'm not sure, when a loud voice says,

"Hey, you. Can you help me for a second here?"

At first, I ignore it because I assume they're talking to someone else, but then they say,

"What, you're too good to help an old guy like me?"

I look up, and 15 feet away is a guy, maybe 55 years old, looking directly at me and smiling.

"Oh!" I say, "I was in my own little world and didn't realize you were talking to me!"

He laughs and asks if I can help him with the wheelbarrow full of dirt he's pushing. I hurriedly get up from my seat and walk over to him. My limp is mostly gone, and Dr. Rai told me I should start doing a little bit more on it to regain strength.

"I've already dumped so many wheelbarrows full of dirt in here today, and my back is killing me," the man says while wiping the sweat off his forehead with the back of his hand.

"By the way, I'm Carrew. I haven't seen you around here before, are you new?"

"I am, been here less than a week. I'm Finley," we shake hands and exchange brief pleasantries.

As I take the handles of the wheelbarrow, he shows me where he needs me to spill the dirt. I push hard up a small mound and then tip the wheelbarrow over.

"Perfect, thank you. You're a lifesaver for my back. Now to spread all this out and be done for the day," Carrew says.

"I'd be happy to help with that, too. I've felt pretty useless the last couple of…" I trail off for a second, "months."

I chuckle to myself, and Carrew says, "I'll take any help I can get. I know they generally don't give new people any work for the first week or two, but I could use a rest!"

We talk for a few minutes while I help spread the dirt around and plant some new seeds and bulbs. He asks if I traveled here with anyone, and I let him know Garven and Esha.

"Oh, I've met them. They're great. I saw them with a couple other people heading out for patrols this morning. Really nice of them to volunteer for that with all the Raider problems we've been having the past few weeks, and with what happened to Annora."

"Yeah, that is really nice of them," I respond. "Did you happen to catch who they went out with?"

"Oh, I think it was Eno, Kian, and a few others," Carrew says.

I finish spreading the dirt and planting, and Carrew thanks me profusely. I look down at my hands and realize I might never get this dirt out of my fingernails. Carrew cracks a joke asking if I'll be here again tomorrow at this time, and I let him know I might. It was nice feeling useful for a bit.

"Thanks again, I really appreciate it. If you're planning on sticking around Buffalo, I can put in a good word for you to get an assignment here in the greenhouse, if you'd like," he says.

"I'm not sure if I'm sticking around, but if I do, I would love that," I say back.

He walks away and I grab my book to start reading again, but I can't concentrate. Why wouldn't Esha and Garven tell me they were going out for patrols? Maybe they were just tired and forgot to mention it. It's not like them to keep something like this from me.

I decide to take a shower since I got pretty dirty from the work in the greenhouse. We get three showers a week if we're not technically working yet. Regular workers get five showers a week. No one really checks, it's the honor system, but for the most part people seem to follow it.

I head over to the shower area, and I can't stop thinking about why they wouldn't tell me. I'm hoping a shower clears my mind. I head back to the room to grab my soap and notice that my backpack is open, which is strange since I'm always careful to close it when I leave.

I look through it and nothing appears to be missing, but it definitely looks like it's been gone through. I sort everything back to where it should be and make a note to myself to ask Esha and Garven later if they were looking for something. I tie the straps up tightly, and place it behind my sleeping area, tucked underneath my blanket, and head back down and out to the showers.

If I was hoping the shower would take my mind off things, it doesn't. Afterwards, I dry off and decide today is the day I'm going to do some laundry on my own. I only have a couple pieces of clothing, so it shouldn't take too long. I want to make sure that if we decide to leave this place, I have as many fresh clothes in my bag as possible.

As I'm walking out of the shower area, I see all four of Kian, Esha, Garven, and Eno walking back in from patrol. I flag them down from about 35 feet away and start to jog over to them, but the concrete under my feet ends up still being a little too painful for my leg to take, so I slow back down to a walk.

"Hey, Fin, how's it going?" Kian asks, as cheery as ever.

"Would be better if you didn't stand me up this morning," I say to him.

Garven and Esha both raise their eyebrows and start laughing. Eno looks awkwardly toward Kian, and Kian starts to blush.

"I know, I'm so sorry. With Annora injured and unable to patrol for a little while, Esha and Garven volunteered to help out. I was out training them this morning and realized I totally forgot! Can I make it up to you?"

"Maybe, maybe not. We'll see, I guess," I respond.

Esha and Garven let me know that they're heading back to the room and are then going to shower and get some early lunch. I'm invited, but I let them know I recently had breakfast, so I'm all good.

Before they leave, I ask them,

"Did either of you go through my backpack today?"

"No, we've been out on patrol since like 8 this morning, and you were still sleeping, so we haven't been back to the room since then," Esha answers.

"Why, did someone go through your bag?" Garven asks.

"I'm not sure. Maybe? It was just all shuffled around weird when I came back to the room a little bit ago. I'm sure it's probably nothing, maybe I knocked it over before I left or something," I say.

"Well, we will try to keep an eye on it while in the room for you," says Esha.

With that, they head off in the direction of City Hall. Eno says his goodbyes to Kian and me and heads toward Niagara Square as well.

I turn to face Kian directly and say, "You could have told me you were training them."

He places his hand over his forehead to block the sunlight and sighs.

"I didn't feel like it was my place," he says. "Let me make it up to you though. I thought maybe today I could finally sneak you in to see the van I was telling you about."

If there was one way to win me back over, this is it. I desperately want to see this van, make sure it's real, and see if we can actually hitch a ride. I go back and forth with myself on whether or not I still want to head to Toronto or if I just want to stay here, but knowing that there is a van ride instead of a hike ahead of me? That certainly helps tip the scales toward Toronto.

"First, I need you to tell me about your dreams," I say, surprising myself with how direct I just was.

His facial expression changes from jovial to serious in an instant. He puts his hand on my shoulder, looks around for a moment or two, and speaks in a low voice.

"Please be careful what you say, and who is around when you say it. We can have a discussion, but it needs to be in private. Please don't say anything like that in public ever again."

His intensity startles me, and I nod that I understand. He tells me that he's going to go get changed, cleaned up, and asks if I'll meet him in his room in about 20 minutes. I agree and he heads in the direction of City Hall.

When he's about ten feet away, I realize I don't know what room number is his, so I yell out and ask.

"I'll let Dev know you're coming, and they can walkie up to me," he yells back. I can count on two hands the amount of people who have that type of privilege inside City Hall.

For the next few minutes, I can't get the image of his face after I brought up the dreams. His scrunched forehead, his narrowed eyes, his paranoid look around. His entire personality changed in an instant. This is the first time I've brought up dreams to someone who also has them, and I was hoping that it would go a little differently than that.

I head to the market at Niagara Square and wander around for about twenty minutes. There happens to be an impromptu lunchtime reading on the entertainment stage. Usually they're reserved for the evenings, but one of the regular performers, Yulia, is here doing a stirring performance for the lunchtime crowd.

The thing I love about Yulia is that she changes her voice for every different character in the book. That takes dedication. Some of these books have so many characters, how does she even remember a unique voice for each of them?

After 20 minutes of watching along with a small crowd of 25 or so people, I walk into City Hall and greet Dev for the third time today.

"Hey, Fin, Kian said to walkie him when you showed up. Give me one second."

She walks a few feet away and speaks quietly into her walkie. After another moment, she nods.

"He says you can head on up. It's a pretty good walk, he's on the 11th floor, room 1104. You gonna be alright with that leg of yours?" She asks.

"Yeah, it's actually feeling much better now. It'll probably be good for me to walk up all those stairs," I respond.

"You say that now, talk to me again when you need a breather on floor six!" She cracks herself up when saying this.

I laugh along too because her laugh is so infectious it's hard not to.

"One other thing I just gotta know, Fin," she says quietly, looking around to make sure no one else is nearby,

"Was it Kian who stood you up this morning?"

She looks at me with one eyebrow raised and a big smile. Her long, curly black hair falls over her face as she shrugs her shoulders. I hesitate, but figure what the hell. If he stood me up, people can know about it.

"Gotta know, huh? Yeah, it was him," I say.

"I KNEW it," she responds, "I just knew you two would be cute together! If he doesn't go and ruin it."

"Whoa, whoa! Slow down there, Dev. We're just friends," I say back, starting to blush.

"Look, Fin, my love life is non-existent right now, so I'm gonna go ahead and live vicariously through yours."

With that, she wishes me luck walking up the eleven flights of stairs and then turns to check in the next person who just walked through the doors.

I make my way toward the stairs, they're on the opposite end of the hallway from the doctor's office about 50 feet down, and start the trek up to his room. When I reach floor 6, I'm about to take a breather, but I remember what

Dev said and could never admit that I actually had to stop there, so I climb one more floor and then take a quick rest.

It's amazing how much endurance I've lost in the last week. Some days getting here, we walked 10 plus miles through tough terrain. Here, I'm just trying to climb some beautiful marble stairs and it's absolutely sucking the life out of me. I make note that I have to start exercising again before we head on out to Toronto. Even if I get to take the van, you never know what's out there.

I use the sturdy railing to pull myself up after my breather and walk the remaining four floors up to his room. I turn down the hallway and notice how much nicer this floor is than any of the others that I've been on. It looks like they knocked some walls down so that daylight can reach the hallway, and it gives some separation between the rooms. I can't help but think that this is a floor that important people live on.

That thought depresses me a little bit.

That's how it used to be in the older times, when the Earth was ruined and lots of people had more than they needed, I think to myself.

After walking for almost the entire length of the hallway, I begin to knock on the door with an "1104" plaque mounted next to it. It's a large, light brown, wooden door with no windows on it and a huge metal plate around the door handle. It swings open before I'm done knocking, and Kian is standing there, half dressed.

"Hey, Fin, sorry about that, just got done taking a bagged shower," he pauses before he finishes his sentence. "Hmm, I guess I've never really thought of how funny that phrase is. 'Bagged shower.'"

For a few seconds I can't help but stare at his chiseled abdomen. I've never thought of myself as someone who is impressed by a muscular body, but, in this very specific circumstance, I definitely am.

Okay, you've been staring long enough, I think to myself and try to look around the rest of his room.

I look around and notice his room is attached to a bathroom where a clear bag is hanging from the ceiling.

Kian notices me looking at it and says:

"It's an old habit of mine. I don't love showering in the common area. I feel like I'm always getting stuck in conversation right before and right after, so I fill up a 5-gallon bag and bring it back up to shower in here. There's a drain there that doesn't seem to be leaking water into anyone else's room, so it works for me."

I'm having the hardest time concentrating on anything he's saying with his shirt still off. Apparently carrying five gallons of water up 11 flights of stairs several times a week is working for him. Looking around the room I realize how nice it is, much nicer than most peoples.

The main living area is about 30 feet wide and 15 feet deep. There's a large, dark wood desk right by the row of windows at the front of the room. The windows themself look out over Niagara Square, and I move closer to them. While looking out, you can see people moving about their day down below. We're also about even with the large, white marble monument in the middle of the square. From here you can really see how thin and narrow it is. There are also gorgeous curtains on the windows, a deep green shade. I assume they're black out curtains so Kian can sleep during the day if needed.

He finally puts on a gray form fitting T-shirt and walks over to the door. He closes it tight and walks back to the bed, about 10 feet away from where I'm standing.

"I need to talk to you about what you started to say earlier. I apologize for being rude, but I needed you to realize how important it was to immediately stop talking about it," he says.

"Yeah, what the hell was that about?" I ask as I take a couple steps closer to him.

Without thinking about it, I cross my arms over my chest and shift my weight to one leg.

"There are certain people here, and more of them than you would think, that really, really don't like people who can see the future in their dreams. Even though there's no way to control it, they don't trust us. So, very few people here know that I can, and I'd like to keep it that way," Kian says.

"Who does know? And who wouldn't like that?" I ask.

"The only ones who know are Dr. Rai, Luna, and Annora. Dr. Rai and Annora took it fine, but Luna has a serious distrust of dreamers. It's taken a year for her to trust me as much as she does, and that's not even a lot. I think she might have told the other elected members, but I can't be sure."

He pauses for a moment in thought, then looks at me again,

"How do you know anyways?" He asks.

"When I was walking into Dr. Rai's office the other day, I heard you talking about it. It was such a casual conversation though; I thought it was okay to bring it up to you. I apologize for doing it out in public like that, I didn't know."

Kian takes a seat on his bed, it's a complete mess of crumpled brown blankets and off-white sheets, illuminated from the light of the windows I was just looking through. I honestly thought he was going to be much neater and tidier than this.

"Yeah, sometimes maybe I get a little too comfortable with Dr. Rai, I guess. That's a good reminder to be more careful on my part," He pauses for a moment, as if to take a mental note, then continues. "So, now that you know, do you have any questions that you'd like to ask me?"

"Yeah, a lot honestly. When did you start noticing that your dreams were actually becoming reality? Also, do all your dreams end up happening, or only some of them. Oh, also, do you sometimes see people in them you can't quite recognize, but it feels like you know them. Oh, and—"

He cuts me off there.

"Okay, okay, I'm going to start forgetting the questions if you keep asking them rapid fire like that!" He takes a deep breath.

"So, my dreams becoming reality has been happening more and more often recently. It used to happen occasionally, but it seems to be, I don't know, ramping up. Secondly, now pretty much all of them do, but not in any sort of order. I could have a dream tonight that happens tomorrow, or it could happen 6 months from now. What were some of the other questions again?"

I have so many I want to ask, but I ask him the one that has kept popping into my mind over and over from the second I found out someone else's dreams come true.

"What do you think it means?"

"That is a good question, Fin. I have no idea. I've been trying to use this ability, as Dr. Rai calls it, for good. Like with what happened to Annora, I used it to help keep her safe but I don't actually know what it all means."

I hesitate for a moment. I want to tell him that my dreams are becoming reality as well, but he's made it seem like others knowing this is dangerous information. Can I trust him to not tell anyone else? I stand there for a few moments debating in my head what to do next.

"You've been quiet a minute. I understand if you feel nervous around me now. Or even if you don't believe me," Kian says.

"It's not that, I promise it's not that, it's just that…" I pause for a long moment, deciding if this is the moment I share with him. "I know this might sound like I'm just saying this to, I don't know, fit in or something, but the reason I needed to know, and why I brought it up out in the street, is because my dreams also happen to me later, in real life, as well."

Kian looks at me with complete surprise. I thought there might have been a chance that Dr. Rai told him already, but the look on his face tells me that he had no idea before now.

"Wait, seriously? I figured there were others like me, Dr. Rai even said there were, but I've never actually met someone. Has any dream recently come true?"

"Yeah, actually. Like you, it seems to be happening more and more often recently, which has been really weird because I've had some really unsettling ones that haven't happened in real life yet. One of my more recent dreams though was me, lying on the ground, surrounded by flowers, with water falling on my face. In the dream I thought it was rain, but I guess it was actually…"

"The mist from the greenhouse," Kian interrupts.

"Yeah. How did you…"

"I know because I had that dream a few weeks back, too." He cuts in again. "I didn't know who was falling on the ground at the time, but as soon as I tried to catch you and missed, I realized I was having déjà vu because I had dreamed it," he says.

I walk a few steps and take a seat on the edge of the bed. We both sit in silence for a few minutes, processing all this new information. How did we have the same dream? Are we connected somehow? Is that why I was drawn to him the whole time? How is his bed this comfortable, and can I get one like it?

I'm now also worried that since all of his dreams come true, mine will too. I've had some unsettling dreams recently that I'm hoping more than anything to avoid.

"So, what were your scary dreams? Maybe by talking about them, we can figure out what they really mean ahead of time," Kian says.

I'm not sure I'm really prepared to talk about them right now, and I let him know. He nods and tells me that when I'm comfortable, he's all ears.

We both continue to sit in silence for a few moments, wondering what this all means. If there are at least two of us here, there has to be more— but how do we find them? How do we talk about it with others when others might be hostile toward us?

I then think of my notebook. I've been writing down my dreams for years. I wonder if there are some in there that later came true, but I forgot about them. I'll have to flip through tonight and see. Not much more we can do now, I guess.

I get up from the bed and walk over to the windows again. I stare down at the people below, wondering who, if anyone, might have dreams that come true as well. The shadow from the building is starting to fill half of the square, and lots of people are taking their meals and moving to the tables in the shade.

Kian comes up next to me, puts his arm around my shoulder, and for a few minutes we look out the window together. I try to hide my smile while it happens, but it's no use. He then slips his hand down to the small of my back and gently rubs his thumb back and forth.

I turn toward him and look directly into his eyes. He stares back into mine and smiles.

"So, you said earlier that to make this all up to me, you were going to show me the van?" I ask him.

"I knew you weren't going to forget," he says.

THE FOURTH DREAM

In my dream, I am being carried away from a road. Someone is whispering to me, but I cannot understand. Without warning, I am placed on the ground and looking up to the sky. There are some dead tree branches in my view, and as I struggle to look around I catch glimpses of thriving trees too.

My body is heavy. So heavy that I cannot move it. I can feel a single teardrop falling from the corner of my eye, down to my ear. It tickles the inside of my ear as it settles. I try shifting my head back and forth but, once again, cannot.

The earth is hard under me, and the wind is blowing dust on my face. I take a deep breath after a deep breath, until after dozens or maybe hundreds of deep breaths I muster all the rage and adrenaline I can and get my arms in front of my body. They're tied together but there's already a knife in them.

In my dream I wonder where the knife comes from. Not how it got into my hands, but where did this knife, in particular, come from. It is not my knife.

I don't fully understand what's happening, but I know what I must do:

Cut myself free. Cut myself free and begin to live again.

CHAPTER 21: WAREHOUSE

It's real. I had my doubts but here it is, right in front of me.

Solar panels covering the entire top of it. A ladder on the side facing us to make any fixes or changes to them. Strange looking wheels. Kian explains that they're not traditional rubber wheels. They fused metal sheeting to them so it can roll over almost anything small and sharp. There's a megaphone on the front corner. Kian says it's so that they can let Toronto know their intentions without leaving them vulnerable.

They've painted it a brown color in order to make it as camouflaged as possible. It has a huge front window and two smaller windows on the side doors, but not a single window in the back. There's also a metal screen over the large front window. He opens up the back doors and there is a bench seating on either side with storage underneath and built-in hooks and shelves above. Whoever is sitting in the back won't be comfortable, but it'll still be better than walking.

On the front they've welded some metal into a small triangle shape. Kian said in the older days, they referred to it as a "cow catcher" but they've made it much lighter, so it doesn't drain the battery. It also has a winch on the front, which would allow larger objects like old cars and concrete barriers to be pulled out of the way.

"We're trying to make it both efficient and functional. It's a difficult balance, but we're pretty happy so far," he says.

It's currently parked in a warehouse several blocks away from the central city area. From the outside of the building, you would never know anything was going on in here and that's the way they want it to stay, for now. No sense getting everyone's hopes up until they can head off for a true test run, Kian tells me.

He then shows me the driver's area. I've never actually seen the inside of a working car before. There are a lot less buttons and knobs than I imagined. It's just a wheel, a couple pedals, and a stick? That's genuinely disappointing.

"So, what do you think? Wanna go for a ride up to Toronto with us?" Kian asks.

Nothing about this experience has made me any less likely to say yes.

"I mean, if I go to Toronto, I definitely want to be in this van. That's for sure," I say.

"If?" Kian says back.

"I mean, yeah, if," I respond. "I know I haven't been here long, but I really like it here."

Kian scrunches his forehead and stares at me for a moment.

"I don't want to assume this would matter to you," he says, "but I'm going to be in the van, and I was really hoping that you would be joining the team heading up there. I know Garven is hoping that his family is coming back for him soon, and I think it would be important for you to be there for him."

He's right, of course. In this moment, I want to tell him about Auryn. What if Auryn actually makes it back, and I'm in Toronto when she does? But Kian and I aren't even a "thing" so, why would I tell him now. There's a lot running through my mind, and a lot I can't talk about with him.

"I know. Garven is important to me, and it would be an amazing trip. I guess I'm just getting tempted by the safety and security here," I finally say.

"There's probably going to be safety and security in Toronto too, and who knows, maybe we'll come back to Buffalo afterwards and have a whole bunch of cool ideas to implement, with your help," he replies.

"Yeah, I mean, I guess you're right. I just need a day or two to think it over. It's really a great opportunity, I just need to make sure that I'm really sure," I say, meaning every word of it.

"I understand," he pauses for a moment, then says, "Wanna go for a quick ride?"

"In the van?" I ask, which I know is a pretty obvious question, "But it's not outside, how is it charging?"

"Well, we have two ways to charge it, while out on the road we charge it with the solar panels up top. In the warehouse we have solar panels outside which lead into the warehouse and to the van. We'd only drive it around inside here, so no one finds out."

How could I possibly say no? I've never driven in any sort of vehicle before. I excitedly tell Kian yes, and we both hop into the front of the van. I swing the passenger side door open and it's heavy. There's a handle on the top of the door frame for me to grab onto and pull myself up by. I land hard on the seat and was expecting it to hurt, but it's so comfortable.

"These seats are so nice!" I say.

"They really are. It makes me wish I was doing the driving on the trip, but we have people who've logged a lot of miles on the inside of this warehouse that will be taking care of that," Kian replies.

He continues,

"Now, I can't let you drive it today because if something were to happen, neither of us would be going on the drive to Toronto. Maybe in the next week or two I can start teaching you."

"I would love that. Then, when we surprise Esha and Garven with it, I can be like 'See, I can keep secrets!' and then hop in the front and drive!" I say. I can feel myself getting carried away with excitement.

"Alright, alright, settle down. You probably won't be driving on the trip unless something terrible happens to…" he pauses, "several of us. In here, we're going to be going five miles an hour for like 30 seconds," Kian says, while chuckling at my energy levels.

He takes the steps of explaining everything he's doing while starting up the car and getting it ready to drive. There's a key to it, but you don't turn it like they did a hundred years ago. They have a two-switch sequence in order to start it, the first switch, according to Kian, brings power to the engine, he flips that and then waits 30 seconds.

He then flips the second switch, which starts the engine up. It's really quiet, nothing more than a light hum to it.

"We want it to be as quiet as possible, so we're less noticeable. That way, even if trouble is ahead, maybe we can avoid it or at least see them before they see us."

There's a handle in between the seats with three notches at the base of it.

"Go Forward! Go Back! Go Nowhere!" Kian says.

He finds this really funny and laughs for a solid 10 seconds about it. I love the way his face looks when he laughs. His hair falls over his forehead until he runs his hands through it. His eyes close almost completely, and the little lines coming off the corners would make you think he's been on this planet a lot longer than the 20 years he has. Whenever he has a hearty laugh, he ends it with one big breath in and then a long exhale.

Once he stops laughing at his own joke, he puts it into "Go Forward" and we start to move. Even with how slowly we're moving, it's exhilarating. A smile grows bigger and bigger across my face, and Kian can see the joy in it.

"So, pretty cool, right?" He says.

I nod and keep looking around at objects slowly moving by us. Kian speeds up slightly and pulls the wheel hard to the left, we do a 180 inside the warehouse and head back in the direction it was parked. We do one more lap around and once we get to the charging station, I look over. In the doorway is Annora.

She's in a black tank top, and her wound, still wrapped up in gauze and medical tape, shows through a hole in her shirt.

"Hey, you crazy kids going for a drive?" Annora asks.

She seems stressed and upset, but also like she's trying to hide it from me. Her lips are pursed, arms crossed, and staring only at Kian as she asks the question.

Kian laughs and says "Yeah, I just had to show someone how cool this thing is. It would be appreciated if you found it in your heart to not tell the electeds."

She looks at him and smiles. I can't help but think in a flirty way. "Yeah, I get it, gotta impress the new people into liking you. It sure won't be your personality that does it."

"Wow, WOW, that's cold!" Kian replies.

They both share a good-natured laugh and then Annora throws her arms around his shoulders and says, "I'll be back with him in a minute, Fin. Don't worry, he'll be in one piece."

With that, they disappear into a side room and I'm left alone, hanging out in a giant warehouse that I probably shouldn't be in. I start looking around and noticing how rough a shape the warehouse is actually in.

Many beams above are missing, which means at some point they crashed 30, maybe 40 feet to the ground. Lots of metal supports that are rusting, and wood walls that are starting to rot. If they wanted a place that looks unassuming, they definitely picked right. I would never in a million years guess what's in here.

For the next five minutes, I wander around this giant place and scope out the wiring that leads to the outside solar panels. They're several different wires that all look, well, a little dangerous. They're well worn, and several of them are wrapped with black tape for long stretches.

Finally, Kian comes back out, but without Annora. He looks a little stressed.

"Well, she's not going to tell anyone that I brought you in here, so that's good," he pauses for a moment. "I do think I'm going to ask Luna, Harlian, Novelia, and Cael tonight if you three can come in the van."

'Novelia' is a name I've only heard in passing up to this point, along with Cael.

"Oh, is it because of something Annora said?" I say, trying to hide a little bit of worry in my voice.

"Maybe a little, but I've been thinking about it the past day or two and it's time," he replies.

With that, he plugs the van back into the charging cables, and we walk out of the warehouse back toward City Hall. We pass "W Huron" and then "W Mohawk" street, and they're bustling with activity. It's a big harvesting day today so everyone has more energy and excitement than usual. Performers are out on nearly every street corner singing, or reading, or performing some plays. It's the most excitement I've seen in the city since we got here. You can feel the energy of the people. Everyone has smiles on their faces, even while doing hard work. It's mesmerizing, honestly.

When we get back into Niagara Square, in the shadow of City Hall, we say our goodbyes. I'm going to do some laundry, and Kian is going to start putting together his pitch for us to come along. It's all I'm going to be able to think about for the rest of the day.

After slowly making my way up to our room in City

Hall, and even more slowly making my way back down the stairs, I head over to the laundry area off to the side of the bathrooms. While hand-scrubbing my clothes with their all-natural laundry soap? I'm thinking about the van.

While grabbing an early dinner with Esha and Garven? I'm thinking about the van.

Watching Yulia perform an old 20th century play all by herself? Honestly, a little bit of Yulia because her voice is smooth enough to lull me to sleep, but also the van.

CHAPTER 22: DECISION

The next morning, Kian knocks on our door. The three of us are already awake and getting ready for the day, so Esha answers. He takes one step into the room and stops; I can tell he's nervous. He taps his fingers on the wall next to the door and clears his throat.

"Hey, everyone. I was wondering if you could follow me, we all have something to talk about," he finally says.

I shoot a glance over to Garven. He shrugs and starts heading for the door, aware of none of the nervousness Kian is showing. Esha starts to get up off her bed before I interrupt.

"Sure, but can we have a minute alone first? We'll be right there," I say.

"Sure, but don't take too long, people are waiting for us," Kian replies.

As he closes the door behind him, I motion for Garven and Esha to come closer. They both walk slowly over to my bed and look at me expectantly.

"I'm pretty sure I know what they want to talk to us about," I say.

Esha and Garven both give me a quizzical look. How on earth would I know what they're bringing us in for?

"So, Kian and I have been…" I pause for an uncomfortable amount of time, "talking a lot, recently."

"Ah! I knew that's where you've been sneaking off too! I told you Esha!" Garven says. Then a realization comes over his face.

"But what about Auryn?"

"Nothing happened like that, Garven!" I protest a little too strongly.

"But we have been talking a lot, and he told me something almost no one else knows."

Garven goes quiet, and Esha sits on the bed next to me. My heart starts racing at the huge news I'm about to deliver to both of them. Esha puts her arm around my shoulder and says,

"What's the big deal? Spit it out."

I look at her, then over to Garven, and then down at the floor.

"They've built a solar-powered van, and they want to drive it up to Toronto for its first long range voyage. Since we're heading up that way, I think they want to invite us to go with them."

"They built a *what*?" Esha says loudly.

I shush her and look toward the door to make sure Kian didn't hear anything.

"They turned an old cargo van into some sort of solar-powered vehicle. Covered the wheels with metal shells, and I guess it can drive for a couple of hours at a time until it needs to be recharged. Most people here don't know about it, but Kian showed it to me yesterday. I just really wanted to see if you guys want to say yes before we get in that room."

"This is so much to take in," Garven responds with. "I mean..."

A pounding on the door interrupts him.

"Are you guys coming or what? We gotta go, these people don't love waiting," Kian yells.

"Seriously, quickly, do you two think we should go or not? Should we go to Toronto with them?" No doubt they can sense the urgency in my voice.

"Hell, I say we go for it. I'm sick of walking. I'm sick of hiding out off-trail from the Raiders. If a whole group of us goes, we are less likely to be attacked. Lots of people can stand guard. I say hell yeah, let's do it."

Looks like Garven is on board.

"Well, I guess it's settled then, Fin. If they ask us, we say yes," Esha says.

That went a lot more smoothly than I had thought it would. I don't know why I had thought I was going to have to convince them, but that was easier than all the imaginary conversations I've had in my head over the last 12 hours.

I walk to the door and open it slowly, and Kian looks annoyed. He's clenching his jaw tightly and tapping his foot on the marble floor. It echoes ever so slightly each time.

We walk with Kian down the hallway and to the staircase. We are meeting on floor five, up a flight of stairs. As we get there, we turn left and pass many different rooms. Kian doesn't say anything as we keep walking, until finally he opens the door to a giant conference room.

Sitting there are two familiar faces, Luna and Harlian. I'd seen Harlian around Niagara Square when Kian pointed him out. He's about my height, 5'10", with brown hair and copper skin. There are also two less familiar faces, Cael and Novelia. I've never seen Novelia in person before, but Kian described her to me once; he did not do her justice.

Her rich, dark brown skin is radiant in the light from the windows, and her dark black hair is in twists down past her shoulders. Her ember eyes lock onto mine as I take a seat.

While taking a seat, I look at Cael. Seeing him now, I realize I had seen him out and about in Niagara Square but I didn't know it was him. He is blonde, and not much taller than I. He wears a jean vest at all times with patches hand sewn onto it. Kian called it his "Battle Vest" and finally being this close, I see it's almost completely full of different patches and fabrics. Some of the sewing has been done poorly and some are falling off. My dad would be appalled at the craftsmanship of it.

These are the four elected leaders of the Buffalo community.

Kian takes a seat next to them, on the opposite side of the table from us. They motion for the three of us to have a seat on the near side. Their backs are to the row of windows, and the sky behind them is beautiful with streaks of blue breaking up the usual stark white canvas.

Novelia welcomes us.

"Hello Esha, Fin, and Garven. Thanks for joining us today." Her voice is smooth and strong. I wish I could ask her to perform with Yulia in Niagara Square. I could listen to both of them all day.

"Kian has brought to our attention that he thinks the three of you would be a good addition for the van voyage up to Toronto. He called you all 'survivors.' But we have some questions for you all."

Garven acts surprised and says ""Van voyage', what do you mean?"

Cael smiles and says "We assumed you knew. We saw

Finley head into the warehouse with Kian yesterday and thought for sure it would have come up in conversation between the three of you by now."

Did Annora tell them anyways, after promising Kian she wouldn't? Or did someone else see us go in there?

Esha and Garven both look at me and act surprised. It takes everything I have not to laugh because they are both terrible actors. Thankfully, everyone else in this room doesn't know that.

"Well, that's certainly a positive point for Finley, being able to keep a secret," Luna says while looking over to Harlian.

"So, what," Harlian begins saying, "do you bring to the table that could be useful on a trip like this?"

"The three of us made a 200 mile walk from Cleveland to here. We survived encounters with the Raiders, terrible weather conditions, and even injury. We can survive anything you, or the trip, throws at us," Esha says.

The five of them across the table nod.

"So, Kian tells us that you two, Esha and Garven, have been doing patrols with us ever since Annora was injured. You haven't been here that long, why would you risk yourselves for a community you barely even know?" Asks Cael.

"It's the right thing to do," says Garven. He shrugs

while saying it.

"And what about you, Finley, how have you been spending your time since you've been here?" Asks Novelia.

"Well, at first I was healing up, but once I started feeling better I started chipping in at the greenhouse."

I look at Kian as I say this, and he looks surprised.

"I was in there one day and Carrew asked for some help, so I dumped and spread dirt, and did planting."

"And how would that help us on the trip to Toronto?" Asks Luna.

"I'm not sure how it would, to be honest. But it shows that I'm willing to pitch in and help the team in any way that I can."

They ask us a series of questions about our skills, abilities, and even about our temperament. They're being especially thorough, and I really can't tell how it's going.

"Last question," says Cael, "Why should we choose all three of you, and not just Garven or Esha?"

The phrasing said all it needed to say, and it hits me like a dagger through the chest. Why would I, an injured, useless nobody, *deserve* to go on the trip? It feels like they're validating all the things I've been saying to myself over the past few weeks.

That I'm dead weight.

That they'd be better off leaving me behind.

That I'm *worthless*.

"Ignoring how insulting that is to Fin – because it is, in fact, insulting, *Cael*," Esha says with a hint of disdain in her voice, "We're a package. It's all three of us or none of us."

Novelia smiles and nods her head once when Esha says this. With that, they thank us for coming in and Kian walks us to the door. Once in the hallway, he closes the door behind us and stays inside the conference room. We turn and start walking down the hallway.

"So, that was awkward," Garven says.

"So, how long have you known they had a van, Fin?" Says Esha.

I vaguely hear her ask the question, but I'm inside my own head so far that it doesn't even register that I should answer. Maybe they would just be better off going without me. I could stay here, tend to the greenhouse, and maybe even make some new friends eventually. No one would ever even have to know I was rejected for this.

Garven then puts a hand on my shoulder and shakes me, gently.

"Hey. I know what you're doing in that head of yours. Cut it out. Esha asked you a question."

"Oh, sorry," I say, "Well, Kian told me like the first night we were here. I didn't fully believe him until I saw it yesterday though."

"The first night? You saw it? Did you see it run? Why did you keep this from us?" Garven asks, rapid fire.

"I did see it, it did run, I actually sat inside of it for a short drive, and because Kian asked me not to," I respond, still in a daze.

As we reach the stairwell, they keep peppering me with questions about the van and anything else I might know about the trip. I answer everything as truthfully as I can as we descend the stairs to our room, as we walk down the hallway, more and more questions. Finally, I can't take anymore.

"I'm sorry. But I can't do this right now," I snap. I don't mean to, but I'm overcome with frustration.

"Whoa, sorry. We're just excited," Esha says.

"I know, I know, but they basically called me useless in that meeting. And you know what? They're right, I am useless," I say as we enter our shared room.

I walk straight over to my bed and sit down, back turned to the two of them. I know how I'm acting right now isn't right. They weren't the ones who insulted me. They had my back and even defended me, but I can't help but feel like some sort of charity case right now.

"Listen, what they said in there sucked. More importantly though, what they said in there wasn't even true. You're not dead weight. We do this together or we don't do it at all. All right?" Esha says.

I turn around and look at the two of them. I expected to see pity in their eyes, but instead I see a steely resolve and confidence from both of them. It does more to help me feel better than any words could.

"Are you sure about this?" I ask.

"We couldn't possibly be surer, Fin," Garven responds.

I stand up off the bed, and walk over to the two of them, then grab them in a big group hug. I hang out for 10 or 15 seconds and finally, Esha says,

"Alright, alright, that's enough wallowing."

I chuckle and return to my bed. I grab my journal and begin writing about the last few days, and how the swings of emotions I'm feeling have only been getting worse. After a few pages, I close the cover, place it back into my backpack, and head out of the room.

The rest of the day goes pretty much the same as the last few have gone. I meet up with Carrew in the "Oh One", learn a little about plants and what it's been like in Buffalo over the past few years. He tells me that it wasn't easy getting everyone on board with some of the more communal aspects of the community.

"But in the end, it made sense that everyone would want to pitch in. It's just us left, no one else can save us, so let's just save ourselves."

"My friend, Garven, he always says 'The only ones who can rescue us, *is* us.'"

Carew looks at me and smiles.

"I like that. Garven's a smart guy. I think I'm gonna steal that saying," he says.

"I won't tell him if you won't," I say.

"Garven's the bigger guy you came with, right? The guy going out on patrols with Kian and them? I've got a bad memory, so I always need to be reminded."

"Yup, that's Garven," I say.

"He's a handsome fella," he pauses for a second. "A good-looking guy like that is going to be snatched up pretty quick around here," he smiles while saying this.

"Oh, god, no!" I say while laughing. "He's my best friend's older brother. Well, more than a best friend, I mean, anyways, no. Garven and I are not a thing and never will be," I say.

"Alright, alright, if you say so! I mean, he's tall, muscular, and has that beautiful dark complexion. My husband would have tried flirting with him every chance he got!" Carrew says.

He laughs and thanks me. We finish up the usual routine of work and he mentions that he's going to head back to his apartment. I ask if it's in City Hall and he shakes his head.

"No, no, I started out there, in a room, but I've been here long enough and put in my dues so that I have a studio apartment over on Franklin Street. Nice little place."

"Do you live with your husband?" I ask.

A sad look comes over Carrew's face for a moment. He smiles a pained smile and lets out a deep sigh.

"I'm sorry, I didn't mean to upset you," I say to him, obviously striking a nerve.

"No, no. It's okay, Fin. He was the love of my life. His name was Elson. The 31 years we spent together were the best 31 years of my life," he takes a moment, obviously thinking about his husband.

"The last few years were hard. I kept up our spirits talking about how amazing Buffalo was going to be for us. How we could rebuild the world and get the medicine he needed to live. Unfortunately…" he pauses again and wipes a tear away from the corner of his eye,

"He didn't quite make it long enough. So now every day, I come to the greenhouse and plant flowers that I hope will heal someone else in his memory."

"I'm so, so sorry, Carrew," I respond.

"It's okay. It's nice thinking about him and sharing him with people," Carew says.

"What about you? Have you eye on anyone here in Buffalo?" He then asks.

I blush a little, and say,

"It's a little complicated right now."

"Love is always a little complicated, isn't it?" He asks.

With that, I give him a hug. He thanks me and asks if he'll see me again tomorrow. I tell him that I wouldn't miss it for the world, and he walks off.

It's a little past lunch time and I notice how hungry I am, so I head over to the food area and grab my normal meal: Oats with fruit. There are other options, but this one fills me up the most, and I guess I still feel a little food insecure so I try to fill up as often as possible.

After lunch, I head back to the room. As I open the door to our room, I see that Garven and Esha are both there.

Esha is pacing the main living area, and Garven is eating something from a bowl on his bed. Coincidentally, it also looks like oats and fruit.

"So, you think they're going to pick us for the van?" Esha says as soon as I enter.

"Oh, honestly, I have no idea. I hope so, though. Even with my leg feeling better, if I can avoid walking 100 miles, I'd love to," I say back.

"We just thought you might have inside information because, well, you know," says Garven.

I sigh and say nothing. I'm going to stay silent until they ask specifically.

"Because of you and Kian," he clarifies.

Ah, yes. Because of Kian and me. It's getting harder every day to pretend like something isn't happening. I don't know what that something is, exactly, but I know we both feel it.

"No, I honestly don't know anything more than you two do at this point," I answer, "We're all on the same page."

They both nod. Esha looks a little disappointed in my lack of helpful new info. For the rest of the day, we all just hang out and catch up on what we've all been up to. It's hard to concentrate while we're forced to wait around for an answer, but it is pretty nice being able to talk to them about their lives for the first time in a few days.

KIAN'S FIRST DREAM

Every night for the last week, Kian has closed his eyes to fall asleep and once he does, he has one dream:

He is carrying Finley through a large, open field. Behind him is the road, and several voices saying words he cannot understand. In front of him is a tree line.

For reasons he does not know, Fin either can't or won't talk to him.

Once he reaches the tree line, he lays Finley down gently onto the ground and puts an item in their hand. When he wakes up, he cannot remember what the item is. All he knows is that they are imperative to Finley's survival.

He then whispers something in Fin's ear, turns, and walks away. Unsure if he'll see them again.

CHAPTER 23: RAMONA

The next morning, as the light barely seeps through the curtains in our windows, a knock comes from our door. I get up, stretch, and try to wipe the sleep out of my eyes. I slowly get to the door and unlatch the large lock, open it, and see Novelia and Luna standing there. The starkness between Novelia's dark black hair and Luna's blinding blonde hair has never been more obvious.

"May we come in?" They ask in unison.

"Oh, uh, sure," I say while simultaneously trying to clear my throat. "Apologies, I'll just have to wake Garven and Esha."

"We're sorry for coming in so early," says Luna, "but we want to give you as much time as possible for, well, you'll find out in a moment."

Her voice is saccharine smooth and, if I didn't know any better, a little fake sounding.

We walk in together, and I wake up Esha and Garven and immediately let them know we have important guests.

Those first rays of sunshine are peeking through the windows right onto Garven's face, and neither of them seem to grasp the fact that they need to get up immediately.

After ten seconds of neither of them moving, I say loudly, "Is there anything I can get for you, Novelia and Luna, while you wait for Garven and Esha to get up?"

Suddenly, they both pop right up. Esha throws on her clean jacket, and Garven does nothing of the sort, keeping his gray tank top and drawstring pants on. As he walks into the room, he apologizes for making them wait.

"Oh, no need to apologize, we know it's earlier than you're accustomed to getting up," says Novelia.

Once all three of us are in the room, she begins speaking again.

"We want to invite you onto the van for its inaugural run up to Toronto. If you say yes, you'll be going with Luna, Harlian, Kian, and two other members, Gates and Coda. The main mission is to make contact with the people in charge in Toronto, share some ideas, and come back with an open line of communication with them."

She continues, "We understand that the three of you may want to stay there once you arrive. Honestly, that was a pro in each of your columns because we're hoping to bring back some new plant life, communication equipment, and other things."

"One other thing," Luna adds, "we're leaving in two days. The van is going to get a surprise sendoff, but I think people might be apprehensive if they knew three new people were going to be in it. So, we're going to have you meet us on the outskirts of the city and catch a ride. I hope that's alright."

"We totally understand. Don't want to ruffle any feathers," I say.

Novelia looks at me, smiles, and says, "Exactly."

She continues making eye contact with me for an uncomfortable amount of time. I can't tell what's happening at first, but Luna, Esha and Garven are all talking to each other and don't seem to notice. As it approaches eight or nine seconds long, she looks at Luna, looks directly back at me, and nods. I notice the tiniest sliver of green wrapped around the ember in her eyes. I can't believe I didn't notice it when we were across the table, but for a brief second it flickers in the light from the windows.

An unsettling feeling comes over my body. I shiver slightly and then nod back. Once I do, she inserts herself back into the conversation in the room and I can no longer spot the green in her eyes.

"Well, I can speak for the three of us when I say we're excited to say yes and whatever you need from us, just let us know," says Garven.

"We'll be in touch over the next two days for sure," Novelia says.

With that, they thank us and then leave the room. As the door closes behind them, huge smiles come across Esha and Garven's faces. I walk over to the door, latch the lock again, and turn to tell them about the weird encounter with Novelia.

"Did either of you notice anything strange while Novelia was talking to me?" I ask.

"Strange? No. Like what?" Garven asks.

"She stared at me for like 10 seconds, looked at Luna, then nodded back at me. It's hard to explain, it was a little weird," I respond.

"There's no way it was actually ten seconds, Fin. I think I would have noticed that," Esha says.

"No, it definitely was. Also, for a moment, there was a green ring in her eyes. It was only in a certain light, but then it disappeared, it was really weird," I say.

"It's not that weird, it happens to your eyes sometimes, too," Esha says.

"What?" I ask, surprised no one has ever mentioned this before.

"Yeah, you never noticed? It just happens with people sometimes; I even noticed it with Kian," Garven says. "Although I guess since there's so few mirrors you don't really get to look at your own eyes all that much.”

With that he shrugs, and he and Esha go back to talking about the trip. I head back to my bed because I’m exhausted, and a little confused about what Novelia meant. After ten or so minutes, Esha and Garven do the same, and over the next little bit, we all fall back asleep.

We wake up around noon and started tying up any loose ends for leaving Buffalo. The next two days were a whirlwind. I said my goodbyes to Carrew and a few of the other people I’ve met in the “Oh One”. As I am saying my goodbye to Carrew, I let him know how much his kindness meant to me.

“Who knows, I might even be back,” I say while I hug him.

“Selfishly, I hope so, Fin. But I have the feeling you’re going to do great things in Toronto,” he replies.

After we stop hugging, I wipe a few tears off my cheek.

The next day, Esha, Garven and I pack up our backpacks with everything needed for the trip the following morning. I put in some water filters, silver foiled food rations, a couple of what Kian refers to as “Ultra Hydration” packs – which you supposedly only need one sip of to last a day – a space blanket for warmth in case of emergency, and then I roll my one-person tent and pad back up and strap it to the top.

As the sun fades and the day turns to evening, we take one last walk around Buffalo. The three of us grab a bite to eat, this time a hot meal of rice, vegetables, and some soy protein. As we grab a seat at one of the picnic tables, Annora spots us from across the way, and comes over to us.

"Hey, mind if I grab a seat?" She asks.

I haven't spoken to her since the warehouse. I can't be sure that she's the one who told on Kian and me, but I have my suspicions.

"So, I hear you're all going on the van up to Toronto tomorrow. That's really great," she says in a hushed voice, low enough for the other tables not to hear her.

"How'd you know that?" Garven asks her.

"Kian told me the good news this morning. I just wanted to come by and say congratulations."

"Thanks," Esha says dryly in between bites.

There's a moment of awkward silence before Annora says,

"Hey, Fin, can I talk to you in private for a moment?"

"Sure," I reply.

With that, we both stand up from the table and walk around Niagara Square for a few minutes. The large solar spotlights that are fastened to the monument provide more than enough light to walk around the square with. Most of the daily vendors have packed up, leaving empty wooden stalls around the outside of the square.

"I just wanted to let you know that it wasn't me who told the electeds about you and Kian in the van," she says.

"I want to believe you, Annora, I really do, but who else would have known?" I ask her.

She stops walking and looks around in all directions, making sure no one is close enough to hear us talk. She then looks up toward City Hall nervously.

"I can't be totally sure, but I have my suspicions," she says.

I look at her intently. If her intention is to be as vague as possible, she's succeeding.

"Listen, I'd love to believe you, I really would, but you're going to have to give me more than 'I have my suspicions,'" I say to her.

She motions for me to keep walking, so I follow her. We exit Niagara Square and turn onto Delaware Ave, heading south. Once we get to a point where City Hall is blocked by the giant, windowless building I saw when we first arrived, she stops and sits on a concrete retaining wall.

"So," she starts again, before a long pause. "I'm pretty sure it was Luna who saw you both go into the warehouse. I've noticed her... I don't know how to put this other than she's been following Kian around. I've seen it for at least a year or so. It's not all the time, but the amount of times I've seen her standing 50 or 60 feet away from him has been concerning."

"Has Kian noticed?" I ask.

"I don't think so, he's so oblivious of his surroundings all the time though, so it's not surprising. I actually brought it up to him a few months ago and he said I was being paranoid; that of course she was around a lot, she was an elected official and she has to meet people and be seen. I just… I don't think that's it."

I take a moment to absorb what she's telling me. With how careful she's been while telling me this, I believe her.

"Why do you think she's following him?" I finally ask.

"Well, Kian has a special…" she pauses while searching for the right word, "ability that Luna has a pretty well-known dislike for. I think she feels like she has to keep her eye on him because of that."

"His dreams," I say.

Annora's eyes widen as she turns toward me. She puts her hand on my knee, and says,

"You know about Kian's dreams?"

"Yeah, he told me about them a few days ago because…" now it's my turn to pause.

My entire life before coming to Buffalo, I had told two people about my dreams: Auryn and Esha. I haven't even talked about them to Garven, although I probably should. Am I really going to tell two people that I barely know over the course of a week?

I steady myself to tell her. If she's kept Kian's secret for this long, she can keep mine as well.

"I have the same ability," I finally say.

Her eyes widen and she takes her hand off my knee. I give her a moment to process, and don't say anything further.

"I see. Does Luna know about this?" She asks.

"Not unless Kian told her, which I doubt," I say.

"You need to do everything you can to keep it that way, Finley. You cannot tell anyone else this, I'm serious," she replies.

She's using the same tone Kian did when he warned me in Niagara Square several days ago.

"She's known Kian for a long time, and she still doesn't fully trust him. There's no way she's going to trust you if she finds out."

"I mean, what would she even do if she found out?" I ask.

Annora stares me directly in the eyes and takes another long, purposeful breath.

"About a year ago, it came out that another member of our community here in Buffalo had the ability to see the future in her dreams. One evening, she was performing on the small stage in Niagara Square and she came out and told everyone. There was a small group of 30 people watching, but the news spread like wildfire. Not just in this neighborhood, but across all the neighborhoods. She said she had a dream the previous evening of a woman in her 30s with striking blonde hair throwing her off a bridge and into the shallow, rushing water far below."

My heart is racing at this point, the only person I can think of with blonde hair that I would describe as striking is Luna.

"She said she had to tell people now because she didn't know how much longer she had to live," Annora continued.

"So, what happened to her? Did she run away? Did people believe her?" I ask.

"Most people didn't, no. But I did. I tried convincing her to leave the city and head to Toronto, but she wouldn't. I even told her I'd go with her. A few weeks later her backpack washed up on the shores of the Niagara River. Inside a clear plastic bag was a suicide note."

Annora wipes a tear away from her cheek and tries to steady herself.

"They never found her body."

I stare at the concrete sidewalk below my feet as we sit in silence for several minutes. It's then I notice a slight sniffling coming from Annora and I look over to see her crying. I put my arm around her shoulder and give her a hug.

"Did you know her? The girl?" I ask quietly.

"I did. She was my sister, Ramona," she replies.

We sit there on the hard concrete for a few more minutes in the increasing darkness of the evening. I tell her that I'm so sorry for her loss, and she nods.

"I just need you to understand how careful you need to be, alright?" She finally says.

I tell her I understand.

"I promise I'll do everything I can to keep both myself and Kian safe on this trip, okay?" I say.

"One other thing you should know, Fin," she says.

"She and Kian were together for a while. Please be careful bringing it up around him, I don't think he ever grieved properly."

It all makes sense now. I can't believe I felt jealousy toward her about Kian. He's like family to her, and she's just been trying to protect her family like we all do. She's taken a huge risk by even having this conversation with me.

She thanks me and we stand up. She gives me a hug but only squeezes me with the side of her body that wasn't injured in the fight with the Raiders.

"Please, Fin, take good care of him," she says as she turns and walks away.

This is likely to be the last time I will ever see her.

"I promise, Annora," I say, hopeful she hears me.

I walk back to Niagara Square by myself, thinking about everything Annora told me. As I get back to the table, Garven tells me that I look like I've seen a ghost.

"It's even worse than that," I say, as I stare at my now cold dinner.

CHAPTER 24: LUNA

The morning that our adventure starts, Esha, Garven and I start walking west. Garven explains that the first half of the trip to Toronto we actually go west and northwest, and then the second half we head northeast. It doesn't make much sense to me until I see the map.

"If Lake Ontario weren't there, this would be like a one- or two-day trip, instead it's five," Esha says while looking at it with me.

The first few blocks we walk through familiar streets, but once we leave the neighborhood, things are very different. We get to a road called "Forrest Ave", which has no trees let alone a forest, and head west. After an hour or so we reach Niagara Street, which is different from Niagara Square, and head south.

To our right we can see a river. The land carved out for it several hundred feet wide, but the river now is only 50 feet wide. I think it's the river Annora was referring to with her sister. I shudder at the thought of it. We walk up to a series of old toll booths and wait. The windows are broken out, and it looks like at some point somebody lived in them.

Harlian said it would be an hour or two before the van arrived, so we find a curb, toss our backpacks down, and get comfortable for a bit.

We talk a lot about how fortunate we are. How none of us could have imagined, during our walk from Cleveland, ever getting a ride up to Toronto. Even though my leg is healed at this point, I shudder to think how sore I would be after walking another 100 miles.

It's already getting hot as we sit on the concrete. I take my jacket off and drape it over my head and shoulders. I pull out my water pack and take a swig, then offer it to Garven and Esha, who both also take a sip.

After an hour, the van pulls up. Esha and Garven are still amazed that it's real and working. The back doors swing open, and we're welcomed into it. We climb in and hang our packs on the hooks.

"Everyone ready for a slow, slow drive?" Kian says with a big smile.

We all nod and take a seat. The smiles on Esha and Garvens faces are infectious, and I grin right along with them.

"Don't get too comfortable though, we've already had to stop once to clear debris from the road. We're probably going to be busy a lot on this trip," says Harlian.

The van starts back up and we begin to cross a huge bridge, five lanes wide by several hundred feet long.

"This is the Peace Bridge and, in a moment, we're going to be in Old Canada," Luna says.

We travel for the rest of the battery life, a few hours, and pull over on the side of the road to recharge for the last couple of hours of daylight. We've been told it's going to be a lot of this, stopping and waiting, but I don't mind; sitting here is better than hobbling through the woods and avoiding Raiders.

Every time we stop, I stay on edge. The way Novelia was trying to get me to notice something about Luna. Annora's sister disappearing after coming out as a dreamer. I have no concrete proof that Luna is up to something, but I stay on guard as much as possible.

That night and the next day follow that same pattern. Drive for a few hours, recharge for a few hours. Occasionally clear some medium-sized debris out of the way. The winch has come in handy to move some old cars out of the way enough so we can squeeze through. Every time we use it, I'm convinced the old metal wire that does most of the pulling is going to snap and we're going to be out of luck. Every time so far though, it's worked.

At the end of the second night, we start a small fire on the side of the road and cook up some food. At the end of the meal, Luna puts a metal bowl over the fire and makes tea. We all take out our small metal cups and she rinses them with a tiny bit of water from our larger bag in the back of the van, then comes out and dries them as the water boils. Once done, I watch as she sprinkles some tea leaves into the bottom of the cup.

I read once that there were small contraptions you put
the tea leaves into, so they didn't just float around in your cup,
but I've never seen one. Even if I had – with my pack jammed
full of food, a med pack, my sleeping mat, my pills that Dr.
Rai gave me before I left, and everything else I packed in here
– there wouldn't have been any room.

After Luna pours the water in, she says,

"A celebratory tea. What we're doing here is amazing,
and we should celebrate that."

We all raise our glasses and toast in unison. I drink
mine slowly, savoring every sip. We won't be able to relax
often on this trip, so the rare occasion we can is special. We
all chat around the small fire for another five or ten minutes
when I realize I'm starting to get tired. The stress of a long
day will do that, so I volunteer to take the first shift of sleep. I
roll out the thin mat and start to rest my eyes for a bit.

Falling asleep tonight is peaceful. I hear the last
remnants of the fire crackling on the other side of the van, and
the rest of the air is filled with low conversation. I stare
upward and can see so many stars, so I look towards where I
think Auryn might be. I notice a comet flying across the sky
as my eyelids get heavier and heavier. I'm falling asleep much
easier than usual tonight.

THE FIFTH DREAM

I see it clearly, glistening from the light of torches on the walls around it. Atop an ancient looking gray stone pedestal, it sits. Almost a foot in length and rectangular in shape, it is the largest emerald stone I've ever seen in my life.

As I stare at it within my dream, I can feel myself drawn to it. I take several slow steps before someone puts their hand on my shoulder. Before now, I hadn't even realized someone was in the room with me. I cannot even be bothered to turn and look who it is, all I can concentrate on is the stone.

I go to take one more step toward it, and everything fades to black. I've never had that happen in a dream before. It's as if something, or someone, isn't allowing me to see what happens next.

CHAPTER 25: FINLEY

The next morning, I struggle to wake up. At least I think it's the morning. I don't even remember doing my lookout shift. All I remember is falling asleep on my mat outside of the van, but as I wake up I can feel the cold metal of the floor of the van underneath me. I'm having an especially hard time opening my eyes. The splitting headache doesn't help either. Suddenly, two other voices start talking.

"Now is the time. We have to dump Finley now," says Luna.

"Agreed," says the second voice, Harlian.

"Finley is a dreamer, and we can't trust them. Get rid of them now. If the other two don't come around, we'll get rid of them too," says Luna.

"What are you guys talking about?" A sleepy sounding third voice says. My eyes are closed, but I can tell that's Kian.

"Ah, finally, you're awake. We didn't think you'd be knocked out this long. We're getting rid of Finley. They can't be trusted, they're a dreamer, but not like you. You, we can trust. Fin? No. They're going to ruin everything," Luna replies.

I am desperately trying to move my body or open my eyes, but I can't.

"How do you know they're a dreamer?" Kian asks.

"I've read through their little journal, and there are all sorts of crazy dreams in there. You all don't even know what they're up to!" Says Luna.

"Wait, you read their journal? How?" Kian asks.

"The first night they all got here, after they passed out, Dr. Rai let me know that Fin would be sleeping for a while, so I snuck in and read some once she left the office. Then, a few days later, Finley was out of their room again, so I did it again. There is some messed up stuff in there. There's a dream about killing Harlian."

I want to scream "Liar! That's not true!" at the top of my lungs, but I still can't move.

Kian sighs an exasperated sigh.

"You guys can't be serious with this, right? Esha and Garven are going to be pissed. They'll never go along with this," he says.

"They will, or they're going to end up dead, just like Finley. When we put it that way, it's not going to be a hard choice at all," Harlian says.

"Plus, Kian, Finley might already know what our intentions for Toronto actually are. They might just be waiting to throw us under the bus. You can never trust a dreamer," Luna says.

I cannot believe she read my journal. I am infuriated. She's known the entire time that I'm a dreamer, but why did she let me on the van to begin with?"

"What exactly are our plans when we get to Toronto? I thought it was to get ideas, some tech maybe, and go back to Buffalo with them?" Kian asks, his voice getting more frantic.

There was silence in the van for a moment. No one answers Kian. Harlian finally speaks,

"Alright, it's settled. We'll pull off here and dump that one on the side of the road. We're still far enough away from Hamilton and even farther from Toronto, so that even if they somehow survive, they'll never find their way up there."

I realize that I have to do something, and quickly, but when I try to move my arms and try to get out of my bindings, they're completely dead. All of me is. I try to scream, to alert Esha and Garven of what's going on, but I can't make a sound. For all I know, they are hearing all this too and can't do anything about it either. I didn't just pass out on my sleeping mat last night. They drugged us.

The celebratory tea. I knew it didn't taste right, but I thought I watched her as she poured it. It must have been when she went back to the van to rinse the cups.

Why did they need me here, though? They could have just left all three of us back in Buffalo and not even taken us on the trip. Did Luna really do all this just to be able to kill me, like Annora's sister? How much of a madwoman is she? She must have read a dream of mine she was in and came up with this plan. I feel so foolish for not taking better care of my notebook.

Slowly I'm able to open my eyes the slightest bit. Harlian is running his hand through his dark brown hair as he paces the van, and Luna is sitting in her seat, looking completely unfazed about leaving me for dead. Kian, though, keeps shooting glances over to my direction.

"Look, we've come too far, the plan has worked exactly how I wanted it to up to now. We keep the soldiers, we leave the dreamer. We can't take the chance of bringing someone who might be the Stonekeeper up to Toronto where the Emerald Stone is," Luna says.

"If Fin really is the Stonekeeper, won't they survive in the wild? We're so close to the Emerald Stone, won't their powers be enough to get them through?" Harlian asks.

"No, from everything I've read about the Keepers, the Emerald Stone doesn't help with survival. That's why we have to do this now," Luna replies.

Stonekeeper? Emerald Stone? What is Luna talking about? None of this makes any sense. The only thing I can occasionally do is have a dream come true. Why are Luna and

Harlian so concerned about me?

"Why don't we just kill Fin instead of dropping them off?" Harlian asks.

"Because, Harlian, some of the Green Cloaks have the ability to tell whether someone is telling them the truth. This way, if we get questioned, we can answer honestly that we didn't kill Finley," Luna says.

She continues,

"Now listen, Garven and Esha are going to want to survive and once we explain how Fin was dead weight, they'll come around. We need as many soldiers and as many strong grunts as possible to put this plan together, so we're going to pull over, get out, and dump Finley on the side of this road."

"What if Esha and Garven don't come around? They're all really close and have been through hell together. They're not just going to suddenly be fine with it, Luna," Kian responds.

"You sure do seem to be siding with the enemy here a lot, Kian. Are we going to have to dump you on the side of the road as well?"

As Luna says that, Harlian turns toward Kian and puts his hand on the gun that's currently in its holster on his hip.

"Of course I'm not siding with the enemy, Luna, I'm just surprised. That's all," Kian responds.

Harlian then glances over at me and notices my eyes partially open.

"Oh crap, look!" He yells as he points at me.

Kian looks over at me and notices my eyes open as well. At that moment, I felt more panic than I had at any point since we left Cleveland. Harlian's face looked worried, Luna's face looked angry, but Kian… Kian's face looked like he was trying to say something to me. His eyes as worried as they are kind.

"We have to do it now. If they're waking up, it means the drugs aren't going to last much longer on the other two, and we cannot have them seeing us do this," Luna says.
She is so cold and calculated in her plan, this has to be what Novelia was warning me about and why Annora was so certain it was Luna who murdered her sister.

"Fine, if this is really what you two want to do, I'll drop Fin off. But it won't just be next to the road, I'll hide them farther away so no one else can save them," says Kian.

"You better not be planning anything, Kian, otherwise you'll be joining Finley, but neither of you will be breathing," Luna says. The way she's talking now would send shivers down my spine, if I could feel it.

"What, you think I'm dumb enough to risk my own life for some people I barely know? You know me better than that, Luna," Kian responded.

"Do I, *dreamer*?" She snaps back. She says the word "dreamer" with such hatred and disdain. It's terrifying.

For an instant, as Luna looks in a different direction, Kian's face looks angrier than I've ever seen it, but it quickly changes. He's trying everything he can to control his emotions.

"Alright, enough chit chat from the both of you. Kian, take Finley and dump them along that dead tree line. We'll keep an eye out for Raiders, and for Garven and Esha waking up, just in case. But make it quick, I don't want to be a sitting duck out here much longer," says Harlian.

Kian starts to grab me, and I am filled with a rage I didn't even know I possessed. I want to scream at him to get his hands off me. He looks at me and I know he can see the anger in my eyes. I did not come this far, I have not survived this long, to die on the side of the road somewhere in Canada. This will not be how this goes down.

He picks me up and slings me over his shoulder. I shouldn't be surprised with the ease it happens, since it's not the first time, but I was hoping my rage had somehow made me heavier and more difficult to move.

He hops down from the back of the van to the road and starts carrying me off. The early morning sunrays are barely peeking over the horizon line. We're in a different spot than we were the night before, which means after we were drugged, they drove for a while. I have no map, no way of knowing where I am, and no idea if I'm ever going to be able to move again.

The tears start welling in my eyes. I know it's not a good idea to cry right now, with no food or water I need to keep hydrated as long as possible, but everything is so overwhelming that I can't help it. Kian must have heard me sniffle.

"Fin, I know you're angry right now. I know you're terrified. But please believe me, I didn't know this was the plan. I'm going to come back to you, I promise. Please just survive a couple days. Stay along this main road but not out in the open. It eventually leads to the lake. On the maps I studied there's a city called 'Hamilton', and an old park there called 'Bayfront Park.' It's by the lake. Hopefully there are still signs there. We'll start our search for you there."

As he lays me down gently under some trees, he looks me right in the eyes while grabbing something out of his pocket.

"The tea they gave you will be wearing off shortly. Until then I've tried to hide you from any people passing by. I'm going to put my small knife in your hands so when you can move your arms again, you can cut these ties. Here's also a small food ration and a hydration pack. It has just a few sips of liquid but that should be able to last you two to three days. I'm so sorry, I have to go now, but we will be back for you."

With that, he stands up and begins to walk away.

I beg my body to do literally anything. I can hear the crunch of his shoes get quieter as he fades into the distance. After a moment, I can hear the van start back up in the distance and slowly roll away, leaving me, for all they know, to die.

But I won't die. Luna and Harlian called me dead weight. The rage of hearing that will fuel me.

As I wait here, unable to move, I am forced to look toward the sky. There are dead tree branches above me, but also some green ones. It's still so surprising when I see real live leaves, or pine needles, but it's something I've been noticing more often on our travels.

After several minutes, I notice the knife placed in my hand by Kian. Not only that it's there, but that I can actually feel it. There is a tingling sensation in my fingers, and I can feel the cold metal of the knife on my skin. I try to wiggle my finger. Slowly, methodically, with a lot of deep breathing and concentration, I move my pointer finger on my right hand.

I feel renewed. However long this adrenaline lasts, I have to use it because it won't be for long. After another hour and a half, I'm able to move both of my hands. Finally, I'm able to use the knife Kian left me to cut the ropes.

After what feels like an eternity, but was probably four or five hours, I'm able to sit up and move all my arms and legs. I try to stand up but wobble, then stumble and decide that maybe sitting for a few more minutes won't be the worst idea.

It'll start getting dark out in just a couple more hours, and this is the first time in years I've been alone. Truly alone. The clothes on my back, a small knife, and food and water for a few days. All alone in a world that doesn't treat strangers or solo travelers kindly.

For the next few hours, I feel the adrenaline slowly wear off, and the stress and anxiety of the situation is making me feel exhausted. Exhausted and lonely. I know Kian said they'll be back for me, but they're just as likely to be killed as they are to ever find me again.

I can feel the panic setting in. Now is not the time, but it never is. I lay back down on the ground, close my eyes as hard as possible, and start talking to myself out loud.

"Let go or be dragged."

"Let. Go. Or. Be. Dragged."

Each time I say it, it sounds angrier until I am nearly screaming it. Then I once again quiet back down for fear of being heard.

My dad used to say this to me when I would get angry that we didn't have tickets for the ships or when we couldn't get medical care for the two of them. He would pull me in close, hug me tight, and whisper "Let go or be dragged" as I broke down and cried into his arms.

Now? Now it's my motto for surviving. It's my motto for trying to lower my heart rate during a panic attack, and I need it right now more than ever.

I breathe in deeply, breathe out quickly, and repeat the process for the next 25 minutes. Eventually the exhaustion overtakes me and, in the same spot I was left for dead, I fall asleep.

Very much alive.

CHAPTER 26: 1600

It's been almost four weeks since the announcement came down. Four weeks that featured a lot of Auryn fighting with her mom and dad. A lot of tears from her younger brother. It's gone from Auryn feeling sad about leaving to counting down the days when she can be on the ship again.

After the official ship roster was announced, there has been a weird vibe around the entire colony. More people than expected wanted to be on the ship back to Earth, which made Auryn especially glad she talked to the assignment officer early. It's also made a lot of people unhappy.

Some families are being split again, like Auryn's, and some people who originally planned on going have come up with injuries or mental health reasons, so they couldn't possibly make another three year-round trip. There's been a lot of uncertainty around the last few weeks, and it's made everyone a little more on edge.

All in all, 1,600 people are headed back to Earth out of the roughly 80,000 that made it to the new colony. Around 500 are essential to the mission: Pilots, engineers, mechanics, and the like. The other 1,100 are a mix of apprentices, people who have enough knowledge and skills that if something were to happen to the essential crew we could still continue the journey, and GSMWs (General Ship Maintenance Workers), which is how Auryn got back on the ship.

She has a ton of usable skills from her parents and from working with Mina the past few months. She knows some coding from her mom and can fix a lot of different parts of the ship from learning from her dad, but being classified as a GSMW has its advantages.

Namely? More time off on the trip. If she wants to go visit the simulation rooms, there is almost no one else on board and plenty of time to do it. She wants to cryo-freeze for a few weeks to pass the time? As long as it's okay with the essential crew, she has that freedom.

Although she'll be assigned as GSMW, Mina has already given her a heads up that every time she is available, she's going to schedule Auryn to work with her. Auryn doesn't mind, she likes working in Engineering. She also likes working with Mina.

There's an ease to being around her. She doesn't feel the need to make unnecessary small talk. They can be in each other's presence and not feel the need to fill the air. There is something comfortable about hanging out with her.

Plus, she is super smart, and Auryn has learned a lot from her over the past couple of months. It'll be good to keep her mind sharp over the course of the journey back.

What Auryn is mostly looking forward to on the trip back. though, is how empty it's going to be. It's an entire ship made to house and entertain 80,000 people. When that many people are actually on board, there are wait times, lines, and you're constantly bumping into people. With 1,600 people?

She can pretty much do whatever she wants, whenever she wants.

Auryn smiles at the thought, which is something she hasn't done much of recently.

CHAPTER 27: LLAMA

I can feel the brightness of the sun through my eyelids as I slowly wake up. The tears I shed from the previous night have dried on my face and the corners of my eyes are filled with rheum, or as Esha so lovingly calls it, "Eye Gunk."

I slowly raise myself up on one elbow, then the other. My body feels weak and, even worse, I feel defeated. As I sit up, a crinkling noise emanates from the lower front pocket of my jacket and helps me remember that Kian placed a hydration pack and food ration there yesterday.

I slowly remove the water from my pocket and I'm careful not to puncture the package. This is all I have now. If I stretch it I can go for three days, but with no water purifier that's all I have. I have to make it to Hamilton in the next three days, which will be especially difficult because I have no map and can't be entirely sure where it is. Kian mentioned it's by the water. Therefore, first things first, I have to figure out my directions and head that way.

Thank goodness I actually listened to Garven and Esha when they were talking about the direction we had to travel in.

I lift the pack up to my mouth and take the smallest sip I can manage. It's impossibly refreshing. It feels like I haven't had a drink of water in years. I'm so dried out that I can feel the drops hitting the back of my mouth and traveling down my throat. I want nothing more than to drink the other two sips in the pack, but knowing I can't afford to do that until tomorrow nearly sends me spinning.

I am about to stand up and figure out which direction I should head in when I hear a sound in the distance. I crouch back down in the spot I was laying and scan the surrounding area the best I can. It's not only blindingly bright, but it's also dusty out. When the wind gusts, the dirt swirls into the air and makes it hard to see more than 20 feet in front of you. I lay still for a few minutes, listening, and can hear voices getting closer. Whoever they are, they are not at all concerned about being noticed.

Finally, I see them walking along the road, no more than 40 or 50 feet from me. There's no mistake to make they're Raiders, seven of them. They are walking on the road heading in the same direction we were in the van. No doubt, they are heading to Toronto.

You can immediately tell Raiders apart by not only what they wear, but how they wear it. They all wear matching dark green bandanas and dark green jackets. While those colors aren't exactly unusual, the left sleeve of the jacket is always either rolled up or cut off entirely.

They're all talking and not paying any attention to their surroundings when suddenly they stop. It's right where the van stopped yesterday to leave me here. They're having a conversation and pointing at the ground.

The footsteps. I wonder if they can see the footsteps leading over here. Two of the men start looking over in my direction and pointing. I don't know if they can see me and I really don't want to find out. I look down at my arms and they are coated in the same dust and dirt that's everywhere, might I be so lucky that I just blend in?

Slowly, I start sliding on my stomach away from where I am. I'm surrounded by dead trees, a lot of them, and if I can just get a little deeper into the wooded area, maybe they won't see me. I take one quick peek over at the Raiders and see the two of them that were pointing starting to follow the footsteps in my direction.

I quickly look behind me and spot a tree with a giant trunk, maybe 10 feet away. That might be my only hope before they get here. I crawl quickly, while trying not to raise my body above the small mound that is now behind me. As I crawl, inhaling face full of dust, I can hear their voices getting louder as they draw nearer.

"These footsteps look fresh. Like they were made in the last day or two," the first voice says.

"Definitely. Since the wind hasn't had a chance to erase them yet, it was not that long ago at all," the second voice affirms.

I manage to get myself behind the tree when the two

Raiders get close to where I just was. I peek around the side of the tree and I see it, glimmering there on the ground where I was: My hydration pack.

"No, no, no," is all I can mutter to myself.

Even if I make it out of this, if they spot that pack and take it, I'm done for. As they approach, I slow my breathing and slowly slide back until I'm laying down, chin pressing against my chest, head leaning against the tree. I glance just barely around the tree and see they're mere feet from where I just was, moving branches and looking around.

I move my head back behind the tree just in time to hear one of them say, "What the heck is that?"

Are they talking about me? The hydration pack? I don't know and I can't move around to check. At this moment I have to decide: Are they talking about me, and do I think I can outrun them?

Right as I'm about to decide, I hear the second voice say, "I think it's a water pack?"

"Well yeah," the first voice says, "but it looks new? What's it doing here?"

"Maybe someone was walking the roads last night, decided to stop here to sleep, and dropped it? If so, we're not going to be far behind them now. We should let the rest of the crew know, maybe we can catch up to them and see if they have any more good stuff."

"Think we should take that pack with us?" The first asks.

"Yeah absolutely. If it's full, that's water for a couple of days right there. The rest of the crew will be super happy with us if we bring back water, and you and I know we need all the help we can get after the incident the other night."

"I told you to stop bringing that up, man," the second man replies.

It takes everything I have not to run after them right then and there. As they start to turn around and head back, I move slightly to see if they're headed back to their group.

CRACK.

When I moved, there was a stick underneath me— a very dry stick that decided it was now time to break into two. I hold my breath, only to hear,

"What was that?" From one of the voices.

"Yeah man, I heard it too, that was loud. Wanna check it out?"

"Alright, you head back to the group, I'll check it out and be over in a second. I'm sure it's nothing," the first voice replies.

I sit up with my back against the tree. He's making enough noise heading back this way that I don't think he'll even notice the noise I'm making. Suddenly, I remember: Kian's knife.

I've never stabbed someone before. Garven and Esha always took care of the rougher stuff. They always showed me different techniques and ways to defend myself and, in this moment, I wish I had paid closer attention.

As these thoughts race through my head, I quietly grab the knife out of my pocket and open it. Better make sure I'm ready, just in case. I feel its cold blade on my fingers. Its handle perfectly fits in my hand. I can feel my heartbeat through my fingertips.

He stops where he was before. I can hear him breathing.

"Anyone out there? If so, we're gonna find you, so you better come out now. We'll take it easy on you, I promise."

Sure, he promises. Anyone dumb enough to fall for that wouldn't have made it to this point after the exodus. I stay more still than I've ever been. No need to peek around the tree this time, I know his eyes are scanning the area, waiting for someone to make a move or make a sound.

"Alright, I'm going to come looking for you and if I have to find you, it's going to be bad, bad news for you."

That, I believe. Everyone knows what the Raiders are capable of. I get one sleep to myself and am suddenly in more danger than I've ever been in my life. The thought of it all makes me want to laugh, but I stay still and quiet.

The desire to laugh vanishes quickly as I realize my second mistake. Maybe it was when I crawled over, maybe it was when I took the knife out, but the food ration has fallen out of my pocket and is laying right next to me. If he looks in this direction, he will see it laying on the ground next to the tree trunk. Should I try and grab it? If he's looking over here, it would give him plenty of time to yell out to the rest of his crew.

I have to leave it there. Glistening in the sun. Why are all our food rations so bright and metallic? Who decided that was a good idea?

The footsteps get closer. I can hear branches crunching under his boots. His steps are slow, measured, and with a purpose.

"Well, well, well, what have we here?"

He is right next to the tree. I can feel him crouching down toward the food ration pack. I can hear his boots creaking as his ankles bend, the sound of his jacket brushing against his pants.

He is, at most, a foot away from me. As I slowly look to my right, he is about to grab the food ration and finally notices me. The horrible smile that takes over his face as he sees me sends shivers down my back. His eyes grow wide with excitement, the sweat from a long morning walk in the blistering heat trickling down his temples, his dark brown beard is wild and unkempt.

As he opens his mouth to say something to me, I plunge the knife into his thigh. Before he can even start screaming, I take it out, move backwards a half a foot, and plunge it back into his calf. My heart feels like it's about to beat straight through my rib cage and out of my chest. I have no idea what will happen next, but I know I have to get out of here, and quickly.

With my first instinct, I grab the food ration and then I notice my first bit of luck in a while: This guy must have been carrying the water pack when he came back to look for me and, after I stabbed him, he dropped it.

I grab both and start to get up. The shock of being stabbed has worn off, and the man starts screaming at the top of his lungs.

"I'm going to kill you!" He screams, while holding his leg.

I have the water and food rations and I'm about to take off running, but he grabs me by the wrist.

"You're not getting away that easily," he yells.

I'm now aware that someone else from the Raiders, no doubt the guy he walked over here with, is yelling and asking what's going on.

I try to squirm away for a second before I realize the

knife, Kian's knife, is in my free hand. I turn to face the man and lift it high into the air. For a moment, as I am winding up, he looks me dead in the eyes.

In my eyes, he can see I am no longer the helpless 18-year-old he cornered. I am no longer the scared loner he stumbled upon.

In my hand, it is no longer Kian's knife. It is my knife.

Finley's knife.

In my eyes, it is no longer fear. It is fury.

Finley's fury.

A half second before I am to plunge the knife into him, he lets go of my wrist. I pause briefly to see what happens next. In another second, I take off. Running faster than I've ever ran in my life, straight into the small, wooded area beyond.

Once I'm ten or so feet away, I hear him calling to the rest of the Raiders.

"They, they STABBED me!"

There were probably some profanities in that sentence, but I wasn't paying close attention. I'm assuming at this point the rest of his crew is running toward him to find out what happened, and now I have maybe a 30 second head start to get away.

There's no possible way I could fight all of them at once, so my best bet is to run and keep running until I can no longer run. I weave in and out of dead trees, branches hitting me in the face and arms, scratches piling up.

After a few minutes, I take a second and hide behind a tree to both catch my breath and see if there's any indication they've followed me. After a few deep breaths, I slow my breathing and look around behind the tree, in the direction of where I ran from. There is definitely a commotion. In the distance I hear two distinct voices slowly getting closer.

I take off running again before they can get too close. 50 feet later, while avoiding a tree branch, a dead root catches my foot and sends me flying hard to the ground.

The thud I make as I hit the ground at full speed echoes through the trees.

I move to get up and as soon as I put weight on my leg, my ankle gives out and screams in agony. Now is not the time for a classic Fin accident. At this moment, I'm pretty out in the open, but there's a small group of trees 15 or so feet from me. I attempt to gingerly walk over to them but collapse again. I am in agony.

I can't get any filthier and dirtier than I already am, so I crawl over to the group of trees and hide myself in the middle of them. I take a look at my ankle and it's starting to bruise, not a good sign.

I'm pretty sure it's not broken, but it could also be the

adrenaline getting me through. Right now, all I know is that I can't outrun them anymore, and if they find me, that will be it for me.

I can hear their voices getting closer. Two of them, shouting back and forth to each other. The woman's voice is getting close to me now. I've had more than enough hiding behind trees in the last half hour to last me a lifetime, but here I am again.

After another minute, I notice they've gone quiet. They're not yelling at each other anymore. Maybe they turned around? Got bored of looking and are heading back. Either way, could I be so lucky?

After allowing myself to breathe for a moment, I hear a voice.

"Please don't scream," she says.

Startled, I turn toward the voice with my arm raised, holding my knife.

"And please, don't stab me with that."

I slowly lower my knife, but still have it gripped tightly in my hand.

"Look, I don't want to hurt you, and I certainly don't want the rest of the group to get their hands on you," she pauses for a moment before saying, "Please stop pointing that knife at me."

My guard is still up, but considering the predicament I'm in, I don't have much choice.

"I'm going to yell out to my partner, but I'm not going to say you're not over here, okay? I just don't want him to get suspicious and come in this direction."

I nod my head slowly and keep my eyes locked on her, still ready to stab if I have to. If I'm going out, I want to take a Raider with me.

"Nothing over here yet, Everton. I'll check out the rest of the area and come over in your direction. There are more woods that way."

"Alright, but don't take too long. We gotta find them quick," the voice echoes back from a distance.

"Why," I pause to collect my thoughts, "why are you sparing me?"

"Because I'm not a murderer and I don't want to be an accomplice to one either. I just joined these guys because I knew I couldn't make it up to Toronto on my own. But now that I see how they really are, I just…" she trails off and stares into the distance.

"You're really not going to tell them I'm here?" I say. I think I'm starting to believe her.

"I swear. But I'm going to have to go in a second. Mind if I take a quick look at that ankle of yours? I can see it bruising from here."

"I-I guess, sure," I respond, still stunned.

"Before all this went down, and the world went to hell, I was a medic. I like helping people. I should probably be helping out the guy you stabbed right now, but I never really liked him anyways," she says, smiling to herself.

"Well, you sure picked a funny group to join up with then," I responded.

As I'm saying this, she's gently moving my ankle in a circular motion. It hurts like hell.

She ignores my comment.

"So, it doesn't appear as though it's broken, but it might be sprained. If you want to put any pressure on it in the next few days, you'll need to tape it up and make a little splint. There's plenty of sticks around to make it, and I see you already have a knife handy, but you'll need some tape."

She swings her backpack off her back and searches through it for a few seconds. She then pulls out two rolls of white medical tape.

"Here, take one. For now, raise your foot off the ground to stop the swelling. In a few hours, make a small splint and tape that ankle up good. Whenever you sleep, make sure your foot is elevated. After two days, replace the tape and make another one. In a week you'll have a limp but be mostly fine. Sorry I can't help more but I have to go."

I hardly have the words to say anything I'm in so

much shock, and so much pain. As she puts the second roll of tape back and zips up her pack, all I can manage to blurt out is,

"What's your name?"

"Oh, I don't think I'm ready to exchange names, but if you see me again in the future, hopefully on better terms, you can call me," she pauses for a moment to think, "Llama Llama."

With that, she stands up, turns, and starts walking away. I thought this situation couldn't get any weirder, but now she told me to call her Llama Llama, so who even knows anymore.

Once she's a few feet away, I notice the two large and colorful patches she has on her backpack. They're smiling llamas. I can't help but laugh a little bit.

A few feet after that, she turns around and quietly says,

"I'd recommend avoiding the roads for a bit, they're swarming with Raiders right now. Good luck, stranger."

She smiles and starts walking in the direction of Everton, while I count my lucky stars that I'm still alive.

CHAPTER 28: ESCAPE

It's been more than a day since Finley was tossed out of the van. Unfortunately for Kian, the solar chargers have been working as expected, and the van has driven around 45 miles. Garven and Esha reacted exactly how Kian expected, so Luna and Harlian decided to keep them bound and gagged in the back of the van.

The same van that is currently pulled over on the side of the road, charging the solar panels with the last bit of light before evening. Kian had expected to see the lake again by now. From all the maps he had looked at before they left, it should have been visible about 10 miles ago. Maybe they hadn't traveled as far as they said they had.

Luna and Harlian, plus the van's two person driving crew Coda and Gates, are outside finishing up their dinners. Kian has been pacing nervously near the back of the van, mostly out of sight, but occasionally making sure that Luna and Harlian see he's not doing anything suspicious back there.

He's been racking his brain the last day and a half, trying to figure out a way to escape, and finally came up with something. On one of his trips by the back of the van, he quietly unlatches the back, swing-out doors, but doesn't open them all the way. He heads back to grab a piece of food off the fire.

"You sure do seem stressed, Kian," Luna says.

"Well, yeah," he replies. "We have two pretty dangerous people tied up in the back of the van."

"Look, if they don't come around by the time we're getting close to Toronto, we'll toss them out of the van— but this time it'll be off a bridge," Luna responds.

Kian wants to shudder with that statement but just nods in agreement instead. He's tried to be purposefully cold toward Garven and Esha the last day to not raise any suspicions from the rest of the crew. After what Luna said to him during their confrontation over Finley, he knows he has to be very careful around them.

Kian again walks toward the back of the van, each step crunching the dry ground below. This time he opens one door part way, so you can't tell that it's open from the front, and leans in.

Garven and Esha look up from the floor of the van with anger in their eyes. They try yelling through their gags, but almost no noise escapes. Kian whispers,

"Look, there won't be a lot of time. You have to listen to me very carefully. In exactly 60 seconds you need to have cut yourself out of the ropes. In exactly 60 seconds you need to slowly open the back doors and run, straight away from the

back of the van. Grab your backpacks, plus mine and Fin's —
they're hanging right there — and go. That'll give you a 45
second head start before anyone notices you."

With that, Kian leans in farther and waves for Esha to
move closer to him. Reluctantly, she wiggles toward him on
the floor of the van and he cuts the ropes tying her hands
behind her back. As she struggles to push herself to a seated
position, Kian hands her a small knife, his last one. Before he
heads back to the front of the van, he whispers,

"60 seconds."

He then slowly closes the door and makes sure it
doesn't latch. While walking to the front of the van, he notices
the crew packing up the last of the food and getting ready to
head back on the road.

"So, what's the plan now that it's getting dark?" He
asks. He knows it's a dumb question, but he's stalling.

"What do you mean, what's the plan? The same thing
we do every night until we get to Toronto: Drive," replies
Harlian.

"Yup, yup, that makes sense. I just have to take a leak
real quick before we go," Kian answers.

Luna rolls her eyes at this.

Kian did not, in fact, have to relieve himself. But
protocol means that everyone must now stand guard pretty
close to Kian to make sure nothing happens to the person

using the bathroom. It's overkill and everyone but Harlian hates it, but he said he learned it in training and makes everyone follow along.

Kian walks off the road, down into a dry ditch, and keeps going for another 10 feet. He goes through the regular motions of using the bathroom since no one is going to be studying him too hard. He's kept count in his head the entire time and knows in about 15 seconds, if Esha and Garven still have any trust left in him, they'll be running away from the van.

There are two main things that could go wrong at this point, Kian thinks to himself.

First, Garven and Esha could try to use the knife to jump the rest of the van when they get in, which would be especially gruesome for them. Secondly, the rest of the van crew notices them escape right away and they get no head start.

He tries not to look in their direction because he doesn't want to give anything away. If all goes according to plan he'll try and convince the team to split up to look for them, then find Esha and Garven and try to find Fin.

Before he finishes pretending, Kian hears Gates yell out to the rest of the group,

"What the hell?!"

Kian turns around and sees that Gates has spotted Garven and Esha running. They didn't get nearly the head start that Kian was hoping for, but it's too late to turn back now.

"How the hell did they get out of the van?" Yells Luna.

"I-I don't know, I just turned around and they were running!" Replies Gates.

Kian runs back to the group and acts surprised the best he can.

"What's going on?" He says.

"They're getting away, idiot! Take Gates and go after them!" Harlian yells in a fit of panic.

Gates takes off running immediately.

"Take this, you're going to need it," Harlian says to Kian.

Harlian hands Kian his gun. While these old things aren't the most accurate weapon from any farther than 10 or 15 feet anymore, they sure will still kill a person. Kian's thankful he gave it to him and not Gates. Gates has always come across as a little trigger happy.

With that, Kian starts sprinting to catch up to Gates. Ahead, Esha and Garven have about a 200-foot lead over them. They're making a beeline toward a small, tree-lined ridge ahead, exactly where Kian was hoping they would go. It'll help block the sightlines from the van for a short while.

Each step while running is uncomfortable. The boots Kian has on are made for hiking, not at all for running, and his knees feel the brunt of the impact.

I'm going to be sore tomorrow, if I'm still alive, he thinks to himself.

Once he catches up to Gates, he slows down a bit. They're slowly catching up to the two of them, Kian tries to buy them as much time as possible by slowing the pace.

"Come on man, hurry up, they're gonna get away!" Gates yells at Kian.

"Sorry man, these boots are awful for running, they hurt like hell," Kian replies.

"That's not my problem, man, now hurry up," Gates replies.

Kian then takes one last chance to slow the two of them down and pretends to trip.

It felt like slow motion to him, bracing for impact on the dry ground. His hands bloodied from absorbing the brunt of it. He lays there for a moment. As he hoped, Gates stops and grabs him to lift him off the ground.

That bought them an extra 15 or 20 seconds for sure, Kian thinks to himself, palms now throbbing.

"Come on man, let's go kill these nobodies," Gates says as they take off running again.

Kian smiles to himself for a brief moment. He has other plans.

CHAPTER 29: RETIREMENT

The last few days before boarding, Auryn's parents started to come around. Her mom could have conversations without breaking down in a fit of tears. Her dad started offering tips on systems that break down often on the ship, and how to fix them. It was bittersweet, of course.

Auryn is 18 and, if all goes as well as possible, she won't see her parents until she's 21 or 22. That's the best-case scenario. For as much as they've fought over the past few weeks, she's still going to miss them, and her little brother too.

"The good news is that you and dad can maybe enjoy retirement now," Auryn says to her mom the day before leaving.

"Well, there's still plenty around here to keep us busy, of course, but it will be nice working half time instead of full time," Her mom responds.

She gives a halfhearted smile along with it to try to cover up the sadness, but it's no use. Auryn walks over to her and gives her a hug.

"Make sure dad's alright while I'm gone, okay? You and I both know he can get pretty stir crazy if there's not enough to do," Auryn says gently to her while still hugging.

"Oh sweetie, he's going to drive me absolutely crazy while you're away," her mom responds.

Auryn and her mom both let out a laugh.

"That's the truth," Auryn says.

"I hear they set up some comms so that the first few weeks of the trip, you can send some video messages back to us. We'd really like it if you did that," her mom says as she puts both her hands on Auryn's face.

She gently pinches Auryn's cheeks and smiles. Alia has done this since Auryn was little. She said her mother used to do it to her as well. Now, as Auryn looks at her mom, she can see the crow's feet from the corner of her eyes, the sign of a life well lived, but she looks tired and there's a sadness in her eyes Auryn will never forget.

"Of course I'll send you videos, and dad and Forbin, too. I'll send one as often as they allow me too. Within a week, you'll be annoyed at how many videos are piling up for you to watch," Auryn says, and she means it.

"Alright, well, you're still here another day, so no need to get all emotional yet I guess. Maybe go spend some time with your father for a bit. He's having a hard time with this."

"I'll go find him, I'm sure he's in the Central Park Dome. Love you mom."

With that, Auryn starts walking down the familiar yet expanding halls leading to central park.

Right before she reaches the dome, she runs into Mina and two people she's seen around but never really talked to.

"Hey Auryn!" Mina says cheerfully, "All set for the trip?"

"As set as I can be," Auryn replies back.

"This is Korine and Waelon, they'll be on the ship with us," Mina replies.

Auryn leans in and shakes both of their hands. She immediately thinks to herself how much she loves Korine's short red hair. Auryn often has her hair in a faux hawk, and some days she just gets sick of having to worry about it each morning. Today is one of those days.

"Mina has told us so much about you," Waelon says. "She said you've been helping so much on the ship to get it ready; we definitely appreciate that!"

"Oh! This is *the* Auryn you've been telling us about," Korine says, "It's such a pleasure to finally meet you, she really has told us so much about you."

Auryn looks over to Mina, her cheeks a deep shade of red. Auryn can't help but smile.

"Yup, that's me," she replies. "I'd love to stay and chat more about all the wonderful things Mina has said about me, but I have to head to the dome."

Auryn says this without any hint of sarcasm, and Korine and Waelon both laugh after she says it.

As they part ways, Mina gives Auryn a hug. Auryn used to tense up when people went to hug her, but she embraces Mina back a little more each time.

CHAPTER 30: MOONLIGHT

It's been several hours that I've been laying here now, my foot resting up on a tree trunk. The swelling has gone down, and it's not throbbing like it was. The last bit of light is starting to fade from the day; as much as I hate traveling at night, that's going to be the only option I have if I want to make any progress toward the lake.

As I slide back and pull my foot off the tree, it starts gently throbbing again. I look around to see if I can find some sticks to shave down so I can make a makeshift brace. Like the woman who called herself Llama said, if I can do two days with sticks and tape, then a few days of just tape, I should be alright, but it's not going to be a fun couple of days.

First, I wrap a layer of medical tape around my ankle and stabilize it. The idea of some sticks right up against my bare ankle for the next two days doesn't seem like the most pleasant time.

Once taped up, I start getting to work on carving down two sticks. It takes longer than I had imagined it would. Once they're smooth enough on two sides to sit on my ankle correctly, I grab the tape again and add another layer. Now, for the real test, trying to walk on it.

I grab a tree trunk and hoist myself up. As I pull on the dead tree, it cracks loudly and I'm certain it's going to give way, but it holds and I'm able to stand.

I gently put some pressure on the ankle, and it's not as bad as I thought it was going to be. The tape seems to be stabilizing it, so it doesn't move around too much. My foot moving around is when it hurts the most.

With that, I put my water and food into my pockets and triple check that they are secured this time.

"No more being careless with my stuff," I say to myself.

With that, I start gingerly walking in the direction I'm fairly certain the lake is. My pace is slow while I adjust to my foot. It hurts a little bit each step, more so when it lands on a tree root or a slight incline. Overall, I feel fortunate not only that I wasn't captured or killed, but that she was kind enough to give me help.

The moon begins filling the sky as nighttime envelopes the day. Thankfully, there isn't much cloud cover, so the light of the moon lets me see what's ahead on my path. I can keep walking for a few more hours through the woods at this rate. Taking the road is way too dangerous; the Raiders are still close by, according to Llama, and I can't chance them seeing me. When I was traveling with Esha and Garven, we spent plenty of time walking through woods and not on a main road, so none of this is new to me.

After an hour of walking, my mind starts to wander. I wonder if Kian was telling the truth, that he's really going to try and escape and meet me at the lake with Garven and Esha. Since the moment I woke up this morning, all I've been able to do is try to survive and get through pain. Now that I'm here, alone, walking into darkness, my emotions are starting to flood my mind.

Are they alive at this point? Esha and Garven are the only people that I consider family that I have left. What if they can't escape, and Luna and Harlian kill them? What if the Buffalo crew finds out that Kian is a traitor and kills him too?

How have I been so selfish to only be thinking about myself this entire day? There are people out there that need me. I don't know how I'm going to do it but as soon as my ankle is healed, I will find them no matter where they are.

As I walk on, I also start thinking more and more about Kian. The range of emotions I felt, first when I thought he was going to leave me there to die, and then as he provided me with a way to live. We had become close in our short time together in Buffalo, and I knew I was starting to have feelings for him. If we all make it out of this alive, I swear I'm going to tell him how I feel about him.

"I like him," I say to no one but the trees. Immediately I start laughing. It feels both meaningless and freeing to say it.

I don't know what I'm going to do if the three of them aren't alive. Even if they can't come find me. I'm hopeful I can fend for myself now. I'm sure that tomorrow there are going to be some houses, or buildings, I can scavenge through and find some supplies. Tonight? Tonight, I'm going to walk for as long as my ankle allows me to.

CHAPTER 31: EXHAUSTION

Kian and Gates are running quickly in the direction the escapees were headed. Garven and Esha reached a small tree line a few seconds ago and disappeared behind it.

"How the hell do you think they got out?" Says Gates between breaths.

"No idea, maybe they slipped out of the ropes? Maybe Harlian missed a hidden knife on them, and they cut their way out?" Kian replied.

"God, Harlian is always messing things up. Luna is going to be so pissed if we don't find them," Gates says.

Kian doesn't have a plan from this point about the escape. It was nothing more than dumb luck that Gates started running before Harlian gave Kian the gun. It's lucky that the tree line ahead partially blocks the view from the van. There's going to be luck in any escape attempt, Kian guesses, but eventually this feels like it's going to run out.

As they approach the tree line they slow to a walk, then, after a few more feet, stop. They scan the area and there aren't many places to hide. It's pretty open except for some occasional trees and dead bushes. Gates mentions splitting up, but Kian reminds him there's only one gun and they should stick together.

In the distance, maybe a hundred feet away, a group of bushes moves and shakes.

"I bet they're hiding in there. They probably got exhausted from running," Gates says, "they haven't eaten in a day and a half."

"Alright, let's approach cautiously, who knows what they might have on them. They've surprised us once already, so we gotta be careful," Kian replies.

"Make sure you have that gun ready, so they know we're serious," Gates says, "and if they say they aren't coming with us, shoot Garven first. Bet that'll get Esha moving."

He does not know Esha at all, Kian thinks to himself.

As they approach the bushes, Kian looks back in the direction of the van. They're a quarter mile away now, maybe more, and from the little Kian can see over the ridge, the van hasn't moved. That's good. They'll need all the time they can get to escape again.

Kian and Gates start wading into the bushes, and there, in the middle, are Garven and Esha each down on one knee, trying to eat a food ration from their bags. They look exhausted and defeated.

"Listen here, you two, you're going to stand up, let me tie you back up, and come back to the van with me. If not, Kian right here has a surprise for you, and it's not a fun one."

With that, Kian shows his gun to the two of them. As Gates continues talking, Kian winks at both Esha and Garven, trying to let them know it's going to be okay.

While Garven and Esha continue listening to Gates, Kian takes one last nervous look back to the van. The entire time Esha and Garven have continued taking bites of their food rations, and Gates is getting progressively more upset by it.

"Alright, get up you two, and grab your bags, all of it. You're gonna have to carry all your stuff back and watch us eat and drink it now," Kian says, making quite a show for Gates.

Really, he just wants to make sure they're ready to run again, and no time is wasted. It's several hundred more feet to some buildings, and as exhausted as they look, he's not sure they have any adrenaline left to carry them.

"Alright, got everything?" Kian says, and Esha and Garven nod to him while each throwing a pack over their shoulder and carrying another in their hands. Four in total.

Kian then swings around and points the gun at Gates.

"Sorry, Gates, but I didn't know I was in a van with a bunch of kidnappers and murderers. I didn't sign up for this," Kian says.

"God damn it, Kian, you let them out of the van, didn't you? Luna and Harlian are going to kill you when they find you, and I'm gonna enjoy every minute of it," Gates yells, spittle flying from his mouth.

"If you just let me tie you up and let us walk away, we can all come out of this alive. No one has to get hurt any more than they already are," responds Kian.

"You know as well as I do, Kian, that if I let you walk away, things aren't going to end well for me. How exactly did you think this was going to go?" Gates is getting angrier and angrier as he speaks.

"You thought the three of you were just gonna walk away from this and go on with your little, meaningless lives? Come on, man, you know better than that. Even if you escape now, where are you gonna run to?"

With that, Gates removes the machete from his clip and in one smooth motion lunges at Kian, who's standing a few arm lengths away. Gates takes his first step, and a deafening explosion immediately follows.

BOOM.

Garven and Esha wince from the pain in their ears. The sound echoes off distant trees and buildings. Once they regain focus, they look at Kian, who is yelling at them to run. Esha takes a look at Gates, who is hunched over and grabbing his leg.

"You, you shot me? What the hell, man!" Gates yells, still in shock.

Esha looks down at Gates' thigh and notices the blood. It's starting to soak through his pants, and he drops to one knee in pain.

"Harlian never should have given you that gun, you traitor!" Gates yells.

Kian quickly grabs Garven and Esha, pulling them in the direction toward the buildings.

"We don't have long until the rest of them come, we've gotta get out of here and hide. Let's go, now!" Kian yells.

With that, Garven and Esha gather every ounce of energy they have left and start running with Kian. Garven looks toward the van and, although it's far, he can make out two shapes running in the direction of where Gates is.

Garven is carrying both his backpack and Finley's, while Esha is carrying her own and Kian's.

"Will you take this already?" Garven says while reaching out Finley's bag in the direction of Kian.

"And take your own bag too, man," Esha adds, while tossing it over to Kian.

"I don't know if I can make it," Garven says in between breaths."

"You don't have a choice, now do you, Garven?"
Yells Esha.

Each step they take on the hard ground is a chore.
Garven and Esha are getting slower every step, and Kian, now
carrying two full packs, isn't much quicker.

Kian turns around to see if they can see who is
running after them. It looks like Harlian and Coda, with Luna
staying by the van. They're not quite at Gates yet, but they're
closing in faster than Garven and Esha can run.

They finally reach a small grouping of buildings.

"Let's get past this building and see if there's
anywhere else to hide, they're going to be looking for us in
this one," Kian says.

"I just want to eat and sit down for a moment," an
angry and annoyed Esha replies.

"Look, I took a bunch of supplies, so when we're in
the clear we can have an entire feast. For now, we have to get
to safety," says Kian.

They scramble past the first set of two buildings. Both
single story and on their last legs. The first is an old garage;
while passing the broken-out window, Kian notices a car lift.
They were made so the mechanics could work on the
underside of a car. Kian is surprised it's still in there. On most
of the popular roads, things like this were stolen and
repurposed long ago.

The second building's white paint has mostly been chipped off, but there's a big metal sign that's half fallen off. It says "E__O." Esha and Garven have passed a ton of these types of buildings, all different companies, all looking almost exactly the same while crumbling. They've seen "S_EL_," and "SU_O_O."

Finley often tried, to the annoyance of everyone, to figure out what the words actually were. Sometimes there was enough of a rust or dirt stain around where the letters used to be. Sometimes Fin would just say words out loud, over and over again, while walking, until Garven asked them to kindly shut up.

There was a gap between the first two buildings and a small group of others. The pavement is cracked and broken, and weeds have grown from the Earth. Kian looks ahead and sees that the next group of buildings are a combination of one and two stories.

"Maybe we can get upstairs in one of those buildings and hide," Kian says to them.

As they struggle along, Kian spots a door on the back of a building. He tries the handle and it spins freely, so he puts a shoulder into the door and it flies open. They all head into the building and Garven and Esha both take a knee to rest and catch their breath. Kian shuts the door and grabs an old, rusted metal trash can to put in front of it.

As he shoves it towards the door, the noise of the metal scraping along the concrete floor is deafening. Now that they aren't sure how far away Coda and Harlian are, they have to worry about making too much noise. Kian makes the final shove and says,

"Even if it doesn't buy us any extra time, it will at least alert us if they open the door."

He then scans the room and spots the stairs to the second level. They're old and falling apart, but it's their best chance at survival. With the broken windows and limited hiding places here, they'd be spotted immediately if they stayed down here.

"Alright, let's get up these stairs, then you can rest," Kian says to Esha and Garven.

"Come on man, you've said that like 3 times already," Garven responds.

"Do you want to be found?" Kian snaps back.

Garven grumbles, and gets back up on his feet, Esha does the same.

"You gotta promise this is the last time we move. If they find us up there, just let them kill us," Esha says while laughing. She's always had a dark sense of humor. Garven chuckles after hearing her say it.

"Yeah, I'll second that," he replies.

"Yeah, alright, fine, this is our last stand or whatever. Now would you please just get up the stairs?" Kian says, quickly running out of patience.

The three of them make their way to the stairs and slowly, one at a time, start walking up them. Esha goes first. You can hear the old wood creaking with every step she takes. On the third stair, the wood cracks underneath her foot and she quickly grabs onto the railing. She manages to put most of her weight on the railing as the stairs sound like they're about to give out at any second.

After she makes it to the top, Garven looks at Kian and says, "Well, this should go well, I'm like twice as big as her."

Esha yells back down and says, "Yeah, but I'm all muscle so it should even out!"

"If I make it up there, you're going to pay for that comment! I'm all muscle, too!" Garven yells back.

"Children, children, we're all very strong, now please hurry up!" Kian says, sounding more exasperated by the second.

Garven tries skipping a step every time he moves up, and about halfway up the 10 stairs, the step he is on starts to break. Just like Esha, he grabs onto the railing. Unfortunately for Garven, he is 6 feet tall and 180 pounds, so when he grabs it, the railing rips off. With that he stumbles and puts a leg straight through a step.

"Son of a…" he pauses. "What a stupid idea this was, Kian."

"Maybe, but it's too late now, be careful and get up there," Kian responds.

Garven pulls his leg out of the hole, and it's bleeding from his shin. He gingerly makes it up the rest of the steps to the second floor, stairs continuing to creak and moan with every step.

When Kian is about to start up the steps, he hears a loud bang outside.

"We know you're in one of these buildings. Say your prayers now because none of you are getting out of this alive. Especially you, Kian."

That's Harlian's voice, Kian is sure of it. He can't tell exactly where it's coming from, but it's close. He takes a couple steps up the stairway and feels the entire thing move under his feet. He pauses for a moment and looks up towards the top of the stairs. There are nine more steps to go, including one with a large, boot-sized hole in it.

He takes one more step and starts to feel the entire staircase shift. He decides to go for it and sprints up the remaining few stairs. As his foot hits the second last stair, it breaks right through and catches his ankle.

The upper half of Kian's body spills onto the floor of the second story while his legs hang off, swaying below, dripping blood from the new gashes on his shin and ankle.

The entire staircase gives way and crumbles to the ground. The sound of collapsing wood hitting centuries old concrete echoes through the cluster of buildings.

As Kian begins to slip, sliding closer and closer to falling from the second story, Esha reaches out and grabs him by the shoulder, his jacket tightly gripped in between her fingers. She reaches a second hand over and grabs him by the arm. Exhausted as she is, she manages one last drop of adrenaline and pulls him to safety, however temporary it might be.

Garven looks over to Kian and says, "Well, they know where we are now," and laughs again. The exhaustion has got to them. Now that all three of them are on the second-floor ground, Kian reaches over and gently closes the door behind them and locks it.

Everyone takes a deep, quiet breath and sprawls out onto the floor. They're all exhausted, hungry, and hurt. Even if Kian had a spare bullet for his gun, it wouldn't be enough to fight off Harlian, Coda, and Luna. They're stuck here, on the upper floor of this abandoned building, hoping that Luna and Harlian decide it's more important to get to Toronto than it is to kill the three of them.

Kian turns on his back and looks up to the roof. There's a big hole in it, and much of the floor has water stains on it. The sun is starting to set on the day, and the rafters below the hole are casting long shadows over the wood planks of the floor.

After a couple of minutes of silence, Esha whispers,

"So, about that buffet?"

Kian laughs very quietly, sits up, and gently gets his backpack off his back. Inside, he grabs two full food ration bars – a day's worth – and a hydration pack for each of them.

"A ration bar?" Esha replies. "I thought you had good stuff. We were eating this in the bushes!"

"Please quiet down! If we make it out of all this, we should have plenty of each for 10 days or more. Including an apple for each of you," he whispers to the group.

They both perk up a bit with the news of an apple being involved.

Esha and Garven take huge bites out of the packs as soon as they've opened them, and after the first swallow they look at each other with such relief. After a few more bites and a gulp of water, their shoulders slump a little less and their head hangs a little higher.

Ten minutes go by, and they can hear the sound of occasional banging and talking coming from around the building. Doors opening and closing, old boards being moved around. Harlian and Coda are being thorough.

Suddenly, a new noise comes into focus. A humming noise. They can't tell what it is at first but it's getting closer. After another minute, Kian realizes what he hears and whispers,

"It's the van, Luna must have driven the van over here to help look."

Esha and Garven nod; Garven finished his ration bar already, and Esha is about to take her last bite. As they continue listening, they finally hear Luna's voice through the bullhorn on the front of the van.

"Alright, traitor, make this easy for us and just come out now. I promise we'll kill you nice and quick. It'll be easy. Either way, you're gonna pay for what you've done to Gates."

Garven rolls his eyes after hearing it and makes a face while Kian mouths the words, "Yeah, right."

They stay still on the creaky floor, not daring to move. Best case scenario is the floor creaks and alerts Luna and Harlian to where they are; the worst case being they fall through the floor entirely. While they are frozen in place, they can hear the metal garbage can rattling around downstairs.

As the door swings open, they hear the can crash to the floor. Kian tenses, his ankle throbbing and chest burning. Garven and Esha remain still on the floor.

"It's dusty as hell in here," Coda says. "Could be from them moving around."

"Could also be from you knocking that damn trash can over too, Coda," Luna says. The anger in her voice near a boiling rage, and her patience near zero.

"Alright, poke around. There's not a lot of places to hide here. So, make it quick," says Harlian to Coda.

Esha, Garven, and Kian can hear them rummaging through everything downstairs: Rusty tool chests, sheets of rotted plywood. The floor below them must be paper thin because they can hear everything, which also means they can't make a single, solitary sound.

Esha, who is lying on her stomach, presses her eye to the floor and can see between two cracks. Luna, with her nearly glowing blonde hair, is right below her, surveying the first floor.

After a few minutes, they hear Coda at the base of the stairs.

"This looks like they might have fallen recently. Maybe that was the noise we heard, Harlian?" Coda says.

"I doubt it," he replies. "If it came crashing down one of them probably would have come crashing with it. Besides, how would we even get up there to check?"

"We could move this toolbox over and stand on it, get a peek up there," Coda replies.

Garven, Esha, and Kian all look at each other nervously. This could finally be it for them. While they have the high ground, two out of the three of them can barely move and are not well equipped to defend themselves against the amount of weapons Luna and her team have.

"They could already be getting away if they kept moving, let's just keep looking and if we can't find them, we burn all these buildings to the ground and go," Luna says.

With that, the three of them move out of the building and onto the next.

"Do you actually think they'll burn the buildings down?" Whispers Garven.

"I don't put anything past them," answers Kian.

For the next hour, they sit there being as quiet as possible. The occasional crashing and shuffling from buildings around them break the silence. Kian and Garven are lying flat on their backs; Kian gave everyone a small camp blanket that they rolled up and put under their heads.

Since the last sound 15 minutes ago, there has been an eerie, unsettling quiet to the air. No feet shuffling on the broken pavement and loose stone outside, no yelling to each other from one building to the next, no loud crashes from cans or board being knocked over.

"Do you smell that?" Esha says, breaking the silence.

Kian's eyes grow wide, and he stands up immediately.

"Okay, both of you, up now, they've done it. They've lit the buildings on fire."

With that, Esha and Garven jump to their feet. As they grab their bags, they hear Luna use the loudspeaker again.

"Hope you enjoy burning, you traitors!"

Kian runs to the busted-out windows at the front of the building and carefully peeks outside, making sure not to be seen. There he sees Luna, Harlian, and Coda using fire starters to light some old, small towels on fire and throwing them into each of the buildings. It's been dry for decades at this point, and these building will go up like paper.

He turns around, runs back to Garven and Esha and yells in his loudest whisper, "We have to get out of here, now!"

The three of them search for a way out that can't be seen from the van. There are no windows that are anywhere close to the ground they could jump out through. Kian realizes that he's going to have to lower them through the hole where the stairs used to be. It would be easy to twist an ankle at the bottom because what's left of the steps are laying down there in a heap, but there aren't any other options.

Kian fills them in on the plan and Garven starts to protest, until they all start noticing the smoke filling the room. Immediately, he is more amenable.

They open the door, and Kian slowly lowers down Esha first by grabbing her arm and getting himself as low as possible. She clears out the area below so it's a safer landing spot for Garven and Kian. Next, Garven grabs Kian's arms, and he slowly gets lowered. When Kian can't get him any lower, Garven lets go and lands hard on the ground. He winces when he lands but looks up and gives Kian a thumbs up.

Kian then drops all the backpacks and gear down to the two of them and slowly lowers himself down as far as he can. Once there, Garven and Esha each grab one leg and help lower him down to the ground.

They grab all the bags and as the fire starts to fully engulf the building, they run out the same door they had come in through.

Once outside, they keep running and use the building as a way to block the van's view of them. Kian's ankle is searing in pain, Garven's shin bleeding onto his pants. After several minutes, they reach the top of a small hill and all collapse to the ground.

"Holy crap. I never want to run another day in my life," Esha says.

All three of them begin to laugh. Relieved that they got out alive. Relieved that they can rest for a moment. Relieved that they can look for Finley.

Esha then crawls up to the edge of the hill and looks out over the strips of buildings now engulfed in flames that are 50, even 60 feet high. Farther away, in the light from the fires themselves she sees the van driving away, no doubt convinced that the three of them were burned alive.

"Alright. How about we set up a little camp here for the night? I think this place is as good as any to get some rest.

Then tomorrow, we head straight for Hamilton and try to find Finley. Sound good to everyone?" Kian says in between deep breaths.

Esha and Garven nod their heads. Before anyone stands up to start making camp, Esha asks the question that she and Garven were both wondering.

"So, Kian. About those apples?"

CHAPTER 32: LORENA

I fell asleep so late last night; I might even call it early morning. Last time I looked at my watch it was about 3:30am, and I fell asleep at least a half an hour past that.

I don't have breakfast to cook over a fire, which is fine because I don't have my fire starter anymore. I have two days' worth of food and water before I start my hike. The important thing is that I am alive, and my ankle allows me to hobble along at a slow pace.

I pack the remainder of my food and water into my jacket pockets and give my foot a good wiggle to see how it's feeling. Not great, but manageable. When I woke up, it was fully asleep because I kept it elevated on a fallen log last night. It took a solid 20 minutes to start getting that tingling sensation in it, and after that? Whew, it did not feel good for a bit.

I stand up to start walking and take a deep breath of air in. I'm going to try and do this every morning now. To appreciate my lungs still taking in full breaths, to appreciate being alive. I don't know what the future holds for me, but I know what I can control in the present.

"Let go or be dragged," I say to myself as I start walking. Judging by what time it is, and where the sun is, I estimate the direction I need to walk in without using the road. I'm still leery of running into Raiders since I still can't run. Staying off-trail and hiding are really my only two options right now.

After a few hours, I start feeling really bored. With how much excitement I've had the last few days, slow, calm, and steady is both needed and also strange. To pass the time, I start singing some songs that my mom and dad used to sing around the apartment when I was little. Unfortunately, my memory doesn't happen to include all the words to the songs, so I'll have to make do.

> *"We were once at the end of the world*
> *But… something something… said it was fine*
> *Something something… never will know*
> *All we've got is time"*

After singing that over and over again, still unable to remember the words, I stop and walk in silence. I wish there was an old gas station sign around so I could try and guess what the company it used to be.

A few more hours into the walk, as daytime is starting to dwindle and evening bears itself, I notice something in the distance, far back in the woods. I come to a complete stand still and focus my eyes on it.

I inch closer until I can see that it's a cabin, and there's a light on inside. Under normal circumstances, I would make a large half circle around the property and avoid it completely, but after breakfast this morning I only have one day of food and water left. With how slow I have to walk, I might be days away from other houses.

I slowly get closer to the cabin, doing everything I can to stay out of view, until I'm about 20 feet from it. I position myself so that I can see through the main window what's going on inside.

I see a woman inside, in her 40s, with shoulder length brown hair, wearing a tan sweater. She is making dinner for herself. I can see a little cook stove inside and a small amount of smoke coming from the top of the cabin. She's also dancing while she cooks and, while I can't hear her, I'm pretty sure she's singing, too.

Whoever she is, I like her already. After a couple more minutes, she disappears from view. I keep watching carefully through the window to see if she comes back. I don't really know what I'm doing here in the first place. Maybe she throws out some food scraps I can scavenge through when she goes to bed? I don't really know. It's honestly just kind of nice to watch someone having a nice time.

As I begin to realize how creepy this is, me, in the dark, watching a woman by herself cook and dance, I am startled.

"I hope you're better at explaining yourself than you are at spying on me," a not so friendly sounding voice says.

I turn around slowly, limping, and the woman from the cabin is standing ten feet away, makeshift bow and arrow pointed right at me.

"I'm so, so sorry," I immediately say.

"Well, that wasn't the response I was expecting. Who the hell are you?" The woman says.

"My name is Finley, I have an injured ankle, and I was nearly killed by Raiders yesterday."

Saying it all out loud like that makes me feel immediately overwhelmed, and a few small tears roll down my cheek.

"Huh, well, what the hell are you doing here, staring in my window like some creep?" The woman replies.

I pause for a moment to try and think of a reason, any reason, that this would be acceptable.

"I honestly don't know. I was trying to stay off the main road for my own safety and saw your cabin. With the light on, I could see you dancing and singing in there and for a moment it was just really nice to watch."

I would be terrible in an interrogation. I'm blabbering on to a complete stranger. Someone with a knife to my throat would get everything out of me.

"Huh. No offense, hun, but you don't seem like someone who would have made it this far on your own."

"I wasn't alone until two days ago. I was drugged and left to die on the side of the road, and the people I was with are still kidnapped and," I can feel the emotions overwhelm me, "I don't even know if they're alive anymore or if I'm ever going to see them again."

With this, I start crying, just a little bit. I am actively trying to conserve any moisture, so crying is not going to help me survive. I wipe the tears off my cheeks and try to compose myself. I look over at the woman, whose demeanor has changed. Her bow is now pointed toward the ground, and her body language is less defensive.

"You know what, why don't you come on in, grab a warm meal. Maybe rest up a bit before you get on with your travels?" She says.

"I-I couldn't possibly impose. I've already taken up enough of your time," I reply.

"I haven't seen another friendly person in months. It'll be nice to have a chat, maybe find out what's going on in the outside world," she replies.

With that, I hobble in her direction and toward the cabin. As I get closer I notice it's unusually tall, as tall as it is wide. When I'm just a few feet from it, I can smell food. Real food. No wonder she was in such a good mood; she's cooking something amazing! She notices me smelling the air.

"I grow a lot of my own stuff, so a couple times a

week I get to have a really nice meal. I'm glad to finally have someone to share it with" she says.

"How do you know you can trust me?" I ask.

"I don't, but the kind of people you can't trust don't usually ask that sort of question."

Fair enough. She opens the door to the cabin and we both walk in. It's really cozy. There's a couch right across from the door we walk in through and a small dinette to the left. The warmth and smell from whatever she is cooking fills the air.

How does she maintain all this, and how does she not get raided? I think to myself.

"I know you probably have a lot of questions for me. Before you start, let's get that coat off, and maybe I have something for that ankle. I can't imagine some sticks taped to your ankle feel very good."

I thank her and toss my coat on the couch. She motions for me to take a seat at the table and she heads over to her wood stove. There's a pot on top; she grabs a ladle and a bowl and scoops in something from it.

"It's a veggie and potato soup. It'll fill you right up. Can't imagine a poor thing like you has had too much hot food recently," she says.

"How is this even possible?" I ask. I didn't notice any vegetable gardens around the outside of her place.

"Well, it took me a while to get my system all figured out. A few years ago, when I first built all these, people would come by and steal my veggies all the time, so now I grow my essentials on the roof. Potatoes, veggies, some berries. It's just me here, so I don't need a lot."

"Is that why the building is so tall?" I ask. I have so many questions for her.

"Indeed. That way people, worse people than you, don't know what's up there. Why don't we save the rest of the questions until after you're done eating? Soup's always the best when it's fresh and hot."

As I bring the spoon to my mouth, I blow on it a little. I can feel the heat radiating on my face. After a moment, I take a bite.

It's the best thing I've eaten in so long I can't even remember. Better than anything on the road, of course, but even better than anything in Buffalo. Better than the apple I have recurring daydreams about.

The potatoes just melt in my mouth. I think there's also spinach? Carrots. Some other veggies. It's so good I want to openly weep, but instead I just make the universal noise for "This Tastes Amazing."

She chuckles. "My name is Lorena, by the way. You said yours was Finley? That's a nice name, has a nice ring to it," she continues.

"I haven't had anyone to enjoy my food since, well,

since my daughter left. Had to be two, two and a half years ago now."

"Where'd she go?" I ask, with a mouthful of soup.

"She headed for Toronto. Tried for weeks to convince me to go as well, but I like this little slice of land right here. I get mostly left alone. Mostly," she looks at me and chuckles.

I blush, knowing that I've turned this woman's life upside down for the night.

"I'm just kidding, hun, you're the nicest company I've had in years. Better than some of the other visitors that have come along."

I'm pretty sure she means Raiders by the tone in her voice, but I don't know if I should pry or not. It's also hard to ask any follow up questions while I'm shoveling soup into my mouth. After I finish chewing and am able to swallow, I ask,

"So, do the Raiders bother you often?"

"They certainly have tried. All sorts of people have come along, looking to take things that aren't theirs…" she trails off for a moment, "but I make it so that it's not worth their trouble."

With that, she smiled and gave a chuckle.

"Wanna see?" She continues.

I nod my head, not having any idea what's about to happen.

She walks over to a rope hanging from the ceiling, looks me directly in the eyes, and smiles. With that, she yanks the cord hard. Immediately, a loud crashing noise fills the room and the cabin becomes darker. I look around and see that everything, windows, doors, all of them, are now blocked by metal sheets.

"And it's not just inside, it's outside too!" Lorena says proudly. "Pretty much as soon as someone comes knocking, if they don't seem quite right, or there's a group of them, I shut the whole place down."

I am truly amazed, and I let her know. Being able to survive like this for a few years, on her own, and set this all up? I don't think I could do it.

"The only problem is, it's a real pain to get everything back open again. Which I'm gonna need to do for the next few minutes here. I guess bragging about it has some downfalls," Lorena says.

With that, she chuckles to herself and then starts lifting the metal sheeting in front of the door. I offer to help but she tells me to rest my ankle and eat up.

After fifteen minutes or so, the cabin is opened back up and she takes a seat across from me at the table.

"So, what's your story," she asks, "besides almost getting yourself killed, of course?"

In between bites from my second bowl of soup, I tell her all about my life. How my parents both passed and Garven watching out for Esha and me, teaching us how to survive.

I talk about our trek first to Buffalo, where I sliced my leg and almost lost it, to the amazing community they've built there. She had all sorts of questions about Buffalo. She admits that she hopes her daughter has the same amazing things happening to her. I tell her I've heard even better things about Toronto than I ever experienced in Buffalo, and a huge smile crept across her face.

"Well, when you get there, if you meet her, her name is Archie. I read somewhere before she was born that it meant 'Brave.'"

"Well, Lenora, if I make it to Toronto and meet her, I will tell her I had an amazing meal with her mom," I say.

"When, sweetie. When you make it to Toronto," she says as she pats the back of my hand.

With this, I know it's probably about time I should leave, so I start to stand up. She asks me where I'm going and I tell her I couldn't possibly impose on her any longer.

"Finley, this is the best night I've had in months. Now I'm not going to keep you hostage here or anything, so if you really wanna go you're free to do that, but it's really late and dark, and that ankle had a long day already. Let me grab you a pillow and you can either curl up on the couch or have a spot on the floor. This way you won't have to worry about what's out there for a night. It's the least I can do."

How could I possibly say no to such an offer? A stomach full of soup and a safe place to stay for the night, and maybe, if I play my cards right, a real breakfast?

"Lorena," I say, "I would love to spend the night here."

CHAPTER 33: MEETING

No one got much sleep last night, as exhausted as they were. Esha and Garven were uncomfortable and sore from being tied up for a day and a half and stuffed onto the floor of a van. Kian has an injured ankle and a deep desire to find Finley. Before falling asleep, Garven noticed several comets streaking across the night sky and wondered what Finley might say about them.

By the time the sun was rising, all three of them were ready to go.

They have a quick breakfast, deciding to eat some food rations over any of the more time-consuming options, and pack up their backpacks. Esha and Garven both have a tough time rolling their mats back up, so Kian helps them. They're both so sore they know the next few days of walking are going to be tough.

Garven puts his map in his pocket and searches for a sign, any sort of sign, to figure out their whereabouts. After limping around in a large circle for 15 minutes, he finally spots a sign for where they are:

"Mohawk Park."

He opens his old map up and searches the area around Hamilton and can't find that name anywhere. He searches a little more toward Buffalo, and nothing. He double checks the sign and confirms that's what it says.

"I can't for the life of me figure out where we are supposed to be right now," he says. "I've checked every town and village between Buffalo and Hamilton and not one of them has a Mohawk Park."

"Let me take a look at that," says Esha. She fumbles with it for a minute and starts looking over every area within a 50-mile radius of Hamilton.

"That's so strange," Esha says. "That's so much farther west from the lake than we should be. We're near a place called Brantford, which is 25 miles away from Hamilton westward. Why would we be this far away?"

"Maybe she had plans to get rid of me as well, or you two," Kian says.

"Why would she want to get rid of you?" Garven asks.

"It's a long, complicated story," Kian responds.

"It doesn't make any sense," Garven starts. "Why did they single out Finley and not either of us? I know they said Fin was dead weight, but that can't possibly be enough of a reason, right?"

Kian looks over at Esha, who catches his glance back. Esha doesn't know that Kian is aware of Fin's special ability. They've never openly talked about it.

"Well," Esha starts, "something that you don't know is that Finley has an ability that they've never told you about. I think myself and Auryn are the only ones who know."

Esha tries reading Kian's face as she says this, but it gives away nothing.

"What? What do you mean by an ability?" Garven asks.

Esha pauses for a long time, trying to find the words to say to Garven. Before she has a chance, Kian speaks.

"Finley's dreams come true," he says.

Esha darts a look over at him.

"How the hell do you know that?" She asks.

Kian lowers his eyes to the ground. He knows Esha is fine with dreamers, but he's not sure how Garven will react.

"So," he begins, "a couple of reasons, really. Fin started asking me a bunch of questions about dreams coming true because I'm also a dreamer."

"What the heck is a dreamer, and why didn't Luna throw the both of you out of the van?" Garven asks angrily.

"Being a dreamer means you can sometimes see the future in your dreams. I earned Luna's trust over the past year; she hated me at first, Garven, but I just kept my head down and kept working, and eventually she started to trust me," Kian replied.

They sit there for a moment in silence.

"Well, if she didn't trust dreamers before, it's only going to be worse now," says Esha.

Garven and Kian nod in agreement.

"Is that why you've always been so protective around Fin?" Garven asks Esha.

"That's part of it. Mostly though, Salia and Burton – Fin's parents, saved my life when my parents were murdered, so I feel like I owe a debt to them," Esha replies.

"I think that debt has been paid back and then some, Esha," Garven says.

"Maybe the time to say that isn't right after we let them get dumped and left for dead on the side of the road, alright?" She replies.

The three of them look at one another with a new understanding. Not just that this was all pre-planned, but the full extent of what Luna was capable of.

Kian interjects, "We're going to find Fin and we're going to start right now. We know where we are now. So, let's get moving."

After walking for a few minutes, Esha breaks the silence,

"If I ever see any of them again, it's going to go very, very badly for them."

"Get in line," replies Garven.

CHAPTER 34: LAKE

In the morning, Lorena gives me a burlap shoulder bag she made herself. She also put a couple fresh vegetables and a chunk of protein in as well. She warns me that I have to eat the protein within the next few hours, or I'll have to toss it.

I don't ask why, or what it is, but I do thank her profusely. It should be enough food to get me through today, she says, and after that I have my food ration bar for another day.

"Sorry, I wish I could give you more, but it's pretty tight around here, food wise." Lorena says.

"You have no reason to apologize. You've done more for me in the last 12 hours than I could ever possibly thank you for. A real meal, a safe place to sleep, and better support for my feet."

We hug, and as I leave through the doorway I turn and say to her,

"When I see Archie, I'll let her know that her mom's doing really well. Maybe I'll even grab her and come visit you again."

She smiles the biggest smile I've seen from her, and tells me, "Well, that would be really nice of you. You can come and visit anytime you like."

With that, I start my trek to the lake in much higher spirits than I was yesterday. My ankle is still sore, and I have to walk carefully. I still don't know if they're going to meet me there, but my belief is renewed. It's amazing what a warm bowl of soup can do for the human spirit.

As I walk, I notice a similar phenomenon as my hike from Cleveland to Buffalo; the closer I get to the lake, the more alive trees there are. When I originally started out yesterday, easily 90% of the trees around were dead.

Now that I've walked 10 more miles? Maybe 25% of them are alive. It makes me think back to Garven and I seeing that group of saplings right along the lake while filling our packs. As much as I'd rather not remember the rest of that day, it was an overwhelming sight.

Two hours into the walk, I remember the protein in my bag and decide now is as good a time as any to rest for a moment and eat it. I pull it out of the bag Lorena made and take a good long look at it.

I have absolutely no idea what it is. Not that that's ever stopped me eating something before, but this is the strangest piece of food I've ever seen in my life. I apprehensively take a bite; it's a little chewy, a little dry, yet somehow delicious.

I savor every bite. There's a smoky flavor to it. I wonder if Lorena had a fire pit where she smokes food. Every bite I take makes me selfishly wish more and more that I could have convinced her to come with me. I really do hope I run into Archie when I'm in Toronto, I'm sure she would love to hear her mom is not only doing well but is a total badass.

After eating, I look into my bag and see a couple carrots and other veggies. I'm plenty full for now, so I'm going to save them for later or maybe snack while I'm on the trail.

My goal is to try to walk 10 miles today. That should get me close enough to the edge of the lake, where tomorrow I'll only have to walk a little bit to make it to Hamilton.

As I walk, I look out for flowers and plants to grab. Ones I recognize from the greenhouse, or from Esha grabbing them before. I would love to meet up with her and show her my own amazing collection of plants she could use.

I think almost nonstop about the three of them. An occasional bird noise, or a pang of pain from my foot, will interrupt me, but oftentimes I go long stretches wondering how they're doing. I don't allow myself to think the worst anymore. I keep replaying all the times Garven has gone out of his way to save us from danger, how his grumpy attitude turned much more into a goofy personality the longer we all spent time together.

How could you not be defensive and a little weary of people when your family left you here, on this dying planet with almost nothing left to your name? The fact that he helped Esha and me, and really became our family, is amazing.

Esha, from the time she came to live with us, was so helpful to my parents. I don't know if I could have gone on living in this world once they both passed if Esha wasn't there by my side every day. Whenever I've brought it up, she's always just said, "You did the same for me."

I turn my thoughts toward Kian. I have no idea if he's actually going to help Garven and Esha escape. I want to believe though, why else would he have left me with the knife, food, and water? He told me to meet him at Bayfront Park, and that's where I intend to head.

A few more hours into my walk, I notice the smell of the air is changing. It's fresher, and a little cooler. That can only mean one thing; I'm getting close to the lake, and the lake should lead me to my destination.

I cross what appears to be an old path and see a sun-bleached sign at the top of a small hill. I decide to head over and read it.

BEAMER MEMORIAL CONSERVATION AREA

Well, at least they tried. Conservation in the 21st century, from what I read, was mostly a small group of people warning everyone of the impending doom, and the rest of the people going, "Eh, probably not?". Now I'm here, because of that, without another soul in sight, reading a sign for an area that almost no one even knows about anymore.

I take a walk up to a sign that says "Lookout Point" hoping to see something encouraging, and in the distance I do. In the far, far distance I see the outline of a city. I hope with every fiber of my being that it's Hamilton. It looks to be maybe 20 miles away, maybe I can walk extra today, since physically I'm still feeling alright.

I start the descent down the hill here at Beamer and notice my ankle not loving a decline. I try taking a slower pace but with the decline and gravity at work, it's harder to slow down than it is to just absorb the impact and keep going. After seven or eight minutes of this, I reach the bottom and already start rethinking how far I'm going to be able to go this evening.

I decide to just let whatever happens, happen. I keep putting one foot in front of another while looking at more and more foliage. They're all small, young trees, but some of them look so healthy. I can't help but smile. For so long we thought nothing was going to be able to grow again, but now that I've seen what they did in Buffalo, and what Lorena did in her cabin, maybe we actually have a shot at this.

Nightfall descends and while I can see Lake Ontario from where I am, I decide I'm going to pack it in for the evening. I search around for a soft spot of grass and find a dead log I can move to put my foot up on. The swelling is less severe but still there after a long day.

I roll my dirty tan jacket up underneath my head and neck and look up at the stars. An occasional comet flies by on its way to disintegration, or maybe to survive, just to leave a large crater on the surface of this mostly empty Earth.

Tomorrow, I will get up with the sun and hike to Bayfront Park, Hamilton. I'd guess it's around 12 miles from where I'm currently camped. Depending on when they escaped, Kian, Esha and Garven might already be there waiting for me. They would have been a lot closer than me, and not hobbling along like I am. Before falling asleep, I realize how hungry I am. I hate trying to fall asleep hungry. I take out the last couple vegetables I didn't munch on while walking and snack on a carrot. It tastes like dirt, but it'll do.

After an uneventful night under the stars, I wake up and immediately think of food again. I have a ration bar and one day's worth of water left. Against my better judgment, I eat half the ration bar and down the water. Being thirsty on the walk is one of the worst feelings in the world.

I have to hope that they made it to the meeting point already, and with some food and water. If not, I'm going to have to search through houses in Hamilton and that can be really dangerous on your own.

I start walking and almost immediately regret not eating my entire ration. I'm still faintly hungry, and it's mostly what I think about for the next few hours of walking. In the early afternoon, I finally stop and allow myself to eat the other half of the ration. The issue now is that my mouth is dry and I have no water left. Thankfully I can see the outskirts of Hamilton just a few miles away, so I march on.

As I reach the entrance to the city, a faded blue sign reads,

WELCOME TO HAMILTON.
Population 535,000. A City of Many Communities

535,000 people. More than the population left on Earth, all in this single place. It's shocking how quickly everything went downhill. Once the ice caps melted, there was no coming back. After the flooding, the drought happened and with it, crops — and humanity's ability to survive — vanished.

I wander my way through the city, dense buildings and high, crumbling skyscrapers. It's bigger than I had imagined. I know that the park I'm supposed to meet them at is by the water, so I walk as close to the lake as possible, looking out for any signs.

As I walk, I can see where the water used to come up to the shore. High retaining walls and boat docks sit a hundred feet away from where the water line is now. All sorts of clearings with signs that say they were recreation areas. I walk by houses, structures that were some sort of industry, and a gas station with a sign that still has all its letters, which is a bummer.

Finally, after two hours of walking, I see it: Hamilton Bayfront Park. I want to run into the park, sprint, skip even, but my leg doesn't allow me to. My head is on a swivel, scanning the area for any sign of them. It's still daylight out and it's easy to see pretty much the entire park, but no sign of them.

"That's fine," I tell myself; I can have a seat and relax for a little while. Or I can walk around and see if they've hidden themselves away.

I do both over the next several hours. No sign of them anywhere. At first, I kept my spirits up but now the more I think about it, the less hopeful I am. They would have been closer. They should have been here already. What if I've been a fool this entire time? The dark thoughts start to creep in.

I decide to try to combat them by being productive and doing something for myself. I need food, I need water, and there are lots of houses close by. I get myself off the bench I'm sitting on and take a quick walk across the street. Initially, I'm looking for a house that isn't too much trouble to break into but also doesn't look like it's been ransacked already.

The first house I walk up to has several broken windows, and the door is already open. It's doubtful anything is left, so I start to walk to the next block over.

"Simcoe St W", the faded sign reads. Might as well start here.

The first house I see on the corner is a beautiful brick building. I can see how it stood the test of time. The side door is closed, so I walk up and turn the handle. It's jammed, probably from all the dust and dirt from storms being whipped around. I turn the handle as hard as I can and put a shoulder hard into the door. It doesn't open, but the handle starts to turn a bit more.

After a couple more shoulders into the door, my arm is starting to feel sore. I'm about to give up and try the next house when I shove it hard one more time.

It opens!

Walking in, it feels like I'm in a museum. Whoever these people were, they weren't around when the ships took off. It looks like nothing here has been touched in 50 years. It doesn't bode well for finding anything useful for me, but I can't help but still look around.

The kitchen is right off the side entryway. It has all the old appliances I've seen in magazines and books. A gas stove instead of electric. A huge table. I wonder if their family had a lot of people, this house is gigantic so they must have. I wander further in and see a staircase that leads upstairs. On the wall of the staircase is a bunch of pictures.

The first picture is of a woman, must be in her 70s, with adorable glasses and a haircut I could see my mom pulling off. The next two pictures are a couple, maybe late 40s. The man has a look on his face that he'd rather be doing literally anything else in the world and the woman looks so nice, like she got dressed up for the occasion.

Seeing pictures of happy families isn't going to lift my mood, so I wander around the house for a bit more. At one point, I knock over a long metal standing rod with several loops at the top. I have no idea what it would be for, but it falls and goes straight through a window, making a loud crashing noise that echoes through the neighborhood.

A moment later I noticed another staircase off the kitchen, leading down into a basement. If there was going to be anything left for me, it would probably be in the basement. I take the creaky wooden stairs down and begin looking through box after box of photo albums, old countertop appliances, and more.

As I dig around, I hear a noise above. I stop moving entirely and listen.

"We heard you break a window; we know someone's in here," the voice says.

How are there so few people left in this world, but somehow, they all keep finding me?

"We're just here to talk. We're not bad people, we're not Raider's or anything," a second voice says.

While I tend to believe them, anyone who is a Raider likes to immediately let you know, I still don't trust anyone, especially someone willing to sneak into a house after me.

I hear them walking around the living room above, so I slowly move to the stairs. I am trying to remember which steps made a lot of noise when I came downstairs, and I try to avoid them on the way up. Otherwise, I slowly take one stair at a time, while listening to hear where they are in the house.

"Come on now, did you go upstairs? You don't have to hide from us. We're friendly," the first voice says.

I have no intention of finding out if that's true or not. I reach the top stair and carefully peek around the side. No one in the kitchen and no one in the living room, they must have both gone upstairs to look. I slowly and quietly make my way across the kitchen, back to the side entryway, and open the door.

It squeaks a little. Enough to alert them? I don't know. So, I take off running.

Well, hobbling really. I head back as quickly as I can toward Bayfront Park. I don't know why I'm heading back there. I guess I'm hoping that maybe I'll turn the corner and see Esha's smiling face, or Kian will run up to me and pick me up off the ground with a hug. I don't know, I just know that's where I want to head.

I get to the entrance of the park as golden hour is ending. It's not quite dark, but it's no longer light out either. Instead of stopping at a bench like I did before, I keep going, keep hobbling toward the water.

I get through a grassy area and into a part that looks like it used to be a beach. A hundred feet out from here, the lake starts. It calls to me, so I walk toward it.

I stand on the edge of the lake and listen to the waves lap just a few feet in front of me. It's not a familiar noise, but it's comforting. I haven't seen Esha or Garven for three days now, the longest time spent apart in years.

Waves crashing.

"I'm not sure I can do this much longer," I say to no one.

Waves receding.

"Even if I find them, what's worth living for anymore?"

Waves crashing.

"I'm just so tired of running, of fighting, of doing everything for the sole purpose of surviving."

Waves receding.

The water is relentless in a way that I cannot be, and I resent it. Waves upon endless waves crashing against the ground in front of me. I take a deep breath and listen. The waves toss in a rhythmic pattern, slightly different every time. It reminds me of the old records my dad used to play, back in the safety of our home. Dust floating through the golden sunrays. Records stacked as high as me.

I didn't really understand what I was listening to, being a kid, but dad loved it, so it meant I loved it too. I could stay here all-night listening, and soon will, because I have nowhere else to go. Nowhere left to search. No hope left to turn to.

Then it starts.

No, it can't happen right now, anytime but now, I think to myself. But there was no stopping it. Not here. Not now.

Heart rate quickening.

Tunnel vision slowly envelops my eyes.

A headache in my temples forming.

No, it can't be. Not right now. Not while alone. One of the things I lost when I was tossed out of the van was my emergency anxiety pills. Dr. Rai gave me a few extras before I left, but they're all in my bag, hanging on a hook in the back of Luna's van.

I want to run or collapse in on myself. The sweating has started. Oh, the sweating. It makes everything even more uncomfortable. I want to run and jump into the water but also dig a hole and bury myself. It's pure adrenaline and I have no idea how long each episode is going to last.

I stand up, take my shoes off in a panic, and frantically jog to dip my feet in the water. Something, anything, to ground my mind and shock my brain into thinking about anything other than the sheer panic racing through it right now.

But it doesn't work, the water of the lake is too warm. I need something cold, but there's nothing around. I crumble to my knees.

My pants, worn and tattered after running through trees and wilderness, are soaked up to the knees immediately. Even though the water is no deeper than a foot, it is overtaking me. My arms are soaked, fingers bracing against the ever-shifting sand, trying to steady a body that's doing everything to fail. My forehead dipping in and out of the water as the waves crash around me, staying far enough out to not drown, but close enough so that it's an option.

Then, the thought occurs. Finally, after hiding those few short moments.

Just dip your face in. The whole thing. Just end it. Right here. Do it. DO IT.

My own mind is trying to convince me of the very thing I've fought so hard against these last few years. But it's right this time, isn't it? It always was. It never was. Every thought is so fleeting I can't catch onto it long enough to say.

There is no Esha, no Garven, no ships coming back to save us. No way to make life any easier than it currently is. Nothing I can do to save this abandoned humanity.

Then I do it. My arms that have been the last line of defense give way. My elbows fold. My face immediately submerged in nothing more than a foot of water. My body is trying to keep the air in its lungs while my brain is making me slowly, but surely, breathe it out.

My eyes could be opened or closed. It's dark, and it no longer matters. The heart racing is there, the headache, the sweating, the nausea, it's all there but it no longer matters. All that matters is that any second now this will all be over.

The pain, the struggle, the endless exhaustion of trying to survive every single day. It no longer matters. I am finally going to be free from all of this.

The darkness I've avoided every chance I could has now closed in around me. The last moments of a dying person, on a dying planet, going meekly into the night. Into the water. Returning to the Earth.

As I ready myself to take a full breath of water into my struggling lungs, my head lifts — not voluntarily — and someone is screaming at me. I can't immediately tell who because I'm using the very last of my strength to plunge my head back into the warm lake.

"NO! JUST LET ME DO THIS," I yell.

"STOP! LISTEN TO ME," they plead.

"I can't. I just can't," I say while trailing off.

Who is it? How did they find me? It doesn't matter. None of it matters.

I feel a second set of hands on me and then, without warning, I am pulled out of the water and I'm being dragged up onto the dry land.

"Please, just let me go. I can't do this," but I don't have the strength to fight anymore.

I'm so exhausted, so over everything, that I just close my eyes and cry with whatever little water I have left in my body.

THE SIXTH DREAM

I am by myself in a mostly gray room. My vision is blurred, and I can only see what's directly in front of me.

To the left, I notice a hibiscus plant in the corner. It's about five feet tall and gorgeous. Lush pinks with stems sticking out in the center, coated with yellow pollen.

I look to the right and see a piece of cloth tacked to the wall. On it, a rhinoceros surrounded by palm trees and olive branches.

I stand there in silence for a few moments, unsure of what I should be doing. There are no doors and no windows in this room. Who would make a room like this? What would even be the purpose? Out of nowhere, a voice I do not recognize startles me as it fills the room.

"Is someone here?" It asks in a low, melodic tone.

It feels like they are talking to me. Not dream me, but *real life* me.

CHAPTER 35: AGAIN

I wake up with a raging headache. It always happens after I have a panic attack that big. Even after Kian gave me my bag and I took my medication last night, I knew it was going to be a terrible morning.

Maybe worse than the headache, I know that I'm going to have to thank Esha, Garven, and Kian for pulling me out of the water. But I'm not going to mean it, at least not yet. It feels selfish of them to make me keep living in this world. Maybe I'm just hungry and thirsty, because I'm always hungry and thirsty, but I'm more upset now than I'd like to admit.

The depression often follows the panic.

"So, do you want to talk about last night?" Kian asks.

"Not really, no," I respond.

I realize this is the first time he's seen me like this. Esha and Garven have dealt with the fallout of a massive panic attack in the past. They know I need some time, but Kian keeps pressing.

"I think it's important we have a conversation about it, Fin. I mean, you were trying to…" he pauses for a moment.

"To drown yourself."

I look up at him, expressionless and unable to say much.

Without warning, Garven steps in between us.

"Listen man, I know you want to help. But you've got to give Fin a little space right now," he says to Kian.

Kian starts to argue with Garven, but Esha cuts him off.

"You've known Fin for a few weeks, I've known them for a decade. Just give 'em some space, dude."

Kian looks over at me and slumps his shoulders. I've never seen him sulk before. He walks a few feet away and grabs something from his bag. He pulls it out and walks toward me. I cannot handle having a conversation with anyone right now.

Esha and Garven tense up as Kian approaches me. Without saying a word, he hands me an apple and walks away. I look down at all its red, shiny, delicious glory, and then watch Kian as he walks back to his seat. I appreciate the gesture and smile at him as he sits. He notices and smiles back. As a group, we all sit in silence for another 15 or 20 minutes. Me, enjoying my apple and some water, everyone else eating a morning food pack. With our bags back, we have the better food packs that we made before leaving Buffalo, not just the silver bagged rations that I had been living off of for a few days.

Garven folds up his garbage and places it into his backpack.

"So, now that we're all back together, I think it's time we finish this trek to Toronto. We can't go back to Buffalo, in case Luna, Harlian and them are going back there. I mean, Kian shot a guy, so no one there is going to accept us on friendly terms," Garven says.

Kian shot a guy? What? I haven't had any time to catch up with what happened to them while we were separated. I've been so stressed thinking about what I have to tell them, that I didn't even think about what they had to tell me. I feel selfish.

"Okay, I'm going to need to hear about that at some point," I say.

"Whenever you're ready," Kian says, "and I'm gonna wanna hear about that ankle. It's like every time I see you, you have a new injury."

"If you think you wanna hear about my ankle, wait till I tell you how I stabbed a guy," I respond.

Esha, Garven, and Kian's heads all snap around to stare at me in disbelief. I smile, nod my head, and tell them it's true.

"Twice, technically," I say with a grin I can no longer contain.

"Screw the ankle, the FIRST thing you're telling us is about stabbing a guy," says Esha.

We all chuckle, and it lightens the mood a bit. I still don't feel much like talking, but it is really nice to have the three of them around again. It feels less lonely.

After another minute, I say,

"Alright. We've made it this far, Toronto it is."

Before starting our trek, Kian pulls out an ankle compression sleeve that I can put over my sprained ankle. It feels so much better than two sticks taped to my ankle, even if they were the nicer ones from Lorena, and I can walk faster right away. I thank him and let him know I'm not mad at him for earlier, but he does have to respect when I tell him I don't have the ability to talk about it all right now. He nods and apologizes.

As we are about to leave the park, we spot two people coming from the direction of the houses, jogging toward us. We immediately tense up. Garven's hand is on his machete, mine on my knife.

"Hey new people! We're friendly!" The woman says.

"We don't mean to disturb you, but we saw you all hanging out over here this morning and wondered if you were the people in the brick house over there yesterday?"

They point toward the house I was, in fact, in last night.

"We just want to know if we have to be worried about Raiders in the area," her partner says.

Kian begins to explain that they just came into the area late last night, but midway through his first sentence, I interrupt.

"Yeah, that was me. I was in the basement when you came in, and I didn't know if you were trustworthy or not, so I snuck out."

They both look at each other with eyebrows raised.

"Wow, you were really quiet, that's impressive! My name is Dahlia, and this is my wife Alvie. Are you all staying here in Hamilton?"

They might be the friendliest adults we've met on the road yet. I feel bad for sneaking out on them yesterday, but I couldn't have known.

"We're actually heading up to Toronto. We hear there's a pretty good society being built," Esha responds.

"Well, that's disappointing," Alvie says, "There's a couple hundred of us here in Hamilton and we're trying to build a community of our own.

We all talk for a few more minutes. They explain how they don't want to travel over to Toronto because they've heard both good and bad about it. They also feel like being founders of a new community here can be a really amazing experience.

We wish them well and let them know if anything happens on the road, or in Toronto, that we'd be thrilled to come back here and help. I can't speak for the other three, but I mean it. Now that we almost certainly can't go back to Buffalo and have no idea what's going on in Toronto, the thought of having another place to set down roots is really appealing.

We finish up talking and let them know we have to be on our way.

After saying our goodbyes, we're on the road once again. It feels really good to be walking with the people I care most about on this world. Eventually, as the fog from the medicine begins to fade, I tell the three of them about my many adventures while we were separated. In return, they tell me about their harrowing escape from Luna and Harlian.

They were most amazed by two things. One, that I could actually stab someone, even in self-defense. Esha sounded like she's never been prouder of me in her entire life, which when I point out to her, she laughs and says,

"That might actually be true!"

I get a good chuckle out of it as well. They were also really fascinated by Lorena. They had so many questions about how her defense system worked, which I couldn't answer, and how much food she could possibly be growing on her roof, which I could.

On day one, we walked for a dozen or more miles. With my ankle feeling better and the compression sleeve, we decided to skip lunch and just snack along the way. We eventually called it an earlier night than normal.

As I lay there in my tent, I start thinking of Kian. While walking on my own, I told myself that I was going to tell him that I like him, and I still will. I just have to find the right time. I do wonder how Garven will take it, considering his sister and I were together for so long. I just hope that he can see that Kian makes me happy when he's around, even if he does have to get used to some of my, how should I put it, *quirks*.

But this morning, he apologized for trying to make me talk and I appreciate that a lot.

After a surprisingly calm night of sleep, we all wake again the next morning. Garven already has a map out and lets us know that in three or four more days, we should reach Toronto and this 300-mile journey can finally be over for us.

All day, I dream about what it will be like. Is it like Buffalo? Is it better than Buffalo was? That, I can't even imagine. All I know is that as long as I'm with these three, everything should end up turning out okay.

After lunch, we begin our journey, re-energized once again.

CHAPTER 36: HOMECOMING

Tomorrow, the four of us make our final hike into Toronto. I can't believe we've made it this far after four days of walking from Hamilton. We've made camp a couple hundred feet away from the last main road into the city. We're pretty well hidden, so Garven wants to make a small fire.

Kian and I are looking around for enough rocks to form the circle of the fire pit. I'm still hobbling a bit, but I'm feeling pretty good considering how far we've walked today. The ankle compression sleeve is a miracle worker.

"So, what are you looking forward to most when we get into the city?" Kian asks me as we're walking. He's carrying an empty bag that we can place small and medium rocks in while we're looking.

"Honestly, I think just having a place to call home again. Taking a couple weeks to get healthy and then figuring out what this life is going to be," I responded.

His face looks a little surprised at my answer.

"Oh, wow. I mean, I guess I was thinking less of the big picture than that. Like, eating a meal that doesn't come out of a silver bag or something, but that's a much better answer." He chuckles a little bit.

I find myself really liking it when he feels a bit embarrassed. His cheeks turn red, and he runs his right hand through his wavy brown hair.

After Auryn left, I honestly didn't know if I'd ever see myself with someone again. It always seemed like things with much more importance, and things that needed much more attention, were always popping up. Now that I've been able to spend some real time with someone again, it's been nice.

It probably helps that he saved the life of Esha, Garven, and me. But even beyond that, there's a magnetism to him that I just can't quite put into words.

"What's with the goofy smile? Find a really good rock or something?" He asks. I realize I've been staring at him for a lot longer than I should.

"Yeah, absolutely. Super good rock," I say back.

With that, I bend down and pick up a rock and put it in his bag. When I place it in his backpack, I give him a playful shoulder bump. He pretends to stumble, which makes both of us laugh.

"Whoa! Whoa! Whoa! Careful there. You don't even know your own strength!" He says.

He wraps his arm around my back and we start walking together again on our rock hunt. It's not fair. It went from him blushing thirty seconds ago to me now. Thankfully, I can turn my face away from him pretending to look for rocks.

He slowly moves his hand to the small of my back and then turns me toward him.

"Look, Fin, I know you've been through a lot recently, more than any one person should have to go through. So, if you don't feel the same, or need some time or space, I totally understand. I just…" he pauses for a moment, takes a step back, and looks at the ground. "I really like you, and if you felt the same way, or, or if…" he starts fumbling his words.

Something about his nervousness is adorable. This is a man who risked his life to save us. Who helped us survive when I wasn't sure we could, and now? Now, he's fumbling his words while trying to tell me he likes me.

He looks up from the ground and directly into my eyes. He's about to start speaking again but, before he does, I kiss him.

So many times over the past few months, my heart has felt like it was beating through my chest: For survival, for panic, for anxiety. Not once has it felt like this for such a good reason. After a few seconds, we release and both look at each other with huge, goofy smiles.

"Oh, so I guess maybe you don't need space or time?" Kian says with a chuckle.

"No, no, I don't think I do," I respond while smiling ear to ear. I move into his body, and he wraps his arms around me. At this moment, I forget everything I've been through the past few months. Heck, I forget everything from the past three years and just melt into him. For this brief moment in time, all feels right with the world.

After 30 or so seconds, we release our hug and resume our rock hunt. Between picking up rocks, we hold hands. It feels like such an intimate gesture.

"So, should we tell Garven and Esha?" Kian asks.

"Yeah, I think so. Garven definitely deserves to know," I say back.

"Wait, why Garven specifically?" Kian asks, genuinely confused.

We're all adults here. I have to tell Kian about my past at some point, so he should probably know the truth about Auryn and me before we tell her brother about any of this. It's only fair.

"Well," I start. I'm more nervous than I thought I would be talking about this. "You know that Garven has family on the second ship that left, right?"

Kian nods his head, listening to me intently, the way he's prone to do.

"So, on the ship were his mom, dad, younger brother, and younger sister, Auryn. She was about my age," I correct myself, "is my age. Auryn and I, well, it's complicated."

"Complicated, how?" Asks Kian.

"So, before the ship left, our families knew each other pretty well. That's actually how Garven and I ended up traveling together, because we had known each other for a few years."

"Yeah, you mentioned that in Buffalo," says Kian.

"Well, what I didn't mention in Buffalo is the reason why our families knew each other. Auryn and I," I pause for a moment, thinking of the right way to say what I want to say. "We were together for four years."

"Together like, dating? Like a couple?" He asks.

"Yeah, exactly. From when we were around 12, 13, to when the ships took off, we were a couple. She was the first person I had ever been in a relationship with, and until their family were granted tickets on the second ship, we thought we were going to be together forever. I know it's silly, being so young and thinking you're going to stay together forever, but we loved each other."

My mind is racing with how Kian is going to take the news. Will he be upset? We've been flirty and had so many long talks, but I have no idea how he's going to feel about this.

"Wait, is that why Garven's been such a prick toward me?"

"Is—is that really your first question?" I say back.

"Well, yeah, I always thought it was just because I was with the Buffalo people and they turned out to be horrible people, but now that I think about it, Garven has been a little standoffish to me almost since day one."

"Well, Garven is standoffish with everyone pretty much all the time, Kian. I think he's been that way toward you mostly because of the Buffalo people thing, though," I respond.

"No, no, no, this makes so much sense now! You and his sister were a thing, and I came in, flirting with you immediately, and it made him angry, I totally get it now."

"Wait, you were flirting with me right away?" I am definitely blushing right now.

"Of course I was, do you think I just pick up everyone over my shoulder and jog them to the doctor when they're not feeling well? But that's not the point, the point is I get why Garven doesn't like me now!"

Kian seems excited to have figured out this great mystery that's been plaguing him for weeks, but I'm more concerned about how he isn't reacting to the news that I dated Garven's sister.

"Do you have any other thoughts about me dating Garven's sister?" I finally ask.

"Fin, we've both had lives before we met in Buffalo. Who you liked, or who you loved, has no bearing on my feelings toward you right now, at this moment. I've lost people I loved, too. I like you for who you are, and a part of who you are as a person in the present is who you were in the past. So, if loving Garven's sister is something that's helped you become the kind, caring, survivor you are today, then I'm glad that it happened."

I feel like saying so much but instead, I bury my face in Kian's shoulder and bear hug him. I had no idea what to expect when telling him. I've been avoiding it for the past few days as we've become closer. I couldn't have imagined this going as well as it has.

"If you want, when you're comfortable, you can tell me about Annora's sister," I say.

The timing wasn't right for me to bring it up, but it never would be.

"Did Annora tell you what happened?" He says, solemnly.

"She did. If you're not comfortable talking about it, I understand," I say back.

"Someday, Fin. Someday soon, even, I'd be happy to tell you about her. For now, let's get some rocks and head back," he says.

I smile at him and let him know I'm here for him, for whatever he needs.

"Alright, so the plan is we find the best rocks we can, and then after Garven hears it from us, we can soften the blow by building the best fire ever. Maybe he'll be worse toward me, maybe he'll be better; either way, at least we won't have to keep any secrets," Kian says.

I really don't want to stop hugging him. Finally, I let go and we stand there smiling at each other for a few more seconds.

For the next few minutes, we find more rocks for the fire pit. Now, for some reason, we've decided to only pick up the best of the best, as if getting better rocks will somehow help with Garven's reaction to us. But we march on and after another 10 minutes, I'm pretty sure we have enough.

As we walk back toward camp, both Kian and I are quiet. We're holding hands as we approach and can hear Esha and Garven talking about what to expect tomorrow.

When we're about 10 feet from them, they both look over at us. Garven immediately notices us holding hands, and I brace for whatever comes next.

"Well, it's about damn time," he says.

Esha looks confused for a second, before realizing that Kian and I are holding hands. She looks over at Garven and starts laughing.

"We've been waiting so long for one of you two idiots to make a move. You've been flirting with each other forever and we were getting annoyed by it," continued Garven.

"So, you're not upset, Garven?" I ask, feeling relieved already.

"Fin, it's been almost three years since Auryn left. We've been spending so much time just trying to survive, and I'm delighted you've finally found time to be flirty with this dope," Garven says back.

"Look, I don't want to make this about me, but is that why you've been such a prick to me since we met?" Kian asks.

Garven looks at me, then over to Esha, before finally fixing his gaze back to Kian.

"No, I've been a prick to you because your face annoys me. Also, your friends tried to kill us."

Everyone goes very quiet with this. As a group we haven't talked much about Kian's role in that entire episode, and there is definitely some leftover tension from it.

After what seems like an eternity of silence but was probably only a few seconds, Garven bursts out laughing.

"I'm just messing with you, man," he says.

"He's just kind of a prick to everyone he doesn't know that well. It's why we love him so much," Esha says.

"Alright, so I guess I shouldn't take it so personally then," Kian says.

"I told you, not everything's about you, Kian," I say to him.

Being able to have these moments is pretty amazing, considering what we've all been through over the past few weeks. We're here, safe, and close to our final destination.

We all keep talking while building the fire. Garven is indeed impressed with some of the rocks we brought back. After he finds some more dry sticks, I pull out my fire starter and get to work setting it ablaze. We decide to skip a long meal tonight and just heat up our packs. We're all pretty tired since we hiked so far today.

"I'm actually getting pretty exhausted. I think I'm going to hop in the tent and grab an extra-long night of sleep. Wake me up when it's my turn for lookout," Kian says. With that, he vanishes into his tent.

Our tent? No, don't get ahead of yourself, Fin.

Either way, the three of us decide to stay up a little bit longer. I can feel the excitement in the air. This long trip is finally almost over. We've been through so much together these past couple of years and I can't imagine anything that happens in the next day or two will break that.

As we sit around the slowly fading fire, a quietness engulfs us. The crackle of slightly damp wood burning in the fire pit. The smell of smoke that always seems to find itself blowing in my direction. The cool breeze off the lake. I can't help but take a deep breath in and enjoy every second of this evening.

Maybe I'm a little love-struck, maybe our luck is finally turning around. Maybe, just maybe, the next few months of our lives will be a little easier than the last few.

Slowly, the three of us lower ourselves all the way to the ground and start looking at the stars, as we almost always did while walking from Cleveland to Buffalo. It feels like decades ago I would always talk about being rescued by one of the ships, and Garven would shut that thought process down.

"The only ones who can rescue us, *is* us."

Without any lights around the fire, the night sky is so vibrant. I am looking out at a million stars. The difference is now, three of those stars might be looking back at us. With everything that's happened, it's hard not to think of Auryn in all this. Would she be happy for me? Has she found someone else?

Did they even make it to where they were going?

I hope they did, and I hope she's found someone. She's one of the best people I've ever met, and she deserves all the happiness in the galaxy.

As we lay here, staring into the night sky, I see a comet streaking across the sky. Still to this day, every time a comet flashes across the night sky, I wonder for a brief moment if that's them coming back for us.

I chuckle to myself how silly the thought seemed now. In a few moments, the comet will burn up in the atmosphere, and we will all crawl into our tents for a night of sleep. I watch it as it streaks across the sky. It lasts longer in the atmosphere than most comets do, it might even be so big it touches down on earth. Some poor desolate rock will get destroyed.

We're all quiet for another minute. I have no idea if they've spotted it as well, or if they've passed out already.

"It's weird that the comet up there hasn't started to burn off in the atmosphere yet," Esha says, breaking through the silence.

"Yeah, I thought it was a little strange myself, honestly," Garven responds.

"It should definitely be burning by now. Maybe it's a super huge comet and life as we know it will change forever?" I say. It was a poor attempt at sounding poetic.

Garven suddenly stands up, and Esha does the same. I follow them up onto my feet and, without saying a word,

Garven starts walking in the direction the comet is heading. It looks like it's heading straight for our area, which would mean everything we've fought through over the past few years would be meaningless. I can't even let that thought into my head.

"It's…" Esha takes a long pause, "*slowing down.*"

"That's impossible," I say. "A comet can't just *slow down.*"

Garven stops looking at the sky and looks right at both Esha and me. Looking as stunned and as excited as I've ever seen him, he realizes we don't quite understand yet.

"You're right, Fin. A comet *can't* just slow down."

He is staring intently at us as he says the words that will forever change our lives.

"But a *ship* can."

(UNKNOWN)

"I swear to you, there was a person right here in the room," a man says.

"I don't know, Abdo, you're getting pretty senile at this old age. What are you, a hundred and thirty now? Sure you weren't just hearing things?" A woman responds.

"I didn't hear them say anything Sun Young! They were standing, right where you are now. I tried talking to them, but they looked startled and then disappeared." Abdo says.

"Hmm, maybe it's true then. Maybe we have another Stonekeeper. It'd be the first new one in what, 90 years?" She responds.

"Be nice knowing we can die in peace, that's for sure." Abdo says, laughing a deep, hearty laugh.

9 798989 751204